FOREVER FREDLESS

SUZY TURNER

 # FREE DOWNLOAD 

Willow Tree Farm

Nestled among a thicket of weeping willows deep in the heart of Dartmoor, lies a house like no other. A house defying the laws of logic—and gravity for that matter. Some might even say it had a mind of its own. They wouldn't be wrong.

Affectionately known as Willow, this house has been an integral part of the Winterbourne family for over 400 years, and it is very, very protective of the Winterbournes, so woe betide anyone who dares to wrong this family of witches…

Compatible with all reading devices.

Exclusively available, and never before published.

Get your FREE COPY of Willow Tree Farm when you sign up to the author's VIP mailing list. Get started here:

www.suzyturner.com/free-book

CHAPTER 1

Standing perfectly still, I watched them dance all around me, arms and legs flailing around like puppets, dressed in high top trainers, faded jeans and oversized, brightly coloured T-shirts. Their parents stood some distance from the dance floor, chatting, drinking and taking photos of their beloved children.

But I couldn't stand still for long. The moment the next song began, a giggle burst from my lips and I jumped upwards, fists banging an imaginary low ceiling above my head. As the music started to speed up, I began to join in the fun.

Singing along and dancing to the tones of Right Said Fred's I'm Too Sexy, I felt something gently brush against my back. When I turned around, my breath caught in my throat as butterflies exploded deep within my stomach. The most beautiful boy stared back at me. His eyes were deep blue, and his jet black hair just brushed above his slim shoulders, while his high cheekbones were flushed a deep pink.

In that very second, it was as though all the other kids disappeared. It was just the two of us, standing still, silently staring into each other's eyes. I felt ever so slightly giddy and light-headed; my face blushed every shade of red, but I just couldn't look away. My body felt as if it would melt into the floor at any moment. Even now, twenty years later, that moment continues to be the most overwhelming experience of my existence.

Suddenly, life seemed to fast forward once more as my dad appeared out of nowhere. Grabbing my hand, he gently pulled me away from the dance floor.

'Come on, Petal, it's time to go. Your mum's waiting for us outside.'

As we reached the exit, I yanked my hand away from his and turned to look back, but the boy had vanished. The song had changed, and kids were now dancing around to the sounds of Snap's Rhythm Is A Dancer, a favourite song at the time.

I scanned the crowd to see if he'd found someone else to dance with, but I couldn't see him anywhere. My dad grasped hold of my hand again and tugged me gently.

'Come on,' he half-shouted above the thud of the music.

Mum stood outside in the drizzle, puffing away on a cigarette.

'Darling, you were fantastic. My lovely little dancing Kate,' she whispered as she bent down and hugged me and kissed my cheek. I could smell tobacco and alcohol on her breath. She must have had another fight with Dad. Arguments were pretty much the norm in those days, but I tried to block them from memory. I'd rather remember all the fun times we'd had together. Although looking back now; they were pretty few and far between. I should have known at the time what was going to happen. Mind you, I was only twelve. A mature twelve but still, I shouldn't have had to worry about things like that.

'You two wait here, I'll just pop round and fetch the car. Just hold on a minute. I'll be right back,' Dad said, in a weak attempt to sound cheerful.

Moments later, the car pulled up beside us and I reluctantly climbed into the back seat. Just as Mum slammed her door, I looked out the window, and there he was, standing by the side of our faded red Peugeot, as the engine chugged into motion. He was staring at me with a flower in his hand with such a sad expression on his face. He must have disappeared outdoors to go and pick one for me. Glancing from his eyes down to his hands, I saw that it was a bright yellow daffodil.

The car began to lurch forward, so I climbed onto my knees, turned around and looked out of the rear window. I could feel my eyes welling up. I pushed my hand against the glass, and several tears slid slowly down my face. He held up his hand and casually rubbed his eye, as if he was rubbing away a tear, too. Our eyes locked together, just for a moment, until the car turned the corner, and he was gone. Out of my life.

If only I'd spoken to him. If only I'd asked Mum and Dad to stay an extra day of the half-term holiday. If only I'd got his phone number. I could be with him now. We wouldn't have lost so many years. So many wasted years. But there were far too many 'if onlys'. I didn't speak to him. I didn't get his phone number. I didn't ask Mum and Dad to stay an extra day. I had done nothing. I had been with my soul mate for just a brief moment in time. I had to live with the fact that I would never find him again. My Fred. My one and only Fred.

You're probably wondering how I know his name.

The truth is, I don't. I couldn't go on calling him the boy without a name', so I made it up. After all, we were dancing to Right Said Fred when we first saw each other; it was only appropriate that I should call him Fred.

Sometimes I wish I'd said something to Mum and Dad about Fred, but I doubt they'd have understood, even though they always used to say that I was much older than my years. When they introduced me to their friends, they'd say, 'this is our daughter Kate, she's twelve going on twenty'. It always made me feel so grown up.

But still, I don't think they'd have taken too kindly to the fact that I'd fallen in love at such a young age. They'd have said it was just a passing phase that I'd grow out of or something like that. Only I knew I'd never grow out of it. I was in love with Fred, and I'd always be in love with Fred. Nothing would change that. Not that it matters. I never told them. I never told anyone. It was best kept to myself.

I did ask my parents if we could go to that same caravan park in Skegness again. We went a few more times when I was a kid, and I even went on my own once I'd moved out. Always hoping that I might find him.

But after Dad ran off with Mum's best friend's daughter, she was never quite the same, and she said she just couldn't face that place anymore because it reminded her of him, I guess.

I rarely see either of them now. Dad's too involved with his recent acquisition – a baby daughter, my half-sister, or should I say, my fifth half-sister. He loves having babies in the house. He really is quite brilliant with them. The trouble is once they start talking and walking, he doesn't really know what to do with them. So his answer is to get the wife pregnant again. I feel sorry for Julie. She's exactly the same age as me. We even went to school together. So she's twenty-eight years old and already has five daughters.

They moved to Newcastle when they ran off together – almost nine years ago – and they've been there ever since. It's too much hassle for them to come and visit me in London and I feel a bit uncomfortable staying with them. The atmosphere always feels so tense. I know that Julie loves my dad, but I get the impression that she feels a bit guilty about it all.

Mum eventually started dating again, but she was never particularly happy until she met the guy she's with now. He seems to be a really decent, honest guy. Like Dad's wife, he's a lot younger than Mum – a year or two older than me. It doesn't bother me, though. His name is Nick, and he's an environmentalist who loves animals and nature. He has to recycle everything and can't waste a thing.

Currently, they're living in Africa. I've no idea where exactly. Every now and again I get a postcard just to let me know that they're alive and well. I'm really proud of her. She gave up everything that she had here – sold the house (she got it in the divorce) and gave much of the money to charity. Now they move from place to place, living off the land, as she puts it. A couple of Nomads is how best to describe them. It's pretty cool, actually.

She sent me a photo a few months ago; she looked so young and full of vitality. I admire her. I could almost imagine doing the same thing with Fred. Although I'd have difficulty giving away all my money. Actually, I don't think I could do what she does. Thinking about it, no... I couldn't stand all those creepy crawlies and mosquitoes. But what if Fred was into all that stuff? No, he wouldn't be. I don't think he would. He didn't look the type.

CHAPTER 2

None of my friends knew about Fred, not even my closest, Jo. I'm not quite sure why. Maybe I just never got round to it, perhaps I didn't want to be laughed at or criticised. In the grand scheme of things, I guess it was so trivial. She'd had enough on her plate without worrying about my pathetic love life – or rather pathetic lack of it. Though I'm pretty sure she'd have understood; maybe I should have told her. Perhaps it would have made her realise why all my past relationships failed.

None of them compared to Fred.

Julian was my first long-term boyfriend. He was such a sweetheart. Very cuddly and loving, and he had always wanted to hold my hand when we were out in public. I went out with him when I was seventeen, for four months. Everything was going fine until we had sex. We were both virgins at the time – not that that had anything to do with it. It was awful and wonderful at the same time – he was so gentle, and it could have been a fantastic experience, if I hadn't made the stupid mistake of calling out Fred's name in the heat of the moment, that is.

I tried to pretend I'd said something else, but I couldn't think of anything that sounded remotely like it, at the time. Naturally, he was rather upset. So much so that he never spoke to me again. I heard from a friend of a friend that he'd been heartbroken. As far as I know, he never did tell anyone what caused us to break up. He must have felt totally humiliated. I would have done too.

He's since settled down with a sweet girl who was in our class at school. I've seen them together in the street, but I usually turn away and cross the road quickly. I'd rather spare him the embarrassment of having to speak to me.

I didn't date anyone for a couple of years after that. It was probably because of the humiliation – and fear that I would give a repeat performance when things got hot and sweaty.

Throughout my early twenties, I had loads of flings – some of the guys were absolutely gorgeous and real sweethearts – but because Fred was always in the back of my mind, I knew I couldn't lead them on. One of them even proposed. It was awful because I hadn't realised he was that serious. Understandably, he was very upset and bewildered when I told him that wasn't what I wanted. I ended our relationship the same night.

Last December, on my twenty-eighth birthday, I met a guy who was tall and slim, with jet-black hair and piercing deep blue eyes. I almost wet my pants when I first laid eyes on him.

It was in a club in Lincoln. A few friends and I were staying in the area (I'm sure you can imagine why I chose Lincoln – it being relatively close to Skegness and all) to celebrate my birthday. I glanced across the room and towards the door when this gorgeous guy walked in. He was wearing a crisp, white long-sleeved T-shirt and a pair of dark blue jeans. His wavy, shoulder-length black hair made his blue eyes stand out like sapphires on a bed of lush black velvet. He was with a couple of friends who were pretty cute too, but not my type.

I could barely take my eyes off him. As he walked up to the bar to get a drink, he turned, gazing around the room until he spotted me. I swear he looked me right in the eyes. It was intense. Ignoring my pals nattering away at our table, I was so completely and utterly mesmerised that I stood up and shook my long dark hair. I was so pleased I'd made an effort that night, wearing my favourite short blue dress. I have to admit, I felt pretty good.

Walking towards the bar, with my hips swaying from side to side, I looked at him and licked my bottom lip. I could tell he was impressed by what he saw. He looked me up and down and, quite indiscreetly, licked his lips too. I had never felt sexual chemistry like it.

I wasn't exactly sure what I had planned to do, or say, but as I approached him, he moved away from the bar and gently placed his hand on the base of my back and gently guided me towards the dance floor.

It was as if fate were lending a hand at the same time because the music changed. No longer the loud thud, thud, thud of the usual club music, the DJ worked his magic to allow a slower, raunchier sound to fill the room. It was perfect for the moment. I couldn't have planned it better if I'd tried.

We moved in perfect unison, with my body fitting perfectly with his. A good mover, he was certainly not afraid to move his hips in time with the sexy rhythm.

It was my idea of heaven. I looked deep into his eyes and imagined that I'd finally found him. As we stood there, gently swaying, our eyes fixed on each other's, he slowly moved in closer until his lips touched mine. A mild electric shock jolted me, and I pulled back momentarily before leaning in for more. It was the most intense kiss of my life.

We were brought back to the present by the sounds of our friends screeching in shock behind us. I could just about hear his friends saying things like 'Go for it, my man'. 'Nice one, mate' and strangely, 'This is your last chance'.

We started laughing, but the lust was too intense for us to control, our lips found each other's again, and we kissed like I'd never been kissed before. I opened my eyes, and he whispered in my ear.

'Shall we get out of here?'

I nodded then quickly waltzed over to where my friends were sitting.

'Look, we're going back to the hotel – Jo, can you crash in Liz and Anna's room?' I asked as I picked up my full-length black coat and handbag.

They were pretty shocked but nodded as they looked him up and down enviously.

I smiled gratefully and rushed to the door, where he was waiting after he'd had a quick word with his friends, who also looked a little shocked at the turn of events. Just as I was about to leave, Jo came running over, 'Kate! Kate!' I turned, and she shoved something into my hand.

'Be careful', she winked, 'These are from Liz'.

When I got outside, I looked in my hand. Condoms. I laughed and discreetly popped them into my handbag. It was then that I noticed it had been snowing. It was freezing, but I didn't care, I barely even felt it because of the chemistry between us. But the way the snow was falling, and leaving a soft white blanket on top of the city, was beautiful. The snow never failed to have that effect on me. I guess it was because I was born in the winter season.

We were lucky to get a cab really quickly, and I reckon we embarrassed the hell out of the poor taxi driver because we couldn't take our hands off each other.

Unfortunately though, as we pulled up outside the hotel, it didn't take long for things to go a bit awry. He suddenly pulled away from me and just held me with an odd look on his face. I couldn't quite figure out what the expression meant.

'Is there something wrong?' I breathed.

'I... I don't even know your name,' he smiled.

'If you tell me yours, I'll tell you mine,' I smiled, thinking how wonderful it would be if he were called Fred.

He grinned cheekily, 'I'm Marc, with a 'C'. It's a pleasure to meet you,' he laughed.

I felt like I was going to explode into a million pieces just by listening to his voice.

Breathing deeply, I said with a smile, 'The pleasure is all mine, I assure you.'

The taxi driver drummed his fingers on the dashboard, reminding us where we were, and Marc smiled, before he looked into my eyes, waiting to hear my name. His eyebrows raised inquisitively.

I would have liked to have told him some totally exotic name like Anastasia, Valentina or Scheherazade but, as I was hoping to see this guy again, I figured telling porkies on the first date was a bit of a no-no, so I said, 'It's Kate. My name's Kate'.

And that's when it happened. The second I mentioned my name – he bolted upright in complete and utter shock.

His mouth fell open, and that strange expression appeared on his face again.

He immediately opened the car door, got out and gently pulled me out after him. He looked so unhappy that I felt like I'd done something wrong.

I just stood motionless as he banged his fists on the top of the taxi and cursed under his breath.

'Hey!' yelled the driver.

'Jesus. Your name's Kate? What am I doing? What have I done?'

I just looked at him, closed my mouth and shrugged my shoulders. They felt heavy.

Confused and shocked, I began to tremble uncontrollably.

'Marc? What's wrong?' I managed to mutter.

He turned and looked so deep into my eyes that I thought I was going to swallow him up. I could have melted.

'I'm so sorry, Kate. This shouldn't have happened. I don't do things like this, and I'm sure you normally don't either. Please forgive me,' then he leaned forward and kissed me. It wasn't like the hot frantic kisses of before. It was different. It was like no other kiss I'd ever had. It was soft, gentle and... strangely loving.

When I eventually opened my eyes, he'd gotten back into the taxi and was zooming off into the distance. I put my finger to my lips and watched as the taillights disappeared. I'd lost all my strength. I was in a daze. That kiss. That amazing kiss.

CHAPTER 3

'Kate. Kate. Are you in there?'

I woke to the sound of Jo's voice and her tapping on the door. Confused, I looked around. I was on the floor in the hotel room.

'Kate – I'm sorry, but I need something from in there,' she giggled quietly as she tapped again on the door.

I stood up and hobbled over, noticing that I was only wearing one shoe.

Opening the door, she whispered, 'I'm sorry sweetheart. I didn't mean to interrupt you and lover boy but... darling! What's the matter? What happened? Oh... God. He didn't hurt you, did he? That... that... bastard!'

I shook my head before bursting into tears.

Half an hour later, after consuming all the contents of the minibar, I was cuddled up in bed with the girls. We were just starting on the booze from the other room. As is usually the case with hotel minibars, though, the contents left much to be desired. One whole bar was barely enough to get a single person drunk, let alone four of us – and we were all up for it. All were feeling desperately sorry for me, while I remained totally dazed and confused. All I kept thinking was 'why?' and 'what on Earth had I done wrong?' But every time I thought about it, I just couldn't work out what it might have been. Everything was hunky-dory until I told him my name. Maybe I should have told him it was Valentina after all. Would it have made a difference? I really didn't know.

'I mean… it was going so well. We were both so into each other, and it wasn't like it had ever been with anyone else. It just seemed so much deeper. I mean, I've never tried to bring a man back to my hotel like that before, it was so out of character for me and then, look what happened.'

'Men can be absolute bastards, sometimes,' said Anna, even though she'd never had a problem with a man in her life. She'd married her childhood sweetheart, John, when she was just nineteen. And he was the world's most adorable guy. He wasn't the brightest spark in the world, but John wouldn't hurt a fly. He was lovely. Everyone adored him.

We all nodded, clinking miniature bottles and downing the last few drops of the alcohol.

Bastards, we all thought.

'You're absolutely bloody right. Bastards. Absolute bloody bastards. All of 'em,' hiccupped Liz, who'd also drank a lot rather at the club earlier, 'I've never never, ever, ever been treated right by one single bloody man. Bastards!'

She was right, though. Even her dad had done a runner, just after she was born. She was 24 and had only had one serious boyfriend – Richard. A total Dick if you ask me. A real two-faced bastard. She was better off without him. Liz was a tad naïve, but to be treated the way she had – it was totally unforgivable.

'Bastard. Just like Richard. Bastard,' she muttered again before bursting into tears.

It's funny how I was the one that was having a crisis, but it was me who ended up doing the consoling.

'There there, Lizzie. I know, I know. Richard's a bastard. I just wish you'd get over the idiot,' I said as I stroked the top of her head.

I guess it didn't really help. Her crying became more intense, and her whole body shuddered uncontrollably, making the bed shake violently. Anna rolled her eyes as if she'd seen it hundreds of times before.

Truth is, she had. We all had. Of course, we were sympathetic, but we'd all seen it coming. We'd warned her about him, but nothing we ever said made the slightest bit of difference. To Liz, Richard had been 'The One'. She had hoped to marry him and have four kids. I shuddered at the thought of anyone having Richard's kids. He didn't deserve them. Liz should have children with someone who worshipped her.

We knew Richard would never settle down. We knew he was a two-timing jerk, who used her for sex whenever he felt the urge.

He had finally 'dumped' her six months earlier. The problem was by how the love rat had done it. He couldn't possibly have let her down gently, with a bouquet of flowers or something like that. Oh no. Richard had to have the last laugh, didn't he? He had to thoroughly humiliate her. Why? We would never know. He was just such an evil man and the way he'd ended their so-called relationship had proved that in more ways than one.

He'd invited her round to his place for a 'romantic, intimate, dinner together'. Liz, being the hopeless romantic she'd always been, took hours to get ready. She bought a new outfit for the occasion. He'd even given her a key to let herself in (first time ever), which she'd done excitedly. Then she'd walked around his enormous penthouse flat calling out his name, looking for him. What she was greeted with hadn't exactly been what she'd been hoping for. She'd actually found him in bed with not one, but two other women. He'd seen her of course; in fact, he'd looked straight at her and continued to have sex while the three of them all laughed drunkenly. What an asshole.

'There's room for one more,' he'd hiccupped, before saying, 'Well... actually this is what I wanted from us, Lizzie, but as you were never up for it, I guess, this is it. You're dumped.'

I mean, can you believe that men even say that anymore? Isn't that what kids say?

As you can imagine, it was taking her quite some time to get over such a humiliating experience. I'd be surprised if she'd ever be able to trust a man again.

It had crossed my mind that Jo hadn't said a word about the 'men are bastards' issue. But then she had no reason to think such a thing. Poor Jo had suffered more than all of us put together. She had experienced something tragic – she had lost her husband to cancer when her daughter was still very young. She'd been totally heartbroken when he'd died. Of course, she'd known it was going to happen; after all, he had been ill for such a long time. But nothing ever prepares you for the loss of the love of your life. And Charles was undoubtedly the love of her life. He had been every-thing to her, and more. Yes, he was a lot older than her, but the age gap had made no difference to their love at all. If anything, it had made it stronger.

It was Charles' illness that had brought me into Jo's life. She had advertised for a nanny to help look after her daughter, Carly when she was just two years old. Jo was twenty-eight, and I was 18. We've been best friends ever since. I helped her cope through her husband's final days and afterwards. The three of us became really close as a result of that awful tragedy.

I guess that night, my crisis wasn't really a crisis at all.

CHAPTER 4

$\mathcal{I}$t was early the following Monday and the snow, which had also fallen in London, had subsided and was replaced by rain, the kind that soaks you from head to toe. Luckily, I had just managed to run down the steps to the tube before it came down really hard, and so I stood, in the dry tube station, waiting for the train that would take me into the city centre to work.

We'd got back from Lincoln the previous afternoon. Poor Liz had been nursing a hangover and had spent much of the train journey running to the toilet to throw up. Fortunately, the rest of us were well enough to look after her and to make sure nobody else tried to get into the bathroom while she heaved and vomited all over the place.

We made sure she'd got home okay. Still living with her mum, we knew she was in good hands.

Anna had phoned John to ask him to pick the rest of us up and take us home.

Jo lived in a lovely big house in Maida Vale with Carly, and I rented their basement flat, which I loved. I'd lived there ever since I'd been their nanny. Jo wanted me to stay there rent-free, which I had done until she no longer needed my services, but when I found another job, I'd insisted that she accepted some kind of rent. I knew she didn't need the money, but it was only right.

Anna lived with John, about ten minutes away from us, and Liz lived in a not-so-nice area a little further afield, so she sometimes stayed with Jo at the weekend.

The train arrived, and as I stepped onto it, someone caught my eye, sitting at the very back. He was reading a newspaper, so I couldn't be sure if it was him or not, but the hair colour was the same, and so was the length. I caught my breath, not knowing what to do. I felt the colour running up my neck to my cheeks. My breath quickened, as did my heartbeat. Marc. What was he doing here? Was it really him? Surely not?

Locating a free seat in the middle, I sat down quickly and just as the train began moving again I turned tentatively, straining to see if it was him or not, but several people were blocking my view of him, making it difficult to make him out. At Paddington, he stood up and started walking in my direction.

Oh, Jesus.

Deciding to be brave, I stood up and turned towards him with a big sexy smile. Only I soon realised it wasn't him. Cringing, I turned back feeling totally embarrassed and then promptly tripped over the briefcase of the person next to me. I fell, smashing my head onto the handrail in front of me.

'Are you alright?' asked the man whose briefcase it was.

'I'm really sorry. Oh shit, you're bleeding. Jesus,' he said as he helped me up and I nodded.

'Yes, yes, I'm fine. No, it wasn't your fault at all,' I mumbled before realising that no, no I wasn't okay. In fact, I wasn't alright at all. And then, of course, I passed out.

oOo

'Kate? Kate? Can you hear me? Jesus, she looks awful. What did you say happened to her? She fell off the tube? No, she fell on the tube. Oh, o...o..k, right.'

I could hear Jo's voice. Where was I? There was an awful smell. I mean really terrible. I couldn't quite place it. It was a really clean smell, but yucky clean. My head throbbed. What the hell? Where the hell was I?

'Jo?' I managed to utter. It didn't half hurt when I spoke though.

'She's awake, Mum.'

I recognised that voice.

'Carly?'

'Shhh, sweetheart. It's okay. Carly and I are here now.'

I opened my eyes. I was in the hospital.

'What the hell happened?' I asked wincing.

'We were hoping you might be able to tell us. The doctor said you fell on the tube – but we're a bit confused, darling. Don't you remember? Mind you, the doctor said you probably wouldn't remember what happened. In fact, he said you might even have mild amnesia from the knock to your head.'

No, she was right. I couldn't remember a thing about being on the tube, except for actually getting on it.

'Miss Robinson? Miss Kate Robinson?' asked a woman in the doorway.

'Yes, this is Kate Robinson,' Jo answered for me.

'Hi, I work at the hospital reception. When you were admitted, a man who said he was responsible for your fall accompanied you. He was really concerned. He waited here until your friends arrived, but had to rush off, so he asked me to give you this and ask you to please call him if you need anything. He was very apologetic. He was really nice,' said the young woman blushing.

She handed Jo the business card and then quickly left the room.

'Paul Walker. Looks like you might have found yourself a boyfriend, Kate,' Jo said, laughing. 'You have a pretty bizarre way of finding men.'

'Paul Walker?' screeched Carly. 'Not THE Paul Walker... the actor,' she added, her eyes wide open with excitement.

'No, sweetheart, sorry to disappoint you, but it says here that he's a web designer.'

I rolled my eyes and shook my head. But it hurt. It really hurt.

A boyfriend? After my little incident with Marc at the weekend, the last thing I wanted was a boyfriend. I'd been put off men for good.

I didn't have to spend much longer at the hospital, so a few hours later I went home with Jo. She made me stay in one of the guest rooms so she could 'mother' me and make sure I was really okay. She'd called the office earlier in the day to let them know what had happened. Everyone was anxious, and they'd even sent a bunch of flowers to the house.

I worked with a great bunch of people at Liberty – a women's monthly magazine. I'd got the job nearly eight years ago, after working for Jo for a few years. Initially, I'd been the office junior, but they soon discovered I had a talent for writing, so I'd been encouraged to write a few articles each month. I loved it.

'Kate, I've run you a nice hot bath. Take your time. There's no rush. We won't bother with dinner until about eight o'clock,' Jo said as she came into the bedroom with some clean pyjamas for me to wear.

'Thanks, Jo, I don't know what I'd do without you.'

'Oh, and Julianne said to take all the time you need to get better.'

'I feel so silly. All I did was fall over, and everyone's rallying around me as if I've just had major surgery or something,' I sighed gratefully.

'Yes, but it was a bad fall. You got a concussion, for goodness' sake. Enjoy the attention while it lasts,' she winked, 'now get in that bath and relax.'

A lovely warm bath was exactly what I needed, and Jo's bathroom was absolute heaven. It was like a vast Roman room with massive circular pillars and a gorgeous roll-top bath, which stood in the centre. I sank down into the water, noticing that she'd put some of her favourite (and expensive) bubble bath in it. It wasn't until the bubbles enveloped me, that I realised how achy I actually was. The hot water began to work its magic, and I slowly started feeling (semi) alive again. I closed my eyes and let my mind wander. Naturally, my thoughts took me to Fred, and I smiled as I imagined him lying in the bath opposite me. Just the idea made my body tingle delicately. I started thinking about what he'd look like now. A thought which naturally led me to Marc.

Marc with a 'C'. Marc, what a gorgeous guy he was. I had come so close to spending a memorable night with an extraordinary man. It could have been the most unforgettable night ever. But then I suppose it was the most unforgettable night ever, just for all the wrong reasons. If only. God, there were too many bloody 'if onlys' in my life. I should have known really. He was too perfect for anything good to happen. The ones who look perfect never are.

Apart from Fred, of course. I bet he looked perfect and would always look perfect. Fred... my personal Adonis. I smiled dreamily.

'A penny for your thoughts,' said a voice in the doorway.

I opened my eyes to find Jo coming into the bathroom.

'Is everything okay? Do you need anything?'

'No, I don't think so, thanks. This is bliss. Just what I needed.'

'So what were you thinking about, just then? By the look on your face, I'd say it was a man.'

I laughed, 'How did you know I was thinking about a man?'

She came and sat down on the edge of the bath. 'Sit forward, and I'll wash your back for you. Well, you just had that dreamy look on your face. I've seen it a million times before, and I think it's about time you finally told me, especially considering we've been best friends for God knows how many years. Neither of us should have any secrets,' she laughed, gently sponging my back and shoulders, easing away the stiffness.

'I'll bet you have a few secrets, don't you?' I asked, turning to look at her.

Laughing, she squeezed out the sponge and handed it to me, 'Everyone has secrets, don't they?'

'Probably. But if you tell me your secret, I'll tell you mine.'

We laughed at the silliness of our conversation.

'Okay, I'll go first,' I said, clearing my throat nervously, knowing it was the time to finally tell her about Fred.

'I'm in love with a guy who I haven't seen since I was twelve years old.'

'Everyone has a childhood crush, darling. That's hardly classified material is it?' she laughed as she handed me the sponge while I lay back down in the water.

'No, this isn't a childhood crush. This is so much more than that. I was on holiday with Mum and Dad, in Skegness, and I saw this boy. He just made my heart flip and my stomach go wild with butterflies. It was love at first sight. I just know it. I know I was only twelve and he must have been thirteen or so, but I just know he felt the same way,' I garbled.

'What's this boy's name?' she asked, fascinated.

'That's the thing, you see; that's the problem. I have absolutely no idea. We saw each other for a few minutes, and then I had to go. It broke my heart. And… and it's never been the same. All I've ever dreamed about is seeing him again and being with him for the rest of my life.'

Jo looked at me, her eyes becoming strangely watery.

'Wow, now that is romantic. I guess he must be your soul mate,' she whispered, rubbing her eyes.

'You mean, you don't think I'm silly and a complete idiot?'

'Of course not. Yes, it's rather odd but strangely beautiful. I think it's wonderful. Wouldn't it be amazing if you found him? Why don't we try to find him?'

I shook my head, 'No. It's useless. I don't even know his name, although I have taken to calling him, Fred.'

Jo looked a tad confused, 'Fred?'

'Well, he needed a name. I got fed up of thinking of him as 'the boy without a name', and Right Said Fred was playing when I first saw him,' I shrugged.

She shrugged her shoulders too. 'Fred it is, then'.

We smiled at each other as I attempted to get out of the bath without my head throbbing.

'Now it's your turn,' I said, facing her as she handed me a towel.

She nodded, 'Okay then. Here goes. I think I might be gay.'

I grabbed the towel so quick that I nearly dropped it into the water.

'Did you say gay?' I whispered.

She nodded her head, looking deathly serious.

'Wow – th… that's some secret,' I said, wrapping the towel as tightly as possible around myself. 'That's kinda sudden, isn't it?'

And then her face suddenly broke out into this massive grin from ear to ear, and she began laughing. In fact, she laughed so much that she fell off the side of the bath.

'You're, you're j...joking, aren't you?' I asked, feeling like the world's biggest imbecile.

She pointed at me, barely managing to speak for giggling, nodding.

'I can't believe you actually fell for that!'

I nodded, an embarrassed smile creeping across my face. 'Yeah, yeah, I know, I know.'

'The way you grabbed the towel. God, I think I'm gonna pee myself. It's so funny,' she giggled as she climbed up from the floor.

I shook my head, wincing from the pain, and tried not to laugh as I walked out of the room, hearing nothing but her incessant shrieks behind me.

That night, as I lay in bed, listening to one of Jo's soothing meditation CDs, I began thinking about the day's events. I couldn't believe I'd made such a fool of myself on the train to work. How I'd managed to end up with concussion was way beyond me. I wish I could remember. Never mind, I guess I'd never know unless I rang that guy who had helped me to the hospital. What was his name? Paul something or other. But did it really matter? Probably not.

Then, as usually happened when I was nodding off to sleep, my mind began to wander back to Fred. The music calmed me as I thought back to that fantastic day, sixteen years ago, and I imagined how he'd probably changed into the most gorgeous tall, dark and handsome hunk.

So Jo finally knew about him. It hadn't been at all difficult telling her. I thought she'd laugh herself silly and tell me how stupid I really was, but instead, she thought it was romantic. It was so strange that after all this time of being her closest friend, I'd received a completely different response to what I'd expected.

It proved to me that I could trust her with anything. I could tell her anything. Why I never did, I've no idea. I felt silly for not doing it before.

I was so completely relaxed that my head no longer throbbed and I knew I was on the verge of sleep when the morning's events suddenly came to me.

I thought I'd seen Marc and I'd tripped over something. I must have been knocked out. God. How embarrassing. And then, at the last second, I'd realised it wasn't even him. God, how humiliating.

I tried to forget all about the awful incident, made somewhat easier by the gentle sounds of a waterfall and exotic birds chirping. Sounds that eventually sent me drifting off into that beautiful world of dreams.

CHAPTER 5

'... *T*hat's right, Syd, Twinkie and Perky have started fighting. No. No, it's the first time. Yes. Yes. No. Boots used to have a similar problem with Pepper...'

A week later, I sat in Julianne's large office, waiting for her to finish a phone call with her local vet.

The managing editor of Liberty was a bit of a cat person. Okay maybe 'a bit' was an understatement. I was actually beginning to think she collected them. Currently, she had thirteen. Yes, that's right. Thirteen cats. And they were just the ones at her penthouse apartment. There were four more in the office (yes, I know, four cats in a London office!). Whenever Julianne interviewed potential new employees, she would always stipulate that they must be keen on cats or it just wouldn't work.

She was such a good client that she was on a casual first-name basis with the vet, Syd. He'd been to the office a few times to give Beckham, Kylie, Johnny and Clooney their shots, so we all knew him quite well. He was always amused at our choice of names for the cats. Everyone in the office was obsessed with celebrities, so it was only apt for these beautiful creatures to be named after their idols. As Julianne considered them to be the office pets, we had all been involved in naming them.

'That'll be fantastic, Syd. Are you sure it's no problem? Excellent. I'll see you around eight tonight, then. Err, why don't I cook you dinner then, as... as a thank you? Yes? Excellent. I look forward to seeing you. Yes, you too, Syd. Bye. Bye.' Julianne slowly replaced the receiver, a smile creeping onto her face.

'He's coming for dinner,' she squealed.

It was common knowledge that she had the biggest crush on Syd, but because he had only been divorced a short time, she had wanted to give him time to come to terms with it before asking him out.

'That's great,' I said, 'you finally decided to do it, then?'

Julianne nodded enthusiastically as Beckham dived onto my lap and began nuzzling my face. I gently put him on the floor and watched him walk around the desk and attempt to do the same to Julianne.

'Who's my beautiful baby Beckhams then?' she said, cuddling the cat before continuing.

'Yes. I finally decided to do something about it. Carpe Diem! Seize the day!' she shouted so loudly and punched the air that it made both me and Beckham jump.

Had she gone completely raving mad?

Standing and putting Beckham back on the floor, she turned to me and laughed, 'I watched that old film with Robin Williams, Dead Poet's Society, last night and it made me think. I mean, it really made me think. I decided: why wait? We only live once, and it's such a short life, so we should do exactly what we really want to do. Don't you agree?'

I nodded, still a bit confused, but I happily went along with whatever she was saying.

'So, that's why I decided to finally ask Syd round for dinner,' she smiled, looking decidedly pleased with herself.

'That's great, Julianne, it really is. But what exactly does Dead Poets Society have to do with this, though?'

'Oh, never mind – it's not important. The important thing is that I've decided to take the bull by the horns a bit more often, to make more opportunities for myself... and others. Which is why I wanted to see you this morning.'

I raised my eyebrows.

'You've been writing articles for us for a few years now, and I think it's about time that you have your own column. What do you think?'

My mouth must have dropped to the floor, and my eyebrows shot to the ceiling because she began laughing.

'I'm guessing you're quite pleased with the prospect, Kate?' she asked, as she picked up a pink watering can and began pouring water into the large green plant in the corner of her office. Funny, I'd always thought it was plastic.

'Pleased… pleased? God no – I'm ecstatic. Julianne, thank you, thank you, thank you!' I yelled, jumping around her office. Beckham looked at me in total disgust and belted out through the cat flap in the door.

'You're welcome. Really, it was about time you were given the opportunity to shine. I've always enjoyed your style of writing, and with Josie leaving us to go to Australia – I thought you were the best woman for her job.'

My face began to ache from the enormous grin I couldn't get rid of. I could hardly believe it. I'd always loved working at Liberty, but to have my own column? Wow. I mean, WOW!

'We have an editorial meeting this afternoon, so we can discuss content then. I'm glad you're pleased, Kate,' she said warmly as she stood and started to put on her pale pink Chanel jacket.

'Right, I'm off into town to buy a new outfit for tonight,' she winked, 'I'll see you after lunch.'

Julianne certainly wasn't your average editor in chief. We laughed after watching The Devil Wears Prada, because even though she is a huge fan of Prada, she couldn't be more different from that bitch, played so well by Meryl Streep. Julianne was the exact opposite, and we loved her for it.

The rest of the day was spent in a daze. I had my own monthly column. It was so bizarre because I hadn't seen it coming at all. A marvellous surprise. Thank you, Dead Poets Society – whatever you are.

The editorial meeting had been great, especially considering it was the first time I was really a part of it from the inside. Usually, I sat in on it just to be told precisely what they wanted me to write. For example, in recent months I'd been told to interview (by

phone) a couple of women who presided over some boring soci-
eties that were hardly worth mentioning in Liberty, but for various
reasons we had to include them – I think one of their husbands
was friends with the director or something like that. It was all
political, really.

Before that I'd had to write about the opening of a flashy new
boutique in Knightsbridge – I didn't even get the chance to go. I
had to do the interview by phone, while one of our photographers
took advantage of the free champagne.

Most of the time, I'd be given press releases and be asked to re-
write them. But now, now I had my own column. Whoopee! Of
course, we'd discussed possibilities for future editions, but Julianne
had pretty much thrown the ball in my court. Everyone was keen
on my idea to focus the next few articles on some of the more
unusual beauty treatments that were available these days. The
possibility of a few free treatments had, of course, crossed my
mind before I'd brought up the subject – why not take advantage?

Researching online, I'd jotted down the names and telephone
numbers of a couple of places and then sat down and tried to think
of an appropriate way to approach them.

'Good afternoon. I'm calling from Liberty magazine. I'd like a
free treatment so that I can review it please?'

Didn't quite have the right ring to it. I tried a few others, but
they weren't quite right either, so I settled on 'Good afternoon. I'm
Kate Robinson from Liberty magazine. I'm currently reviewing
beauty treatments and would like to know if you would like to
feature...' By the time I'd got that far they were practically begging
to be involved.

So far, I was booked in for a day of Thalassotherapy treatments
at a nearby spa, a day at a new sports, fitness and relaxation centre
and a free Chinese massage with a fabulous new masseur who had
just got off the plane from China.

I couldn't believe my luck.

'Good morning, Miss Robinson. I'm Giselle Noiseau. Welcome to our Thalassotherapy centre. I do hope you enjoy your day. If you have any questions, please don't hesitate to let me know. If you'd like to go through to the changing rooms, please change into your swimsuit. Here is a bag for your belongings, a key for your locker, some slippers and a robe. And finally, here is your schedule for the day. Have fun. Just ask for me at reception, if you need me. I shall see you later.'

Clearly, Giselle was a very busy lady, so I simply nodded, smiled and said very little, anxious to get started on the pampering session. So, after changing into my bathing costume and placing my belongings into the bag and locker provided, I headed out to find what exciting treatments beckoned.

Glancing at my schedule sheet, I read 9am - Treatment Room 5.

Wandering around the vast, peaceful centre, that resembled an enormous swimming pool, with its beautiful pale mosaic tiles and soothing white ceilings, I eventually found room number five. It wasn't quite nine o'clock, and about seven other people were waiting outside. No-one said anything. Not a look, not a smile, not a word. What a lovely bunch.

A few obviously weren't new to this Thalassotherapy lark, armed with novels or magazines; they sat on posh white leather designer chairs, oblivious to everyone else, waiting for their treatments to begin. I peered around the door of Treatment Room 5 and saw a small swimming pool. I hoped it was heated.

I turned back around and looked at the bored faces of the others as I sat down into the oddly uncomfortable chair. If this was supposed to be exciting; why did they all look so miserable?

There was a girl who looked to be about thirteen, reading a rather thick hard-backed novel. She looked frightfully upper class, with her open robe revealing an Armani swimsuit and Versace slippers (I work at Liberty, it's my job to know what people are wearing). Her long dark brown hair was immaculately tied back in a perfect French braid. She stretched out her long, slender legs, accentuating her sickeningly perfect figure. I self-consciously pulled my feet under my seat and pulled the robe tightly around my stomach. I know my body was pretty good, but compared to that young Megan Fox lookalike, I felt positively frumpy.

Sitting next to her was a short, balding man, with a permanent grimace on his face. He also had a book in his hand but didn't bother to open it. Instead, he did nothing but stare at the many mosaics opposite, with an occasional glance at the clock on the wall above me.

Utterly oblivious to everybody else were an elderly couple, who sat bickering about something or other. I couldn't understand a word, as they babbled in Russian. He was trying to read a newspaper and she kept pushing it to one side. It was easy to tell the couple were wealthy – both were dripping with gold, even though the receptionist had pointed out to me that jewellery should not be worn during treatments.

A middle-aged gay couple stood by the entrance to the treatment room. I imagined they were in the 'honeymoon period' of their relationship, as they appeared to be unable to keep their hands to themselves – and clearly were not worried what we thought about it, either.

Lastly, there was a somewhat normal-looking woman of about 35. She sat next to me, fidgeting with her fingers nervously. I had noticed her in the changing room and had nodded good morning. She'd smiled back but not said a word. She was very short but pretty, with short blonde curly hair and a curvy figure. She was clearly nervous about something.

Finally – dead on nine o'clock, a young man appeared, hurrying towards us. He clapped his hands and smiled, revealing the most perfect set of gleaming white teeth I've ever seen.

'Allo, my name is Renée. Please follow me, but first, remove your robes and slippers and valk through ze small vater pool by ze door, to make sure ze feet are clean. Ve zertainly don't vant any grime getting into ze pool!'

I stepped into the water, which was freezing cold and quickly out again the other side, silently cursing.

Once everybody was inside Treatment Room 5, Renée closed the large thick glass door behind him.

'Pleaze place your swimming caps on your 'eads and zen hop into ze pool. Ze water is lovely and varm.'

He was right, the water was positively divine – like soft, warm milk. I sank down, looking forward to some form of relaxation, when Renée suddenly yelled, 'Run! Run! I vant you to run as fast as you can all ze way around ze pool, okay? GO, GO, GO!'

I got such a fright that I bolted as fast as I could, overtaking everyone.

"Okay, miss? Miss? Vhen I say run as fast as you can, I prefer zat you don't create a tidal vave, no? Okay?'

I slowed considerably and mouthed 'sorry', hoping no-one else had really noticed my faux pas. Well, he had said run fast.

We carried on running for a few more laps until he finally slowed us down and, eventually, we stood still.

'Now, I vant you to put one leg on ze side of ze pool. Yes, yes, that's it, that's it!' he yelled, clapping his hands as he walked around the edge of the pool, checking on everyone's progress.

Fortunately, I was relatively fit, after starting aerobics quite a few months before, but I could see the elderly couple were having some problems with this exercise. Renée gave them a hand but not before the poor woman nearly drowned after her husband accidentally used her head as a grab rail.

Another twenty minutes later and Renée clapped his hands excitedly, telling us the class was over and we could get out of the water. I allowed everyone else to exit ahead of me, so I could enjoy a quick relaxing swim before my next 'treatment'. After this, I wasn't sure what to expect.

'Tout vite, miss, please. Quickly, quickly,' he clapped again. Somehow he always managed to make me jump. I shot out of the pool, afraid of getting into trouble with Colgate there.

Checking my schedule, I noticed I was immediately due in Treatment Room 6. Next to this was the name Renée. Joy.

Quickly grabbing my things, I skipped into the next room, not forgetting to splash my feet and flip flops into the ice-cold water by the door first.

Inside this room was another pool, smaller than the first. The same group of people and Renée stood staring at me with raised eyebrows.

Mumbling my apologies, I rushed down the three steps into the water. Again, it was delightfully warm. Before anyone had the chance to warn me, I bashed my leg against a metal object under the water.

'Ouch.'.

'If you were ere a minute ago, you would have eard me tell you to be careful of ze bars in ze vater, miss,' he smiled falsely.

What an ass. Him, not me.

I smiled back and heard the lithe young model to my side, tut. I turned and looked at her in disbelief and she rolled her eyes, shaking her head at me. She probably fancied him.

'Everybody, please face ze vall in front of you. Hold on to ze bars by your side and ve vill begin,' he gestured, walking around the pool and turning on the jets.

Erupting in a mass of bubbles, the jet streams began their work of pummelling each and everyone's bodies. Renée reached into the water to adjust the position of the jets.

'Okay, now ve start. I vant you to turn to your side, so zat ze jets push into your side. Now move ze body up and down, up and down, up and down. Ze jets should massage every part of ze side of your body, okay? Up and down, up and down. Zat's it. Yes, yes. Now move your arms, so you massage ze arms and shoulders. Up and down, up and down, up and down. Yes, yes, yes.'

Clearly, he was starting to get a bit excited. I noticed that every time he said 'up and down', he focused on the girl beside me. I sneaked a look, and she smiled sexily back at him. God, she was only about thirteen for goodness' sake. Paedophile.

Unfortunately, he saw that I'd noticed, so he bent down in front of me.

'Oh dear, miss, I don't zink your jet is in ze right position. Let me move it for you,' and he tweaked the jet so that it caused me a little problem.

Firstly, it was now in the perfect position to virtually remove my swimsuit without any assistance from me. Every time he told us to turn around or to the side, I was forced to hold on to it for dear life. It was rather embarrassing. I know very well that he'd done it on purpose, as he kept smirking. As did she. However, I did manage to get my revenge on her a few moments later, when we had to face the jet so that it focused on the lower stomach area...

I certainly didn't do it on purpose, but it pummelled my bladder to such an extent that I peed myself. It was only a little bit. At first, I was totally and utterly embarrassed, as you could see a few yellow bubbles bobbling around within the water. I tried to ignore them until I noticed that the bubbles were headed straight for the pompous little cow. I tried hard not to laugh, especially when she spotted it and couldn't get away from it. What a lovely warm feeling.

As the session came to an end, I found myself hoping that I wasn't in for any further 'treatments' with Renée and his side-kick. Fortunately, when I'd gotten out of the water and checked my timetable, I didn't have anything to do for an hour – during which time, I could use any of the spa's facilities. First, I popped into the shower to rinse off any remnants of pee.

Wrapped in my robe, I decided to have a wander around the spa. The only thing I really disliked about it was the fact that it was so quiet. Some meditation music wouldn't have gone amiss. I peeked into a few of the rooms, noticing odd-looking large baths full of dials and knobs. There were tiny little rooms for massages, a large airy room for T'ai Chi, a gym (which I shied away from because Renée was in there, with his little friend), swimming pools, Jacuzzi, Turkish bath, sauna and, thankfully, a bar. That's more like it.

I decided to have a small fruit smoothie (they didn't serve real drinks) and jot down some notes for my article while I waited for session number three, which was called 'Jet Shower' and was with someone called Cherie.

Cherie turned out to be a vivacious American girl with love for sadomasochism. At least that's the conclusion I came to, after our little tête a tête in Treatment Room 10. I made sure I got there well in time for my session. I didn't want to be frowned upon again by anyone I'd already met (or not met, as the case was) that morning. I stood waiting outside the door; I would have sat, but there was no chair. I also noticed that the glass door was thicker and not transparent like the others had been. Also – I was the only person waiting this time, leading me to believe I was in for a much more enjoyable experience.

Out of nowhere bounded a tiny, yet butch young woman. 'Well, hello there. You must be Miss Robinson?' she yelled as if I were standing a mile away.

I nodded, newly apprehensive and a little scared of what this woman was going to be doing to me.

She clearly saw the fear on my face and laughed.

'Oh, silly. I'm not gonna hurt you, y' know? Come on in. There we go. Now let me just close this here door behind us. Now, if you'd like to take off your swimsuit, we can start up this invigorating jet shower. It does wonders for your skin. You'll lurve it. I assure you,' she hollered as I stood, cowering in the corner of the room.

Had she told me to remove my swimsuit? Had I heard right? Surely not.

'I'm sorry, err Cherie, did you tell me to take off my swimsuit?'

'That's right honey. Just whip it off, and we can begin,' she winked.

Oh, God. A butch woman was telling me to take off my swimsuit and then she was winking at me. I kept thinking to myself, be brave, be brave. It'll make for great reading in the Liberty article. After all, that was the reason I was there in the first place.

I slowly and tentatively removed my one piece.

'That's it, honey. I've seen it all before. Don't worry. I ain't gonna bite ya,' she winked again as if biting was the first thing on her mind. Yeauch. God, give me strength.

'Right, if you'll just stand at the end of the room there. That's it. Face me. Good girl.'

I stood, butt naked, at the end of a strange long room that was completely tiled – floor, walls and ceiling, and I looked towards her. It seemed to happen in slow motion from then. Cherie pulled out a considerable hose and aimed it right at me and turned it on. Freezing cold water shot out, hitting my feet, legs and stomach.

'Aargh!'

'Don't worry, honey. It'll only be cold for a few seconds,' she shouted above the sound of the gushing water.

The water soon became warmer and, every now and again, Cherie would yell at me to turn to my side or to face her or to face away from her. Standing totally naked being hosed down by a butch woman with a fully flexed fire hose, has got to top my list of most humiliating experiences ever.

It may be particularly suitable for circulation and cellulite – but I'd rather stick with the orange peel, thank you very much.

I was beginning to believe that the staff of this place had neglected to be told that I was a Liberty magazine reporter and should be treated with the utmost respect and given the best treatments possible. After a few more similar experiences, I was glad to be back in the changing rooms, putting my clothes on, to get the hell out of there. I understood why that other woman had looked a tad nervous, earlier.

Admittedly though, my skin did feel invigorated.

Naturally, my colleagues were later thoroughly entertained by my encounters with Cherie and Renée, and no, I doubt I'll ever live that one down. But the upside to the whole experience is that Julianne was over the moon with my article.

'I absolutely love it, Kate. It's fantastic. It's got exactly the right amount of humour and that perfect personal touch. Your column is going to be a hit with our readers. I can feel it.'

And it was.

I had lots of response from readers who shared my sense of humour, some even wrote to tell us about similar experiences they'd had. We ended up writing a 'spin-off series', interviewing some of the readers and visiting spas all over the south. Our readership increased by twenty-five per cent after only two months. Liberty was becoming a huge hit.

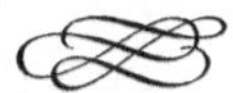

CHAPTER 7

I didn't think my life could get any better. My career had blossomed so much that even Fred couldn't keep my thoughts away from my next article. Until that is, the most bizarre, life-changing, jaw-dropping thing happened to me. Me!

Lying in bed, indulging in a much-needed lie-in one Saturday in mid-May, there was a knock on the door. Yawning, I sat up and looked at the clock. 9am.

'Is that you, Jo?' I yelled, 'Come on in!'

But there was a knock again.

Begrudgingly climbing out of bed, I pulled on my fluffy pink dressing gown and matching slippers. 'Hang on. I'm coming!'

I opened the door to be greeted by a man in a suit facing the other way.

'Hello?'

He turned around, and I actually gasped, out loud. He was easily one of the most gorgeous men I'd ever seen. He wasn't exactly tall, but taller than me, with cropped dark brown hair and brown eyes. He wore an expensive dark blue suit with a pale blue shirt and tie. Armani, I think.

'Good morning. I'm looking for Miss Kate Robinson.'

His voice was deep and smooth. The kind of voice you could listen to for hours.

So lost for words, I completely forgot that I'd just got out of bed and must have looked hideously terrible.

'Are you Miss Robinson?'

I nodded, 'Err…ye..yes, that's me. Kate R….R…Rob…in..son.'

'May I come in, Miss Robinson?'

I managed to compose myself before asking with a smile, 'And you are?' just as I realised I'd yet to brush my teeth. I closed my mouth quickly, not wanting him to get a burst of morning breath.

'I'm sorry, Miss Robinson, I should have introduced myself. My name is Tony Fonseca, I'm a solicitor with Fonseca & King. I'm terribly sorry to bother you at the weekend, but I have some important news for you. May I come in?'.

Curious what business a solicitor could possibly have with me, I let him in. Suddenly utterly embarrassed at the state I was in, I wrapped my dressing gown tightly around my waist and blushed.

'If you'd like to make yourself comfortable, I'll just go and change,' I said, leading him into my cosy little lounge.

'Thank you.'

'I won't be long.'

I dashed into the bedroom, throwing open the wardrobe doors, ripping off my dressing gown and falling over my pyjama bottoms as I tried to get them off. Not wanting to look like I'd made too much of an effort, I slipped on a pair of Tommy Hilfiger jeans, my favourite white Hard Rock Café T-shirt and brown boots.

Rushing into the bathroom, I scrubbed my face and teeth, gave my hair a quick brush, threw it up into a messy ponytail and then applied mascara and eye-liner as well as a few squirts of perfume.

I stopped for a moment, checked myself in the mirror before taking a few deep breaths. Then I walked back to the lounge.

'Sorry about that.'

'That's quite alright, Miss Robinson, no need to apologise,' he said with a smile.

'Would you like a cup of coffee? Or tea?' I offered, realising I hadn't had anything to drink yet.

'A cup of tea would be lovely, thank you.'

He followed me into the kitchen.

'May I?' he asked, pulling out a stool at the breakfast bar.

'Of course, please sit down. How do you like your tea, Mr Fonseca?'

He looked up; clearly impressed I hadn't forgotten his name already.

'White, no sugar, thank you.'

'Well, Miss Robinson...'

'Please, call me Kate. Nobody has called me Miss Robinson since I was at school, apart from that time I was stopped by the police when I...' I stopped myself and blushed, 'just call me Kate.'

'Okay, Kate. Please call me Tony. I'm sure you're wondering why I'm here. Well, I'm saddened to inform you that your uncle, Sam, has recently passed away.'

'My Uncle Sam? But I didn't even know I had an Uncle Sam. You've come to tell me that? That's a little odd, isn't it?' I asked, passing him his tea.

'He specified in his will that when you be told of his death, he be called 'Uncle Sam'. He is not, in fact, your real uncle. His real name is Samuel Jorge Rui Encarnação Pinto Oliveira Simões. Apparently, he knew you when you were a child.'

I didn't think I'd ever heard such a ridiculously long name and it certainly wasn't even vaguely familiar. I had absolutely no idea who this man was, and I said as much to Tony.

'Well, Kate, he obviously knew you well, because he has left you his entire estate.'

'I'm s..s..s..orry. He's left me his entire estate? Didn't he have any family of his own?'

Tony shook his head sadly.

'I'm afraid not. He was never married. His will indicates that almost everything he owns should be left to you.'

Tony placed his briefcase on the kitchen worktop and pulled out a folder. He stood and turned to look at me.

'Kate, Mr Simões has left you his house in the Azores, his apartments in New York and Toronto, his resort in Skegness...'

'Wh..at?'

My eyes opened wide, 'Of course. Uncle Sam. Now I remember. We used to stay at his resort in Skegness. He looked after me a few times when Mum and Dad wanted to go out on their own.

And he often kept Mum company when Dad went fishing. Yes, even before I was born, Mum and Dad knew him. God, how could I forget him? He was such a sweet man. Hang on a sec. If Mum knew him before I was born, and he's leaving all this to me,' I gasped at the thought.

'What if? What if he's really my father?'

Okay, perhaps I was a bit melodramatic, but you never know. Why else would he leave me everything he owns?

'I don't know, Kate. Perhaps that's a question for your mother. But perhaps you shouldn't jump to conclusions just yet.'

'How did he die?' I asked.

'Cancer.'

Tears welled in my eyes as I thought about the poor man, whose apparent only source of happiness was the odd time spent with a little girl and her parents so many years ago.

'But I haven't finished yet, Kate. As I was saying, he's left you the house in the Azores, the penthouse in New York, the apartment in Toronto, the resort in Skegness and the amount of,' he glanced down at his paperwork, 'just over a hundred and forty-seven million pounds sterling.'

The room began to sway, I heard a crash, something warm and wet dripped down my chest and then...

'Kate? Kate?'

I opened my eyes to find an angel looking down at me.

'Are you alright, Kate?' the angel said.

I felt as if I was dreaming.

'I'm rich, aren't I?' I asked as I slowly stood up before sitting down in the little sofa in the corner of the room.

'Yes,' he laughed, 'you're a very wealthy woman. Are you feeling alright? Can I get you something to drink? Perhaps you need something a little stronger than tea?'

I nodded with a grin.

'I don't have anything, though, I really need to go shopping. Could you pop next door and call Jo for me? It's okay, she owns this flat. She's my best friend. I'd really like her to be here. Plus, she'll have something strong to drink,' I said in a slightly giddy tone.

Tony stood up, nodding, and went out the front door.

I sat up and noticed that I had tea down my favourite T-shirt.

'Oh, shit.'

Jumping up, I grabbed a towel and began frantically rubbing at the stain before realising that I could now afford to buy millions of T-shirts just like it. I stopped rubbing and started laughing.

Within minutes, Jo and Tony walked back into the kitchen.

'What's going on, Kate? Are you alright? And why do you need something strong to drink so early in the day? It's not even 10 yet… and why are you laughing?'

'T-Tony, te.., tell her, please.'

Half an hour later, Jo and I were both drinking brandy. Tony, sensibly, stuck to the tea.

'I can't believe it. It's just so surreal, isn't it? I'm a millionaire. Kate Robinson, millionaire. Do you think it sounds right?'

Jo nodded, 'Of course it sounds right. It was meant to be.'

'Well, while the two of you come to terms with all this, I'd better leave you to it. Kate, we obviously have some paperwork to attend to, shall I come back later today or tomorrow? I'm here until Monday morning, then I'm flying to New York. What suits you?'

Jo answered for me. 'Why don't you come back later, Tony, and we'll have a celebratory dinner. We'd love you to stay for that, wouldn't we Kate?'

I nodded, 'Absolutely, that would be fantastic. If you come round here say, about 5.30 and when we've sorted out the paper-work, we'll go upstairs to eat.'

A warm smile spread across his face, 'That would be lovely, thank you. I'll see you at half past five, then. Don't get up. I'll see myself out.'

He shook my hand, then Jo's, picked up his briefcase and was gone.

Jo looked and me, and we both shrieked with laughter.

'You're rich, you're rich!'

'I'm rich, I'm rich!' I yelled back, clinking our brandy glasses together.

CHAPTER 8

*J*o threw a dinner party that evening, inviting Anna and John, Liz, Julianne and her new man Syd (yes, they were officially a couple).

One of those rare people who could concoct a delicious meal from the sparsest of ingredients, Jo was a real whiz in the kitchen and that evening managed to create the most delicious prawn roulade, followed by chicken à la king (Jo loved to 'play' with 70s recipes) with one of her traditional twists and finally, the pièce de la resistance, Baked Alaska. She was amazing. Truly amazing.

A few bottles of champagne had already been polished off by the time we'd gotten to the dessert, and most of the conversation had revolved around my staggering news.

'So, tell us, Tony, how did Kate become lucky enough to have you as the solicitor handling Uncle Sam's estate?' Jo asked as she lazily leaned over to re-fill everyone's glasses.

'No, Carly, darling, a half glass of champagne is more than enough for you,' she winked at her daughter, who stood up and said she'd had enough adult talk for one night, anyway.

'I'm going to watch TV in my room,' she leaned over and kissed my cheek after kissing her mum. 'Congratulations, Kate. Good-night, everyone.' She was such a sweet kid. I felt genuinely proud to have had a small hand in her upbringing.

Everyone mumbled their 'night nights' as she shuffled her feet out of the room.

'Sorry, Tony. Go on,' said Jo.

'That's alright. I'm actually Portuguese myself. I moved to the States to study law, and I now work between there and the UK. Samuel Simões was looking for a solicitor based in New York and London, who could speak Portuguese,' he answered.

'But Uncle Sam spoke perfect English,' I said.

'Yes he did, but he wanted someone that could speak Portuguese to handle the estate after he passed away, particularly to help you deal with things in the Azores. He assumed that you would at least visit the house there, before deciding whether to keep or sell it. In either case, you'll need my help. Portuguese bureaucracy isn't the easiest to deal with, especially if you can't speak the language,' he said, as he took a small sip of his champagne.

'So, you'll be visiting the Azores? Wow, how exciting,' giggled Liz. 'You're so lucky. I've never even been abroad, I haven't even got a clue where the Azores is – are I mean – is... whatever,' she slurred.

'I haven't had the chance to even think about anything, yet, but yes, of course, I'll be going over. Why don't you come with me? In fact, why don't you all come with me? On me, of course. That'll be fantastic. A holiday for my closest pals. What do you reckon? Please say yes.'

Eyebrows rose inquisitively.

'I'm totally and utterly completely serious. We'll have a fabulous time. Say yes. All of you say yes!'

'Yes, yes yes!' shouted Liz at the top of her voice, giggling and almost falling off her chair.

'Well, it goes without saying that Carly and I would absolutely love to come,' winked Jo.

'Kate, darling. I would love nothing better than to join you in the Azores, but I don't think I'll be able to, what with work and everything. And who'd look after all my pussy cats?' breathed Julianne.

'Oh go on, Jules. I'd be happy to look after them. At least you know they're in good hands. You could do with a holiday,' offered Syd as he gently kissed her cheek and rubbed her back.

'Yes, come on, Julianne, just for a week or two. I'm sure we can work something out at the office. That's what the assistant editors are for, aren't they? To fill in for you, every now and again?' I coaxed.

'You know, you're absolutely right. Okay, I will. I will come with you. But only if it really isn't a problem to take care of my harem of cats, Syd?'

He reassured her with another kiss and a loving smile, and she beamed at everyone around the table.

'So, what about you two,' I said, looking at Anna and John, who smiled shyly.

'That's really sweet of you, Kate, but we couldn't. We couldn't expect you to pay for our holiday,' he answered, gulping down what was left of his can of lager.

'John,' I shouted, 'I've just inherited millions, for goodness' sake! The least I can do is treat you to a holiday. Come on. Please come. It just wouldn't be the same without the two of you. You must come. I won't take no for an answer,' I decided.

Anna jumped up from her chair, holding her glass high, 'Here's to Kate – the best, most generous pal anyone could ever wish for. Congratulations, Kate – and thank you,' she yelled. Everybody followed suit, standing up and clinking glasses, laughing and giggling and looking forward to an impromptu holiday in the Portuguese sun.

'What on Earth is going on?' asked Carly, rushing into the dining room wearing a pair of girlie pink pyjamas, 'What's all the noise about? I'm trying to watch Gossip Girl, and I can't hear a word... AT ALL?'

'Here, Carly, have a drop more champagne – we're celebrating going on holiday. You're all coming on holiday to the Azores with me,' I giggled as I handed her a drop more of the delicious liquid, which she took and sipped sensibly.

'Cool! When are we going?' she asked.

Jo tutted with a smile, 'Always the eager teenager.'

I told her we needed to find a time that suited all of us, so we weren't entirely sure yet.

'Don't worry, we'll give you plenty of time to pack,' I laughed, 'I'll take you clothes shopping too,' I whispered, out of Jo's earshot. Even though Jo was very well off, she didn't like to spoil her daughter too much.

Carly beamed and put the glass down before repeating goodnight and returning to her bedroom.

Later that night, when everyone had gone home on a champagne high, and I'd returned to my cosy flat, I finally had time to think about the day's surreal events.

I knew I would never have to worry about money matters ever again, but it left me feeling strange and a bit preoccupied. For the first time in a long time, I really wanted to speak to my mum. There was something bugging me that had stuck in the back of my mind since Tony had given me the news. Had my parents kept something from me? Was Dad really my dad? Was I actually half Portuguese?

The thought stayed in my head until I gradually drifted off to sleep. That night was the first night since I was twelve that I'd fallen asleep without thinking of Fred.

<h1 style="text-align:center">CHAPTER 9</h1>

The sound of my mobile phone ringing woke me up. Diving out of bed, I tried to follow the sound of the jingle before it rang off. I soon found it, hiding under a cushion, in the lounge.

'Hello?'

'Katie, sweetie is that you?' asked a distant voice.

'Mum! Oh my god – how weird. Just last night I was thinking about you. I really wanted to...'

'Listen, darling. What is it? What's wrong?' she asked, without allowing me to answer. 'I just knew something was wrong. I felt it last night. Well, okay, it wasn't me that felt it, but an African witch doctor told me you needed me.'

Temporarily lost for words, I was shocked by how a strange person in Africa could possibly know I needed my mum.

'Are you alright, sweetie? You're not hurt or injured, are you? Do you need money or something?'

That made me laugh out loud.

'Darling? Why are you laughing?'

'Mum, you're never going to believe it but...' suddenly my phone beeped to tell me the battery was running low, 'Mum – hang on. The battery's running out. Just a sec,' I screeched as I rummaged around in a drawer desperately trying to find the charger before it ran out. Plugging it in I held the phone to my ear, 'okay. It's in,' I sighed.

'Oh my god – you're pregnant, aren't you?' she shrieked down the phone.

'Sorry to disappoint you, Mum, but no, you're not going to be a grandmother any time soon. I'd need a man for that,' I sighed as I listened to the almost audible disappointment on the other end of the phone.

'But, speaking of being pregnant, I wanted to ask you about when you were pregnant with me...'

'You did? Why?' she asked, without sounding at all guilty.

'Mum, I'm completely serious here. Is Dad my ...' I stopped for a deep breath, 'real dad?'

There was a pause on the other end.

'Mum?'

'Darling, why on Earth are you asking such a thing?'

'Please, Mum, can you just tell me the truth? Is Dad my real dad?'

'Well, of course, he is. What makes you think that he wouldn't be?'

I explained everything that had happened the previous day, eager to find out the truth about Uncle Sam. The odd thing was that she didn't seem at all surprised that her only daughter was now a multi-millionairess.

'Darling, even though your father and I have our differences, I don't ever want you to think that he's not your real father, because he is,' she sighed, 'but... I guess there's no reason why you shouldn't know the whole truth now.'

The whole truth? My knees became weak and, afraid of what I was about to discover, I bent down and curled up on the carpet, 'Go on,' I muttered.

'Samuel and I had an affair,' she admitted.

I gasped. Even though she hadn't been a part of my dad's life for many years, the thought of her cheating on him hurt. It really hurt.

'For how long?' I managed to ask.

'Years. I'd be with him every time we went on holiday. He was the reason we went to Skegness.'

'But I thought I was the reason we kept going back? I was the one that always begged for us to go back,' I said, suddenly realising that all that time, we hadn't gone to Skegness because of me, but for her to have a sordid affair.

'Your dad always wanted to go somewhere else for a change but, with both of us wanting to go back, he always agreed in the end. Although I never really understood why you were so desperate to return, year in, year out. You were always so miserable. But I wanted to go because of Samuel. He was a wonderful, loving man. When I became pregnant with you, we did wonder if you were your father's or his. We knew when you were born that you weren't Sam's. You were the image of your father.'

'Did Dad know about you and Sam?'

'I don't know. If he did, he never said anything. Your father loved me, and even though we fought like cat and dog sometimes, he didn't want to lose me. In the end, though, we just couldn't make it work. But he doted on you. Don't you forget that, Katie.'

I smiled, yet I was confused. There seemed to be so many questions, but nowhere to start.

'But if you were so in love with Sam, why didn't you stay with him, instead? Why didn't you marry him and have his kids? Why didn't you go back to him when Dad left you?'

'Sam never wanted to hurt anyone. Even though what we did was wrong, he didn't want me to leave your father. He couldn't bear the thought of him being responsible for the end of someone's marriage and, more importantly, he didn't want to hurt you. I know, it was mad. That's probably why he left you everything in his will. You were the child that could so easily have been his.'

'But why didn't you go to him when Dad left?'

'I did, briefly. Don't you remember? You'd already moved out.'

'But why didn't you stay with him?' I asked, confused.

I could hear her catch her breath as if she was trying not to cry.

'He... he knew he was dying. He didn't want me to see him deteriorate. He didn't want me to see him die,' she sobbed, 'God, I wish I'd have just stayed with him. But he pushed me away. The thought of me seeing him like that tore him apart. He wanted to spare me the pain, too. He must have been so alone. I'm sorry, Katie. I'm sorry to be such a disappointment to you.'

The intense emotion crawled up the insides of my stomach like a caterpillar on speed.

'You've never been a disappointment to me, Mum. I love you,' I cried.

I could hear her sobs on the other end of the phone. I felt for her more than I ever had before.

She managed to clear her throat and laugh a little.

'Listen to us grown-ups, crying like little babies. I wish you were here, darling. I could really do with a hug right now.'

Funny how we could be thousands of miles apart, yet we were having such a significant mother-daughter moment together. We'd never been particularly close, but in the space of a few minutes, I felt closer to my mum than I'd ever been.

'You've got Nick, remember, Mum. If you'd stayed with Sam, you wouldn't have Nick now. Sam obviously wanted you to be happy and watching him die wouldn't have made you happy, would it? He wanted to allow you to find love again. And you have,' I smiled as the tears rolled down my face and moistened my lips.

'Thanks, darling. You're my angel, you do know that, don't you?' she said quietly.

She hadn't called me her angel since I was about twelve years old. I felt warm and fuzzy all over.

We talked for a little while longer. I offered to send half of the money over to her, but she was adamant that she didn't want any of it.

'Donate some of it to some African charities, Katie – that would mean more to me than anything,' she'd said.

I was still so shocked about how calm she was about the money. Since being with Nick in Africa, she'd come to achieve what most of us can only dream of: complete unadulterated happiness, something that comes from inside, something that can't be changed by any amount of money. I realised that's what Sam had wanted for her. It must have been the hardest thing for him to do, but only he knew that it was for the best.

We finally said goodbye with me promising to visit, as soon as I'd sorted out everything with the inheritance. I stretched out on the floor feeling calm; a flood of happiness washed over me as I realised that my mum was indeed one in a million. It had only taken me twenty-eight years to realise it.

49

CHAPTER 10

A month after Tony had first visited me, the arrangements for our holiday had been organised, and we were finally on our way to the Azores for two weeks.

We'd picked up a flight from Gatwick Airport and were spending three nights in Lisbon, before catching our next flight to the islands.

It was the first time Liz had ever been on a plane, and she was absolutely terrified. At the airport, even though it was very early in the morning, she'd had to be calmed down with a couple of stiff drinks. And on the plane, she'd looked like a corpse - sitting bolt upright with her eyes wide open, barely blinking. She'd refused to peer out of the window and wouldn't eat a thing. Before we took off, she carefully watched the flight attendant as she demonstrated the safety points. She screeched at everyone to shut up and gave anyone the evil eye if they weren't listening. The landing was clearly the most painful part of the trip; all I can say is, I'm glad I wasn't sitting next to her because she almost broke poor Carly's hand.

Being exceedingly grateful to have landed safely, she thanked the stewards profusely as we made our way down the aisle towards the exit. The moment we stepped out onto the steps, I had to shield my eyes from the bright sunlight that instantly kissed my face. A smile spread across my lips as I looked up at the intensity

51

of the glorious blue sky. Even the scents differed wildly from the country we had left behind.

'It's Oleander,' smiled a well-dressed elderly man to my side. 'The smell. Oleander.'

'Oleander?' I repeated, turning my eyes from his. I followed his gaze and noticed a lovely hedge plant in the distance, covered in pink flowers. Somehow, the smell reminded me of my childhood. It's weird to say so, but it smelt like, like...

'Wow, it smells just like Play-doh!' giggled Carly, who was still rubbing her hand, trying to get the blood to return to it.

'That's it, that's exactly what it smells like. It's gorgeous,' I laughed as we began moving down the stairs towards the airport arrivals hall.

We were all booked into a five-star hotel on the outskirts of the city and, for a treat, I'd arranged for a couple of limousines to take us wherever we fancied.

Julianne, a keen photographer, had brought along a very expensive camera to take photos for possible future editions of the magazine, so she and Carly headed out to the city centre to take pictures of the many beautiful sights Lisbon had to offer.

Jo and Liz decided a pampering session was in order so were whisked off to a nearby spa. Anna and John decided to go for a romantic wander through the city streets, which left me alone; yet I was content to sit and do very little by the hotel pool, other than laze about and read the latest gossip magazines, one of my favourite pastimes.

'Do you mind if I join you?' said a familiar voice approaching me.

I put my sunglasses on top of my head and looked up.

'Tony! What a lovely surprise. I thought you were meeting us in the Azores?'

'I had some business to attend to here, so I thought I may as well tie it all in with your trip. I hope you don't mind.'

'Mind? Of course not. It's really good to see you. How are you?' I asked happily.

'I'm fine, thank you. And you? How are you enjoying your new life?' he asked with a grin as he sat down on the lounger next to me, taking off his sunglasses at the same time.

I smiled, knowing that 'my new life' hadn't really changed much... yet. I knew it would soon, but I hadn't wanted to do anything too drastic until I really felt ready. After my chat with my mum, I'd decided to take things slowly, one step at a time.

'I'm great, thanks. Still a bit overwhelmed, actually, to tell you the truth.'

'That's completely normal, under the circumstances,' he said kindly.

'Would you like a drink, sir?' asked the young, dark-haired waiter who jaunted over from the impressive pool bar just a few metres away.

"Uma bica e uma agua das pedras, faz favor,' he responded fluently, before turning back to me 'Would you like a drink, Kate?'

'A martini and lemonade please.'

The waiter smiled, nodded and promptly turned around and headed back towards the bar.

'I forgot you're Portuguese,' I said as I closed the pages of the magazine and dropped it into my bag, 'It sounds like such a beautiful language. Perhaps I should try and learn a few words.'

Tony smiled, 'It's not the easiest language to learn, but it is worth the effort. Maybe I can give you a few lessons?'

I laughed, 'I'd like that. I was always quite good at French at school, maybe that'll help.'

Our drinks arrived, and I was quite surprised that Tony had ordered fizzy water and an espresso.

'Nursing a hangover are you?' I asked curiously, eyeing his drinks.

Laughing, he quickly drank his miniature coffee and shook his head, 'No, no hangover. This is typical of what the Portuguese like to drink. And being Portuguese myself,' he shrugged his shoulders. 'I miss the coffee. English and American coffee doesn't quite do it for me,' he smiled.

'Do you come back here often?' I asked curiously.

Since I'd met him, all I knew was that he was a solicitor, he was Portuguese and lived between New York and London. I presumed he was divorced because he didn't wear a wedding ring, but did have a faint mark on his ring finger.

Shaking his head, he told me he rarely had time to return to Portugal.

'Perhaps now I'm working for you, I might get more opportunities to come back,' he suggested with a grin. 'But seriously, one day I'd quite like to buy a second home here. My wife talks about it all the time.'

So he was married.

'Your wife?' I said, looking at his hands.

He rubbed his ring finger with his other hand. He had long, perfectly formed fingers with lovely clean pink fingernails. I looked at his face, waiting for a response, and for a moment, he seemed rather sad.

'Yes, I have a wife. Zara. She's Portuguese too. She came with me to America when I began studying law.'

'You must have been together for a long time then?'

He nodded, 'Yes, you could say we were childhood sweethearts. We started dating when she was twelve. I was fourteen,' he said with a smile as he reminisced. 'That was a long time ago, though.'

I was hooked, curious to know why he looked so sad. I wondered what had happened, if anything, but certainly didn't want to pry. He was my lawyer. Yes, he was becoming a friend, but we hadn't quite got to that stage where I could ask about his private life. I hoped we would become good friends, though, because I found myself drawn to him easily in that way. Not romantically though, of course not.

'I don't know about you, but I'm feeling rather hot. Shall we go for a swim?'

Clearly glad of a change of subject, Tony smiled, 'I'd love to, but I have something that I really must attend to. Perhaps later?' he said, standing, as I messily wrapped my hair into a bun and removed my sarong.

'Okay, then. I plan on staying here all day anyway, so I'll see you later on,' I said as I walked towards the edge of the pool and slowly lowered myself into the cold water.

Tony called out até logo and was gone.

I swam for half an hour. It was bliss because there were very few others lounging around the pool; it was utterly peaceful. No children were screaming or splashing about, just a handful of other adults, clearly enjoying the quiet and the perfect afternoon sun. The waiter quietly hovered, waiting for the odd order for drinks or snacks, but other than that there was virtually no movement within the confines of the pool terrace atop our hotel roof.

I lay down on a lounger and must have dropped off to sleep because, before I knew it, I was woken up by the trickling of cold water on my stomach. It didn't make me jump though, it was far too pleasant.

'Wakey, wakey, sleepy lady,' giggled Carly.

I opened my eyes to find Julianne standing above me with her camera.

'No – don't take a picture of me. I probably look awful,' I grimaced.

'On the contrary, Kate, you look lovely and relaxed. A perfect picture to accompany the article you're going to write about your new found life,' she winked.

'I'm writing an article about what?' I asked.

'Well, don't you think it would be a great feature for our 'Real People' section? An 'It Could Happen To You' type thing? I think it would be wonderful. Of course you'll write it, won't you Kate?' she asked with her eyes open wide and one finger on her lips.

I shook my head vehemently. 'No way.'

I didn't want the world and its wife to know about my fortune. That would be a nightmare. Unless, of course, I wrote it anonymously.

As if reading my mind, Carly suggested the very same thing.

'It would make superb reading, and it could be anonymous if you really don't want your name on it,' Julianne pouted.

'I'll think about it. Now, are you coming for a swim?'

After my first day of relaxation in the sun, we'd had a lovely long night's sleep, chilled out the next day and then gone out clubbing until the early hours of the following morning.

Jo didn't want to leave Carly alone at the hotel, so we carefully dressed her and did her hair and makeup. In the end, she looked about seventeen, not the youthful thirteen that she was. Jo was so amazed at the transformation that she actually cried, muttering something about her baby no longer being a baby anymore. It was both amusing and touching.

The club some of us had ended up staying in until 4am was actually a strip club. Not a tacky one, I might add, but a tasteful one. Yes, the strippers were all female, but there was a great atmosphere. Anna hadn't been too keen on going. She'd whispered to me that she really didn't like things like that, so John suggested that they head back to the hotel.

Julianne took Carly back too. She might have looked seventeen, but she had a few years to go yet.

The following day, we'd all gone sightseeing together. We'd visited a beautiful palace in the hills, called Sintra. It was stunning. Lovely and cool, a refreshing change from the hot sun outside.

The mood soon changed though, as Liz started getting nervous about the upcoming plane ride to the islands. In fact the night before, she'd barely slept, downing a couple of large brandies while the rest of us drank coffee the next morning. As we boarded the flight to head for the islands, all our attempts to calm her failed miserably when she saw that the aeroplane being used to take us there was quite a bit smaller than the one we'd travelled on from London.

'I can't get on that,' she screeched, 'It's just… a… a… toy. We're all going to die,' she sobbed.

I felt the eyes of all the other passengers descend on us heavily, as we repeatedly asked her to calm down, but to no avail.

'I don't suppose you've got any strong tranquillisers on this plane, do you? You know, the ones used to knock out elephants?' I joked to the flight attendant with an embarrassed grin.

She clearly wasn't amused.

'Madam, you're going to have to calm down. There are children on board who can hear you,' she said crossly, 'Let me get you a blanket – maybe that will help.'

She turned to me and whispered from the corner of her mouth, 'I think she's frightening them.'

Looking around, I noticed a couple of youngsters on the verge of tears.

'Liz, sweetie, this is a perfectly safe plane – think how much lighter we must be than the big plane we were on the other day. Surely that must mean we've got a better chance of staying airborne,' I said, desperately trying to think of something, anything, that might shut her up.

Clearly, she wasn't quite that naïve, as she gave me a sarcastic look before turning to look at the stricken little girls. Seeing how frightened she'd made them seemed to do the trick. She smiled, somewhat falsely, at them and turned back around.

'Sorry,' she mouthed to the attendant as she was handed a small blanket and a pillow which she took and clung onto.

Take-off was clearly very difficult for her as she gripped poor Carly's hand again until it was white. Within fifteen minutes of take-off, Liz was snoring like a trooper with her mouth wide open. Good job there were no flies onboard.

The rest of us breathed a sigh of relief as we sat back to enjoy the few hours' journey in peace. Little did we know that we were heading to paradise.

e were so relieved that Liz slept through the entire flight because, on our approach to the island, even we were astounded at the apparent length (or lack thereof) of the runway. If she'd been awake, she would have screamed blue murder. What appeared to be a runway looked more like a short, little country lane that dropped straight off into the vast ocean beyond.

Of course, there was nothing to fear as the landing was perfect, without a single bump.

As we exited the aircraft, the smell of the hot summer sun gently enveloped us, giving us that wonderful feeling of relaxation that can only be achieved on holiday, when you can finally leave all your troubles behind. I took a deep breath and looked around. A tiny arrivals lounge awaited to one side and everywhere else were the most stunning sea and mountain views. There wasn't a single cloud in the sky. Strangely, I felt at home, even though I'd never stepped foot on the island before.

Wow, my life was almost unrecognisable.

Jo patted me on the back and smiled as if reading my thoughts.

'Come on, Kate, your new house beckons.'

I linked arms with her on one side and Carly on the other, and we almost skipped into the airport, following the rest of the gang who had eagerly already entered the building. Liz was the first, of course, the further she was from the plane, the better.

Once we'd collected our luggage, we headed straight to the car hire desk where we picked up two jeeps. Tony drove one and John the other as we headed in the direction of my new house. Butter-flies bubbled in my stomach. It was such a strange sensation knowing that the house belonged to me, even though I'd never been there before. What would it be like? Would it be huge? Would it be small? Was there a pool? Honestly, though, it wouldn't have mattered if it was just a shack; the island was so beautiful, I could imagine never wanting to leave.

I did have a slight inkling as to the size of it though because Tony had assured us there was room enough for us all to stay there. He'd said he'd stay in a nearby hotel, but I was adamant he would do no such thing. He was becoming more of a friend than your typical solicitor, and I'd made it quite clear he was welcome to stay with us. In fact, I'd insisted on it.

As we drove through tiny white-washed villages, with little hill-top churches and barely a soul to be seen, the group began to get into the holiday spirit.

'Wow, isn't it the most gorgeous place? Talk about a world away from London,' yelled John, above the sound of the wind rushing through our hair. Tony's idea of hiring open-topped jeeps was just fantastic.

'It's incredible,' shouted Anna as she squeezed his hand tightly.

I smiled fondly at the couple as I took in the beautiful vistas all around, barely able to believe this could be my future home – or one of them, at least! But not in the very near future. Even though I was rich beyond my wildest dreams, I had no intention of leaving England. I loved living in London and couldn't imagine living anywhere else.

I also had no plans to stop working at Liberty either, especially now it had just started to become exciting. I realised that having this much money could entitle me to live the most exciting life possible, but, apart from my lack of Fred, my life had been pretty good up until then. I didn't want to change it that much, and I'd read so many stories about people who'd won the lottery and whose lives had changed, beyond recognition, and not in a positive way, either. I would try and avoid that happening, at all costs. At least I hoped it wouldn't change me. I sighed quietly to myself. It was the strangest thing, this feeling of not quite being me anymore. No matter how much I didn't want to change, I just felt different. And not in a way I could explain.

Before I could dwell on my strange thoughts any longer, we stopped in front of a massive black gate, made from the most intricately designed wrought iron. It must have weighed a tonne. Beyond it was a long, twisting avenue, dotted on either side by huge green palm trees. When Tony stopped the engine and hopped out of the jeep in front, we pulled up alongside him and climbed out.

'Well, this is it. Welcome to Casa Linda. I believe he re-named the house after a lady he once knew,' said Tony as he looked at me knowingly. Linda was my mother's middle name. 'It also means 'beautiful', and I'm sure you're about to understand why,' he added.

Anna was practically bouncing up and down with excitement as the others peered through the gate, clearly astonished at the impressive entrance.

'Can we go in, can we go in?!' exclaimed Carly.

Tony nodded his head and said, 'Yes, we're meeting someone here who has the remote controls to open the gate. He should be here any minute now.'

I wandered up to the gate and gently stroked my hand along the wrought iron. I almost felt like I was on another planet. I wondered what was beyond that point. Where did the palm trees lead? Had Sam designed this place? Had it been his favourite home or had he lived most of his time in Skegness, New York or Toronto? I wished I could find out more about him. The man had given me so much, and I had no way of even thanking him.

He must be buried somewhere, I thought, making a mental note to ask Tony some questions before we returned home. The least I could do was visit Sam's grave and tell him - well, his spirit - how grateful I was. I wish he'd have got in touch with me while he was still alive. I wondered if he actually knew anything about me. Had he tried to find me? Had he tried to at least find out about me?

An overwhelming feeling of sorrow engulfed me as I stood there, both hands on the gate, peering up that long tree-lined avenue. Oh, Sam, I thought sadly.

Suddenly the faint sound of bells tickled my ears. Turning around, I spotted a little old man on a white donkey coming up the road towards us. The bells were dangling from the animal's neck, jingling as he moved from side to side.

'Ora bom dia,' yelled the friendly-looking man with the biggest grin on his face.

We nodded, laughed and saluted him, not knowing how to greet the man in his own language. He struggled to get down from the animal but wouldn't accept any assistance from John or Tony.

His jolly, rotund face was covered in wrinkles that had no doubt developed from years in the hot sun. His eyes were of the brightest blue, and they twinkled naughtily. It was easy to see he had probably once been very handsome, in a cheeky sort of way. He rambled on for a little while to us all, but he soon realised we had absolutely no idea what he was talking about, so he focussed all his attention on Tony, who smiled and returned his questions fluently. It was fascinating to listen to – almost musical.

'Wouldn't it be great to actually be able to understand?' said Liz as she giggled flirtatiously at the old man.

We nodded at the thought of learning a new language. Maybe I would. Especially now I had a perfectly good reason to.

After struggling to get back on the donkey and yelling his goodbyes (or so we were told), he didn't turn around to go the same way he had come but carried on up the hill in the opposite direction.

'His name is Manuel. He used to be the gardener here,' said Tony, 'but when Sam died, he decided to finally retire. He is nearly ninety years old. Remarkable, isn't he?'

I was flabbergasted. Goodness, I hoped I would look that good at that age. I hoped I was still alive at that age!

'Wow, does this place hold the secret to eternal youth or something? Maybe we should immigrate here, John,' laughed Anna.

'No need for that sweetheart, you will always be young and

beautiful,' he said as he hopped back into the driver's seat. 'After you, Tony,' he yelled.

The rest of us got back into the jeeps as the gates creaked and slowly opened, reminding me of the grand entrance to Aladdin's cave.

'It's actually like something out of a horror film or something, isn't it?' Carly exclaimed, more to herself than to anyone else.

'I certainly hope not,' I whispered to myself with a grin.

CHAPTER 13

That long twisted avenue, lined with those stunning, colossal palm trees, couldn't possibly be the driveway to just one house, could it? It was more like the road to a five-star resort or something. After what seemed like ages, we turned the final bend, and the house appeared in front of us. And my…what a house it was.

Nobody said a word, and I couldn't even bring myself to get out of the jeep. Like everyone else, I just sat and stared at the magnificent building.

After a couple of minutes, Tony laughed beside me, 'It really is something special, isn't it?'

I nodded; my mouth felt like it must have been hanging beneath my knees.

'Come on, we can't sit here all day,' he said as he slid out of the jeep to go and chat to the others while they waited for me to compose myself if that was at all possible.

I slowly stepped out of the jeep and looked up at the massive property in front of us. The long, winding driveway had culminated at a large paved area, surrounding an impressive circular fountain. In the centre was a beautiful naked woman made of stone. She was holding a large pot from where, presumably, water would pour when the fountain was turned on.

To stare at the house itself, sunglasses were a necessity as it was painted such a bright shade of white. Four tall, Romanesque columns stood either side of a large Oak front door.

'Well, what are you waiting for?' asked Tony, grinning as he handed me a set of heavy keys. 'This one here is for the front door.'

I took it, laughing, and rushed up to the entrance. My hands shook as I took a deep breath and placed the key into the keyhole. I turned back and looked at the others anxiously.

'Go on then, Kate. Open it. Open it!' they shouted as if I were opening the best ever Christmas present.

I laughed and pushed open the door to what felt like a whole new life.

I gasped. I'd never seen luxury like it. The front door opened onto a large round entrance hall, where a grand staircase beckoned upwards. I felt as if I'd just stepped into one of those old-style musicals, expecting a multitude of feather-clad dancers to appear, dancing around me and hiding me from the audience with their huge fan-shaped feather boas. I had visions of little orphan Annie sliding down the bannister with Daddy Warbucks in tow.

'Oh. My. God. It's awesome,' said Carly, snapping me out of my trance.

'It's bigger and more impressive than any five-star hotel I've ever stayed in,' exclaimed Julianne, 'It's unbelievable. Wow, this will make the most fabulous set for many of our shoots.'

I looked at her sideways, and she laughed.

'Did I just say that out loud?' she giggled.

'Of course, you'd have to pay big bucks to use this place for a high fashion photoshoot,' I replied, momentarily forgetting I actually owned it.

'Well, of course you'd get paid. I just hope you'd give us a good discount.'

Smirking, I hugged her. 'You can use it any time you want, and it won't cost you a penny.'

Keen to continue looking around, I left everybody inspecting the intricately-designed entrance hall and headed deeper into the house. The first door I came to lead into a vast sitting room, furnished with ornate dark wooden furniture. Not to my taste, but it was very fetching in its rightful place nonetheless. A huge marble fireplace was the room's focal point, above which hung a large framed painting of a beautiful dark-haired woman. I stepped back, thinking she looked somewhat familiar. Turning my head to one side and squinting my eyes, it suddenly dawned on me who it was. Mum. It wasn't an exact likeness, but she was recognisable.

Goodness, this man must have been obsessed with her. They really should have got together after Dad left. I sighed. Uncle Sam was clearly besotted with her. But then, Mum wouldn't have such a wonderful life with Nick now, would she?

Starting to feel a little uneasy, my knees gave way, and I stumbled, holding on to the nearest chair for support. I caught my breath and decided I needed some air, so I pushed apart the heavy velvet curtains and opened the closest sliding door. It led out onto a covered terrace, and as I looked up, I lost my breath once again. The view was spectacular. The tree-lined driveway up to the house had hidden the fact that we were perched on the edge of a cliff and I was surprised to see a vast green, overgrown lawn, literally disappearing into the deep blue ocean beyond.

It was so beautiful that I cried, literally cried. And I couldn't stop. The tears fell and fell. I don't think they just fell for the view, of course, they fell for Sam, they fell for my mum; they fell for a relationship that may or may not have worked. I was confused. I was so happy, yet so sad at the same time.

I don't know for how many minutes I sat there crying my heart out, but when I turned around to go back inside, I noticed everybody standing sadly behind me.

Taking my hand in hers, Carly pulled me inside. 'Don't be sad. Sam really wanted you to have this,' she whispered.

For such a young girl, Carly often surprised me with her words of wisdom. Losing her father so young had given her something you don't often see in people her age, a maturity that you don't even see in some adults.

'Sorry, everyone,' I smiled, a little embarrassed, 'just got a bit emotional for a minute there.'

'Don't be sorry, it's completely natural. Never be sorry for that,' Anna said, as John patted me on the back kindly.

Pulling myself together, we had a proper look around. We

found more and more huge stunning rooms and each had the most awe-inspiring view to go with it.

My favourite room, though, was the kitchen. It seemed to be a little more traditional Portuguese than the rest, even though its size could only be described as massive. A large Aga-type oven sparkled to one side; it looked like it had never been used. There were plenty of free-standing wooden cupboards along each wall, and a huge stainless steel fridge loomed above everything else.

A large, family-sized long Oak dining table was the focal point of the room, which made me think of those feel-good American movies, where several generations gather together for Thanksgiving and such. After watching those kinds of films, I'd always wished my family had been like that – you know, six or seven siblings, all happy with kids of their own and all getting together for special occasions to make even more special memories together.

Of course, I realise that rarely happens. Families get together, and there's nothing but trouble. Arguments and fall outs. You can't choose your family, but you can choose your friends, I thought. On cue, the others waltzed into the kitchen, all still oohing and aahing about the beauty of the house.

'I don't know about you guys, but I'm starving. Shall we all have a quick shower and then head into the nearest village for a bite to eat?' asked John, patting his stomach.

We nodded, gathered our belongings from the jeeps and rushed upstairs to wash and change. The others waited for me to choose my bedroom before the excited madness of getting ready began. The room I chose sat directly above the main sitting room and had a large terrace that looked out across the ocean. Inside was a simple yet massive, four-poster bed. Other than that, and a large free-standing dark wooden wardrobe, the room was quite bare. The walls were painted white and simple white drapes hung from the windows. A door next to the entrance revealed a large en-suite bathroom with a walk-in shower made from cream and white mosaic tiles. It was beautiful in its simplicity.

Less than an hour later, Tony and I were first out and waiting down in the main sitting room.

'You look very nice,' he complimented as I walked in wearing a new white linen maxi dress. I smiled, did a little twirl and said 'It's new. From eBay!'

He laughed and shook his head as I twirled.

'I'll never stop buying clothes from there,' I giggled as we heard the others rushing downstairs, ready to head out to get some food.

We piled into the jeeps and headed to the nearest restaurant in the nearest village. It was a traditional Portuguese place, with tiled walls indoors and out, that served all kinds of fresh fish and meat dishes.

'Benvindo. Welcome,' nodded the waiter as we walked in and asked for a table for eight. The man, who was in his mid-fifties, smiled brightly and led us onto a terrace with a fabulous ocean view, to the best table.

'This is a beautiful restaurant you have here,' I said, sitting down and ogling that breathtaking vista.

'Thank you, madam. It has been in my family for many years. You are English, no?' he asked with a warm grin.

I nodded.

'You are the young lady who has inherited Samuel Simões house, no?'

I laughed; clearly, this was a small community.

'I am,' I answered, smiling, 'I'm Kate. It's a pleasure to meet you.'

Delighted, he clapped his hands together with excitement. 'I am Paulo. Welcome to the Açores. It is a beautiful house. Is so sad about Samuel. He was a wonderful man. Everybody here loved him. We miss him,' he said sadly. But before he could dwell on the thought, he clapped his hands again and said, 'You must please allow me to serve you our finest dishes this evening...' and he continued to explain the day's fresh fish and seafood dishes.

After he'd finished and taken our orders, he returned with another young man, both carrying glasses of port. 'Please accept some white port... on the house, for you all,' he said.

'Oh, thank you. Thank you so much,' said Anna, 'That's really very kind of you.'

The man nodded and smiled. 'This is my son, Filipe. If there is anything you need, please, just ask Filipe or me, okay? You enjoy your evening.'

Carly blushed as the attractive young man handed her a fresh orange juice as the rest of us held our glass of port up to him and Paulo. 'Cheers.'

'Thank you, Paulo,' I added before he left us to continue serving his other customers.

Hours later, we headed back to the villa. It had been a wonderful day. One that had ended on a high, with us eating and drinking like kings, thanks to Paulo and his family-run restaurant.

CHAPTER 14

For the next few days, we relaxed like we'd never relaxed before, spending hours and hours dozing by the fabulous infinity pool. It was the most beautiful swimming pool I'd ever seen, with its deep blue water seemingly cascading off into the softly glistening gentle waves of the Atlantic Ocean below.

But, on day five, we decided to stop being so lazy and chose to do a bit of sightseeing. Not before a quick swim after brunch, though.

As I stood beneath the shower, rinsing off the remnants of chlorine, I reached for the shampoo and lathered my long brown hair while letting my mind wander to old memories. Or should I say an old memory? It had been some time since I'd thought of Fred and, as I pictured his face (how I thought he would look now, not then), I was reminded of my not so memorable evening with Marc. I sighed and tried to push the thought from my mind as I stepped out of the shower and dried myself off.

It wasn't as easy as that though (pushing Marc aside, not getting dry). All I could see was his face. The more I tried to obliterate it from memory, the brighter and more appealing it became. That gorgeous face. Those blue eyes. The black hair. I sighed again.

Why couldn't I be normal? Why couldn't I just forget about all that nonsense and just move on with my life? I mean, come on, my life was undoubtedly changing at an alarming rate, surely I could change my love life as well. Find someone decent to settle down with, perhaps? Someone who didn't 'fit the bill'. The Fred bill.

'Are you ready, Kate?' shouted Anna from the bottom of the stairs. 'We're all waiting for you.'

'Almost!' I yelled back before rushing to get dressed and apply a little make-up.

A few minutes later, I put on a pair of cut off jeans and a pink vest top, grabbed my Fit Flops, cardigan and handbag, and rushed down the stairs as fast as I could.

'Sorry,' I said as I climbed into the jeep before we set off to check out a little more of the island. As we began a slow drive along the coast, Julianne was almost hyperventilating with excitement.

'Oh my goodness, it's stunning. Just stunning. Stop.... stop now!' she yelled.

As John slammed on the brakes in a panic, Tony narrowly missed hitting us up the back.

'What? What's wrong?' he asked as he turned to look as she jumped out as quickly as she could with her camera in hand.

'It's just so beautiful. I need to take some shots,' she said.

'You do realise we nearly crashed, Julianne?' I asked, shaking my head in disbelief.

'Oops,' she said simply, before ignoring the rest of us and continuing to take the photos as if nothing had happened.

Tony's raised eyebrows and John's shrugged shoulders proved how relaxed they were. Had we been back in London, it would have been a different story. It was then that Carly began to giggle. A giggle that spread like wildfire among us. Before long, we were all laughing. Deep belly laughs, that gave us a stomach ache.

Julianne stopped taking photos of the spectacular views and turned to look at us with furrowed eyebrows.

'What?' she asked. 'You guys are crazy,' she muttered with an embarrassed smile before graciously climbing back in and letting us continue our drive.

There'd been several signs dotted along the road indicating that a volcanic crater was nearby and, from what I'd read in a leaflet I'd picked up from the airport, the location was known to be one of the most spectacular spots on the whole of the island. None of us wanted to miss it so we continued to drive all the way up, excited as to what we would see at the top. The temperature began to cool a little on our ascent.

Arriving at a rather large car park, we jumped out and surveyed the scene around us. It was certainly breathtaking, there was no doubt about it. Armed with cameras, baseball caps and even a towel (John had an odd thing about going everywhere on holiday with a towel around his neck) we wandered to a nearby information point which clearly showed how the crater had been created, thousands of years before. I very carefully leaned on an old, rickety wooden handrail and let out a deep, happy sigh. The others joined me as we took in the view beyond. The vast hole in the ground was surrounded by a massive amount of shrubbery in varying hues of green. The depth was difficult to gauge from our position, but it was certainly a long way down to the bottom, which was filled with sparkling blue-green water. Although beautiful, it did scare the living daylights out of me.

'Why don't we have a walk around the edge of the crater?' suggested Anna, 'It would be good to get some exercise.'

My distaste for anything remotely higher than a few feet put me off immediately. I can't even climb a stepladder without coming over all dizzy.

I was clearly the spoilsport of the bunch, but it didn't bother me. I preferred to wait in safety, and the comfort, of the jeep than risk a potential fall to my death.

'Oh, Kate, you're such a coward,' laughed Jo. 'But we love you for it.'

'We won't be long. We'll be back before you know it,' added Julianne as they ambled off, looking very much like the tourists they were in their flip flops, cameras around their necks and John with his towel over his shoulder.

I chuckled as I watched them wander off into the distance while I settled comfortably down into the seat, rifling through my handbag to pull out the novel I'd recently started reading. It was lovely, sitting up there alone, with that awesome view and a great book to keep me company. I noticed it was 2.45pm.

An hour later, they were still walking, and I was still enjoying my solitude.

Two hours later, I looked up from my book and felt a slight chill. Looking around, I noticed it had become a little misty. But I thought nothing of it, assuming they'd be back soon.

However, at 5.30, I started getting rather preoccupied. Where on Earth were they?

A few minutes later, I heard a strange sound. It sounded distinctly like sirens, which seemed to be getting closer.

Sure enough, three cars zoomed past where we'd parked. Each one had a flashing light atop it with the alarming sounds of sirens blaring loudly. I jumped, wondering what was going on. Had something happened? It couldn't be with my lot, could it? How would the authorities know? No, it must be something else, I figured.

I watched as men jumped out of the vehicles. One ran over to me and spoke to me in perfect English, though with a slight accent.

'We have had a call from a man who has become lost. Are they with you?'

I breathed a sigh of relief.

'No, it can't be,' I said, 'I have five friends out walking. They'd all be together.'

'Okay, thank you, madam.'

I watched as he ran back to his colleagues and shook his head. They continued to talk to other people on walkie talkies and mobile phones. Soon their cars were joined by an ambulance and a fire engine.

It was only then that I became fully aware that the mist had become a thick, dense fog. Jumping out of the jeep, I wrapped my cardigan around my shoulders and quickly approached the man who had spoken to me.

'Excuse me. I'm really very worried about my friends now. I hadn't realised that it had become so foggy.'

'How long have they been gone, madam?' he asked with concern.

I told him it had been a few hours, and he nodded.

'Don't worry. We will find them. You stay close, okay?'

As I stood amidst the chaos, my thin cardigan did little to keep my teeth from chattering. How had I not noticed this cold? And the fog? What if something terrible had happened to them? And Carly. Oh goodness, she was only thirteen. I began to sob quietly when I was approached by a fireman with a very kind smile.

'You no worry, miss. This happens much in the Açores. We find, okay?'

I smiled at his broken English, grateful for his kindness. It was then that he removed his heavy coat and placed it carefully over my shoulders. I took it gratefully and felt instantly warmer.

He led me to the fire truck and opened the door.

'You sit in here. You wait in here. Everything okay, yes. You no worry.'

I did as I was told and climbed aboard. It's funny, most people (okay, most kids) want to sit in a fire truck. It would have been kind of cool had it been under different circumstances. But it certainly wasn't an experience I could enjoy.

Minutes passed, and I was just wiping a few more tears from my cheeks when I heard a yell of some kind.

The friendly fireman ran towards me and said 'one person, they have one person.'

Just one, I thought, what about the others?

I watched as a lone figure appeared from the mist. It was Tony. I hopped down from the truck and rushed over to him. He hugged me tightly.

'Are you alright?' I asked, 'I've been so worried. You've been gone so long. Where is everyone?'

Tony explained that when the mist had thickened and several hours had passed, the group had become more concerned for me so they'd decided that Tony should split up from the rest and try to come and tell me they were on their way.

However, with the mist developing into more of thick fog, it had become increasingly difficult to see in front of them.

'I'm so sorry, Kate. You must have been worried sick. We hadn't intended to go off for so long. I hope the others are found soon. It's become quite cold out there as well,' he said as we stared off into the distance, not seeing anything.

'I knew that if I just kept walking, that eventually, I would come out somewhere... even if it was the edge of the cliffs below,' he said, semi-joking.

Moments later, shouts and voices could be heard. Tony left me momentarily to see what was going on. He returned, looking decidedly relieved.

'They're all there. They're all okay, although someone has twisted an ankle. I'm not sure who it is though. You can breathe now, Kate. They're fine. We're all fine,' he smiled awkwardly.

As the group appeared, I rushed over to them, very much wanting to scold the lot of them for being so silly in the first place, but when I saw them all looking guilty and tired and worried sick, I decided to let them off the hook.

'Where's Liz?' I asked, suddenly realising she wasn't with them.

Carly smiled cheekily, 'Oh she's right behind us, and she's not alone.'

Sure enough, Liz appeared in the arms of a handsome young fireman.

Even after everything that had just happened, I couldn't help but smile. I could tell by the look on her face that she was smiling too, inside and out. I looked from Liz to the fireman, and I could see that he was smiling too. My, my. Could this be love at first sight?

For the next few days, we barely saw Liz. She and her own personal fireman appeared to have fallen instantly in love. Liz and Jorge, happily ever after. I certainly hoped so.

She'd even travelled back down the 'mountain' with Jorge, in the fire truck, because they clearly didn't want to lose sight of each other. Talk about working fast. I'd never seen love work its magic like it... well, unless you count Fred and me, of course.

I wished he were there with me. Would he ever be? I tried not to dwell on it but, seeing Liz and Jorge all loved up just brought that precious memory swimming back, which then led to thoughts of my near-miss with Marc, with a 'C'. It wasn't even a one night stand, I sighed.

'That was a deep sigh,' said a voice behind me as I lay sprawled on a wooden sun lounger by the pool.

Jo plonked herself down beside me, crossing her long tanned legs.

'What's on your mind?' she asked, smiling and squinting in the sun.

'Oh, the usual, I guess.'

She nodded, 'Fred's on your mind again, is he?'

Isn't he always? I thought.

Shrugging my shoulders, I relaxed and lay back down, shielding the sun from my eyes with my arm.

'You know, there were a few moments when we first arrived when I hadn't given him all my attention,' I smiled, 'but finally seeing Liz so happy and in love just reminds me of what I'm missing.'

She nodded as she uncrossed her legs and spread out on the sun lounger beside me.

'Well, that I can certainly understand. I miss Charles too.'

We both closed our eyes, not saying another word, just allowing the heat to penetrate deep into our skin, making us sleepy.

But it wasn't long until we were rudely awakened by the feel of something cold, while the sudden sound of giggling and splashing came from the swimming pool.

'They must be awake by now,' giggled Carly as she, Tony and John doused us in the cold stuff.

'Okay, okay,' I said, jumping up off the sun lounger and throwing myself in at the deep end.

'You got us, and now I'm gonna get you,' I screamed, by which time I'd completely engulfed them in water.

Failing miserably to pretend to still be asleep, Jo moaned and followed suit, narrowly missing us as she dive-bombed into the water.

'Come on in, Anna! You're the only one left out now,' called her adoring husband.

Muttering to herself, she mumbled and turned on to her back, trying to ignore our cries.

'All right, that does it!' shouted John, 'I'm coming to get you!'

And with that, she sat bolt upright and screamed.

'Noooo!'

But it was too late. He'd picked her up and jumped into the fresh water.

'John, you bugger,' she shouted the moment they appeared from beneath the surface.

'Well, well, well...' came a voice from indoors. 'It sounds like you're all having a wonderful time.'

Liz and Jorge appeared out of the lounge sliding doors, holding hands and grinning at each other like love struck teenagers.

'Come on, you love birds, come and have a swim,' I shouted, splashing them as hard as I could.

Moments later, they were in the water splashing about with the rest of us. Soon though, we all calmed down, letting the sun dry our faces and shoulders before we immersed ourselves beneath the sparkling surface.

Breaking the silence, John sighed and said what we were all thinking.

'I can't believe we've only got a few days left. We ought to make the most of it. What shall we do this evening?'

'Let's have another barbecue,' yelled Carly, who slowly pulled herself out of the pool, before diving back into the deep end.

When she re-surfaced like a sleek dolphin, she continued. 'That way, we don't have to do anything, we can stay around the pool for the rest of the evening,' she giggled.

Agreeing, Tony and I volunteered to pop into town to buy a few groceries and food for the night's feast.

'Don't forget the wine!' shouted Anna and Jo, half an hour later, after we'd dried ourselves off and were heading towards the jeep.

'As if!' I yelled back.

Laughing, we hopped in as Tony started the engine and we drove down the winding driveway, slowing to a standstill while the grand gates opened.

As we ambled around the local supermarket, picking up tomatoes, chickpeas, potatoes and a host of other stuff for our dinner, Tony's mobile phone rang.

I couldn't help but hear snippets of conversation.

I guessed it was his wife. She was clearly not happy. Embarrassed, he looked at me, raising his eyebrows, reminding me of a naughty schoolboy being scolded by his teacher.

"No, don't be ridiculous... how can you say something like that? It's just business... honestly Zara.... no... look I'm sorry... look... I'll be back in a few days... let's talk about it then. Okay? Yes, alright. See you then. Of course.... bye.'

I looked as if I hadn't heard a word but obviously failed miserably.

'My wife,' he said.

I smiled. 'Is everything okay?'

'Yes. Fine. Fine,' he answered unconvincingly.

I didn't really want to pry so I said no more, and we continued shopping. We carefully chose a few bottles of wine and a crate of beer before paying and loading everything into the jeep.

As we hopped in, Tony turned to me with sad eyes.

'Actually, everything isn't okay. I know it's not my place to talk to you about such things, but I do feel that we have become good friends over the past few weeks.'

I nodded, and he continued. 'It's just that things haven't been quite right between Zara and me lately. Admittedly, it's one of the reasons that I was so keen to come here with you guys. I needed to get away for a while and sort my head out.'

Again, I nodded, not saying anything.

He hesitated for a moment, before shrugging his shoulders. 'Jesus, I'm so sorry, Kate. I shouldn't be pouring my heart out to you.'

'Tony, please don't be embarrassed. I'm actually quite a good listener, you know. Or so I've been told,' I laughed.

He smiled, relieved.

'Thank you. I guess I needed someone to talk to. All my friends in London are 'our' friends, so it's very difficult to talk to them. Zara and I have been together since we were very young. Thirty odd years is such a long time, really. I guess I just feel like I may have missed so much,' he shrugged, staring ahead.

'You may think you've missed so much but look at it from the other side. Look at all those wonderful years you've spent together. If you hadn't got together back then, you might have spent years searching for her, it could have been thirty years wasted. It could have been thirty years of kissing a lot of ugly frogs before finding your princess. Yet, here you are, thirty lovely years all spent with the woman of your dreams. Thirty years of fantastic experiences and memories. Don't look back to what you might have missed,

Tony. Look forward to everything you still have together. Do you love her?' I asked.

'I've always loved her, it's just that I'm not sure that I am still in love with her, you know?'

'When was the last time just the two of you took a holiday together?' I asked.

He looked around, his mind ticking.

'You know, I can't even remember.'

'Perhaps there lies the problem. You're not spending enough time together. Tony, think about Zara. Think about the first time you fell in love with her. Think back to how she made you feel. Think about how she must be feeling this very moment. She probably thinks she's losing you. Don't lose something worth keeping, Tony. Grab it with both hands and hold on tight. You never know what will happen in this life so you should treasure every moment. Every single damn moment,' I said, banging my fist on the dashboard.

I looked up to see tears in Tony's eyes, just as mine began to well up too.

'Jesus, Kate, you're right. You're so very right. I've been such a fool. Thank you. Thank you!' he said as he leaned in and gave me a hug.

Together we laughed and cried, as passers-by looked on as if we were mad.

'Come on, let's get back. The others will be wondering what's happened to us,' I said as he started the engine and we eventually pulled away from the car park.

'Kate?' he asked, startling me out of my little daydream for a second.

'Hm?' I answered.

'You know everything you've just said?'

I nodded.

'I hope you don't think I'm prying into your life now, but it just sounds like you've loved and lost. You really don't have to talk about it if you don't want to but, just to let you know that I'm here if you need a shoulder, okay?'

Had I been that obvious? For a split second, I panicked, not sure I wanted anybody else to know about Fred, but I suddenly realised I was fed up of having such a big secret weighing me down. I was finally ready to open up. In fact, I decided that I was finally, just maybe, inclined to think about moving on.

Woah there! Had I just thought about moving on? Crikey. This was some day we were having.

I chuckled, and Tony looked at me, smiling, 'what's so funny?'

So I told him, explaining everything about my beloved Fred.

CHAPTER 16

It was so miserable and grey, considering it was July. The drizzle was coming down at a constant pace as I reminisced about those memorable days in the Azores, where the sun had been scorching hot and the skies glorious and deep blue.

A lot had happened in those last few days.

Not only had I poured my heart out to Tony, but I'd told the rest of the group too. They were my closest friends, and they deserved to know the truth about me. They'd often asked why I'd never felt the need to settle down, and I'd said nothing, keeping Fred a secret, so close to my own heart for years. I'd felt oddly liberated, almost as if I could finally move on with my life.

But just as I was finally starting to think about moving on, they'd tried to encourage me to continue searching for him. Alone, I'd tried and failed. Now they wanted to help. They honestly thought that he could be found, bless them.

But even though I'd love nothing more than to find him, I certainly didn't want to start a nationwide manhunt, and had expressed my concern at some of their more outlandish plans, including launching an appeal in the media!

I'd thanked them for their enthusiasm but turned them down. I had to put my foot down somewhere.

So the subject hadn't been mentioned again, though I knew it wouldn't be forgotten. I now had a group of friends determined to find him. What had I started? Had I created some kind of monster?

This wasn't the only thing to have come out of those last few days of our holiday. Julianne had insisted I write a 'Real Life' feature for Liberty magazine, telling everybody about my extraordinary story.

I only agreed provided I could remain anonymous. I didn't want everyone to know that I was now a millionaire. It was unnecessary, or at least I thought so anyway.

She had also taken some stunning photographs of Casa Linda that would be published alongside it. 'Especially as we can't use any photos of you,' she'd pouted with a wink.

The other major thing that had happened was Liz and Jorge's engagement. It was the quickest romance in history, but it was clear for all to see: they were completely and utterly in love. Even an idiot could see it was real.

Due to work commitments, Liz had returned home, where she would stay until a replacement beautician was found for the salon where she worked. It also allowed her to tie up any other loose ends before moving to her new life on the island, with the man of her dreams.

We were a little concerned. She was moving from the UK, a buzzing place with people everywhere, with a multitude of things to do, to a little island in the middle of the Atlantic Ocean. It's the most fantastic place for a holiday, but to live there? She was so brave to even consider it.

What we do for love, I sighed to myself as I crossed the road, avoiding a massive puddle that was spreading fast towards the pavement. But I wasn't quite quick enough and, just as I reached the other side, a large lorry sped past and soaked me from head to foot in dirty brown rainwater.

I screamed silently and hurried out of the way before it happened again. At least I was on my way to the office, where I knew there would be something I could change into.

'Oh. My. God. What on earth happened to you?' yelled Jasmine, the receptionist, as I pushed open the big glass door to the Liberty office.

'Bloody lorry just soaked me,' I muttered, shivering.

'Oh, you poor thing, go straight into the bathroom and I'll get you something warm and dry to put on,' she said in her warm motherly Caribbean tones. Although Jasmine was only twenty-three, she had a real maternal side to her and loved caring for people. Whether we wanted it or not. In this case, I did.

'Thanks Jas, you're an angel, you really are.'

As I plonked my bag down on the sink in the ladies' loo and stepped out of my dripping wet long pink denim skirt, which was no longer pink but a nasty shade of brown, in walked Julianne, cuddling Beckham.

'Jasmine just told me what happened, you must be freezing! They're bloody arseholes, those lorry drivers. They don't give a damn about us poor souls on the pavements,' she screeched, frightening the cat so that he catapulted out of her hands into the nearest sink basin, before hopping to the ground and purring by my bare legs.

'Beckham loves me, though, don't you, darling?' I asked, bending to stroke him.

But as soon as the door opened, he bolted.

'I guess not,' I said, feeling sorry for myself.

'Here you go, sweetie,' said Jasmine as she handed me a lovely thick towel and a fuchsia coloured Juicy Couture tracksuit in size twelve.

'Jasmine, you're a star. I'm so glad we keep a stash of clothes in the office for times like this,' I said, feeling refreshed and much more comfortable.

'Thank you, Jasmine,' Julianne said as we exited the bathroom. Jasmine nodded happily and rushed back to her desk, where the phone was ringing. I was just about to sit at my own desk when Julianne asked me to join her in her office.

'Can I get a coffee first?'

She laughed. 'Of course. Can you bring one for me, too?'

With two cups of the hot stuff, I pushed open her door and sat down, joining several cats who purred in various hiding places; bookshelves, waste paper bins, handbags. These cats were wonderfully good at finding the perfect spots to curl up and go to sleep.

It certainly is a cat's life.

'I just thought we'd have a little chat about your article for this month,' said Julianne as she closed the lid to her laptop and looked up.

I nodded, taking a big gulp of hot coffee at the same time, which led to a bit of a coughing fit. Julianne waited a moment before realising I was literally choking, my face becoming redder.

She jumped out of her chair, sending it spinning behind her, knocking the waste paper bin over, which in turn sent a cat hurtling, meowing as if it had been kicked.

She rushed to my side and patted me gently on the back, but nothing seemed to help.

She pressed the intercom on the telephone, panicking 'Jasmine, Jasmine! Hurry. Kate's choking and can't stop!'

Within seconds, Jasmine was in the office, rubbing my back and, bizarrely, blowing on my forehead. She also encouraged me to take small sips of water in between taking slow deep breaths.

'There, there. That's it. It's finished now. Calm down,' she whispered encouragingly.

Feeling like a child, I slowly returned to normal, taking deep breaths and smiling, embarrassed.

'Oh, God, Kate. I thought you were going to keel over and die. You scared me,' screeched Julianne.

By now, the cats had become so freaked out by the commotion that they were trying desperately to hide. That's when I noticed many of the office staff were standing behind me, watching in horror.

'It's okay, guys. Cancel the ambulance, she's fine,' I heard someone say disappointedly.

'Jesus,' I gasped, red in the face, 'I seem to be today's entertainment.'

'Come on, everybody out. She just choked on her coffee, that's all. The show's over,' said Jasmine as she shoved them out the door.

'I don't know what I'd do without you, Jas, you really are a star. An angel,' I smiled, my colour slowly returning to normal.

She smiled and nodded before rushing off as the phone began ringing again.

'Are you alright?' asked Julianne, real concern in her voice.

I nodded, 'I'm okay thanks. It's terrifying when that happens, though,' I answered, still shaking from the shock. 'But I'm okay. Really. What were we talking about?'

For the next half hour, we discussed everything I should include in my article before she showed me some of the most beautiful photographs she'd taken of Casa Linda.

'Have you given any thought as to what you're going to do with the house yet?' she asked as she relaxed back into her chair.

'I'm still considering all my options. It's a beautiful place, though, and so peaceful, but I don't think I want to live there. It's certainly not the kind of place to live on your own. Speaking of which, how're things going with you and Syd?' I asked nosily.

The mere mention of his name brought a grin to Julianne's face, and she blushed.

'Well, between you and me, things seem to be moving quite quickly. So quickly, in fact, that he's asked me to move in with him,' her voice seemed to increase a few octaves at the end of the sentence, and she blushed even more.

'Wow, that is fast,' I grinned. 'Are you going to?'

'Of course I am,' she yelled, suddenly aware of how loud her voice had become. She looked down, straightened her skirt, cleared her throat and blushed.

'Julianne, that's wonderful news.'

She'd fancied Syd for such a long time and, after getting together, she was clearly head over heels in love with him. It was incredible how all my friends were suddenly meeting the men of their dreams and settling down. Soon it would be just me. All alone. A sigh slipped out from my lips, and I looked at her in embarrassment.

'Oh, Kate. I'm sorry. It's thoughtless of me to be telling you this, especially considering your... predicament.'

Her comment made me chuckle, and once I'd started, I just couldn't stop.

Julianne looked at me, and soon, she began to giggle too.

'Pred...ic..a....ment!' We giggled and giggled, shaking our heads violently.

My stomach began to ache, and as I held it tightly, I noticed the door being pushed open secretively and several heads peered in. A few staff members looked at us then looked at each other, shrugged their shoulders and closed the door again.

Minutes later, the phone rang. Julianne was barely capable of picking it up. 'Ye...s... Jas....mine,' she giggled, 'oh... err... I don't.... think... I can take... it. Laughing... too... much. Huh? Yeh... yeh... okay'.

She put the phone down and shook her head. '

Stop... Kate.... stop. Have to... work.'

We laughed for so long that we could barely even remember why we were laughing in the first place, so we soon began to calm down, and I decided it was a good time to leave. I motioned to her that I was going and she nodded, almost as if pleading me to get out.

Closing the door behind me, I leant against it and looked up, wiping the tears of laughter from my eyes. I suddenly realised how silent the office was, and as I looked around, just about everyone was staring at me.

'Private joke,' I said before making a quick exit to the bathroom.

Looking in the mirror, I was totally red-faced. My eyes appeared swollen as if I'd been crying instead of laughing, and my mascara was smudged around my eyes. I looked a mess.

The door opened, and somebody's arm appeared, holding my handbag. I took it gratefully.

'Thanks, Jasmine,' I whispered.

I emptied my make-up bag into the sink and began reapplying my mascara and eyeliner as well as a dash of lip gloss.

I stared at myself in the mirror.

'Predicament,' I whispered to myself. Was I in a predicament? Had I spent my life in a predicament? Was it time for me to finally accept things and move on with my life? Should I try and forget all about the man of my dreams and see if there was Life After Fred... LAF. I smirked to myself. LAF... Maybe someone was trying to tell me something.

CHAPTER 17

The September edition was out. My life story. It felt bizarre, seeing it in print, yet a feeling of relief came over me, especially knowing it had been written anonymously. Although our readers would know these kinds of miraculous things do happen, they didn't have to know who they happened to, did they?

Only a select few knew who the story was about and they were my closest friends, Jo, Carly, Liz and Jorge, Anna, John, Julianne, Syd and Tony (and, of course, my mum). My dad, on the other hand, didn't know. I had barely spoken to him in months, but I couldn't bring myself to tell him about the amazing thing that had happened to me, the amazing thing that had completely changed my life in every way possible. It wasn't that I didn't want him to know, it was because of whom the money and the property had all come from.

But, deep down, I knew I needed to have a conversation with him. I was just putting it off. I would do... soon. I just needed a little more time.

In the meantime, I was just enjoying my life one day at a time. I knew there was much to do, but again, I didn't feel quite ready to start making huge decisions that would affect the rest of my life, like what to do with Casa Linda, when to visit the penthouse apartment in New York (and what to do with it), when to visit the apartment in Canada and what I should do with the now-derelict caravan site in Skegness. There were lots of other things I had to do as well but on a more personal level. I wanted to find out more about Sam, for example.

Even though I was now seriously rich, I was still yet to succumb to buying my own house, or even my own car. I was content using public transport and still happy to live in Jo's basement flat.

In fact, I was on the bus on my way home that day when I noticed two young women reading Liberty. Because it was the latest edition, I couldn't help eavesdropping.

'Oh my god,' said one. 'Have you read about this woman who inherited millions?'

'I know,' the other answered as she flicked back to the pages.

'God, can you imagine having that sort of money?'

They continued chatting about what they would do if they were rich, including buying a large yacht, having liposuction and hiring George Clooney.

I suppressed a giggle.

As my stop loomed ahead and I stood up, I heard one of them say, 'But the first thing I'd do would be to buy a nice car and stop using public transport. This is so gross. Look at that, someone's been sick over there,' she pointed to a load of stinky vomit in the corner of the bus.

Hopping down the steps, I watched it drive off into the distance.

Perhaps she was right. Maybe it was time to splash out on my own car. It wasn't as if I didn't drive. I passed my test, the second time, around ten years ago; I just never really needed a car. I guess it was about time. It wasn't like I couldn't afford it.

That evening, as Jo and I sat eating a Chinese takeaway in my cosy living room, we pondered over what car to buy.

'I certainly don't need anything big,' I said, stuffing the most delicious Singapore noodles into my mouth. 'But then I don't want something too small, either. It needs to be able to sit four, including me.'

Jo nodded, unable to speak as she chewed on a rather large mouthful of sweet and sour pork.

'So you don't fancy anything flash, then?' she eventually asked.

Shaking my head, I couldn't think of anything worse. I didn't want anything too sporty, and I didn't want anything that would draw too much attention to myself.

'It should be nippy though, I can't be doing with a car that's got no guts to it,' I laughed, remembering my dad's old Peugeot that was so slow it was embarrassing. We used to get hooted at traffic lights, people thinking he hadn't noticed the lights turn green. He had, of course, it was just that the car was so slow to get going. Mind you, it was an enormous vehicle, far too big for its' engine size.

Jo had a BMW X5. It was fantastic, but I didn't want something quite so big.

'How about a Mini?' she suggested, taking a sip of wine.

Hm. That wasn't a bad idea, although Minis were a bit common.

As if reading my mind, she said, 'You could get one sprayed a different colour to make it a bit more unique.'

Nodding, I pictured a pink mini with cream leather interior. I loved it. I guess I would have a mini, then. That was easy. Although considering I didn't want one that drew too much attention to myself – a pink mini probably would do just that. But, what the heck.

The next day I planned to look for my nearest dealership and see if I could get one in pink. My favourite colour!

'You're so predictable,' Jo moaned. 'You and Carly, with your pink,' she said, smiling and shaking her head.

Carly would go nuts when I told her about my plans. I was excited about telling her, but it would have to wait until after the weekend, as she was spending a few days with a school friend. She was growing up so fast. It only felt like yesterday when Jo and I were changing her nappies.

The next day I woke up bright and early, eager to get out and order my new car. Jo was too busy to come along so I'd roped in

Anna and John for extra support. After all, I'd never ordered a new car before.

Unfortunately, ordering a new car wasn't quite as straight forward as I'd hoped. Because I wanted a particular shade of pink, I'd have to have it especially made.

I told the dealer that I wanted a different shade of pink, with cream leather interior and cream stripes on the bonnet – not black, nor white. But cream.

As the words tumbled from my mouth, I realised I sounded a bit of a diva, and so I looked away in embarrassment.

Anna burst out laughing while John was far too busy inspecting all the other cars for sale to have even noticed.

'Sorry,' I blushed, 'I really don't mean to sound like a drama queen. I'm not usually like this,' I giggled nervously like a youngster. God, it was embarrassing.

'That's alright, my love,' he replied. 'If you really want to have the car specially made to order, it's not a problem, you just have to be prepared for quite a wait. To have one made will take a few months,' he said confidently.

There I was, hoping to be able to drive the car almost immediately, well okay maybe not straight away but I thought it would only be a few weeks, not months. I sighed, ignoring everyone around me, thinking about what to do.

'Let's go and have a cup of coffee and think about it, Kate,' said John, who had re-joined us.

'Erm. Okay. We'll be back. Thanks for your help,' I said as they dragged me away outside.

As we settled down in the café right next door, John ordered three cappuccinos and a couple of chocolate brownies before we talked about what I should do.

'Another option is to buy one of the ones in there, in another colour and take it to a local garage to be re-sprayed,' suggested John. 'At least then you wouldn't have to wait, would you?'

'No, that's not what she's going to do at all,' said Anna, matter-of-factly, as she took a bite out of her brownie.

I looked at her, confused.

'I'm not?'

'You're going to order one with every spec that you want, and it's going to be completely and utterly yours. Made precisely for you,' she said, smiling as a few crumbs fell out of her open mouth before continuing. 'Come on, Kate,' she looked around surreptitiously and lowered her voice. 'You're insanely rich, and so far all you've spent is a couple of thousand on a holiday to the Azores. Don't you think it's time that you splashed out on yourself? You deserve it,' she looked around again secretively, making sure she hadn't been overheard. Confident that no-one was listening, she leaned back and grinned.

She was right, of course, and what better way to treat myself than on a car that would be completely me?

I slowly grinned back.

Unbeknown to me, the office had begun receiving lots of phone calls from the press wanting to know the identity of the woman in September's main feature.

Julianne had called me into her office that morning and confessed.

'Kate, don't be alarmed but...' and then she told me all about the fact she'd had the BBC, ITV, Sky News, Elle Magazine, Marie Claire, all the well-known weeklies and lots of other journalists on the phone. They all wanted to know who I was.

I panicked, terrified I was going to be hunted down by all those scary people. I hadn't even put the television or radio on for a few days; I'd been too busy talking to Tony about Sam, daydreaming about my new car that would take months to be delivered and pondering about how on Earth I was going to talk to my dad about all of this.

It turned out I was fast becoming front-page news. My story had generated so much interest that almost everyone was asking 'Who's That Girl' (a particularly popular headline, apparently).

That night I convened an emergency meeting at Jo's house – my flat wasn't really big enough for everyone. I invited Julianne and Syd, Anna and John, Jo and Carly and Tony and Zara (I thought it best that Zara came too, considering it was an evening thing). Sadly, Liz and Jorge couldn't make it considering they were thousands of miles away. I decided I would call her the next morning to discuss the problem.

As everyone began arriving, wondering why they had been summoned at such short notice, I stood alone in the bathroom, staring in the mirror. I wondered what would happen if the press did find out who I was. Would they hound me? Would I start getting letters from everybody, asking for money? Begging letters? I shuddered at the thought. I had never wanted to be famous, not really.

Pulling myself together, straightening my spine and taking a deep breath, I went out to greet my closest friends.

'Hi everyone!' I called out. 'Thanks for coming. Sorry about the short notice. Oh, thanks, Jo,' I said as she handed me a much-needed glass of white wine, and squeezed my arm encouragingly.

I spotted Tony, and with him was a small, exquisite-looking, dark-haired beauty. She had long, straight black hair, down to her waist, and the features of the most beautiful china doll. She smiled as soon as she saw me. I knew instantly we would become good friends.

'You must be Kate,' she said, lightly pushing Tony aside so she could kiss my cheek. 'It's such a pleasure to meet you, at last. Tony has told me so much about you,' she said huskily.

'The pleasure is really all mine, Zara. I've heard a lot about you, too - all good, of course!' I laughed, thrilled that the couple had clearly overcome their problems. They were very much in love, and it pleased me, secretly knowing that I may have helped bring them back together again.

'Thanks for coming, Tony. I'm so glad you brought Zara along, she's lovely,' I whispered as we exchanged hugs.

He smiled back, knowingly and thankfully.

'I think I might know why we're all here,' he said to everyone, surprising even me. I wondered what he knew.

Everyone turned to him, each gingerly sipping at their wine, except Carly, who drank from a can of Coca Cola and John from a can of lager.

'If anyone has read the papers or seen the news over the past few days, they'll know that everyone wants to know our Kate here.'

I cringed and blushed at the same time, aware that the eyes of my closest friends were on me.

Clearing my throat, I nodded. 'Yes, it seems that everyone and I mean everyone, has read Liberty this month, which is absolutely fantastic. It's given us major coverage. It's just what the magazine needed. The bad side though, is that everybody does seem to want to know who I am. Honestly, guys, I don't think I can cope with everyone in the UK knowing my name, knowing my face and knowing that I am... erm... well, rather well off,' a little laughter ensued. 'Do you think we can keep this to ourselves? Is it physically possible? Can you all keep my secret for me?' I pleaded.

Everyone began nodding. 'Of course, Kate, we wouldn't dream of telling anyone. You're our best pal. We will always protect you,' answered Jo.

'I'm sorry to have dragged you all here just because of this, but since Julianne told me about it earlier, I've been worrying myself silly. Thanks so much for coming, you guys. But fear not... I have ordered some food, so at least we can eat well,' I laughed.

As if on cue, the doorbell rang.

'Pizza!' shouted Carly as she rushed to open the front door.

Sure enough, pizza had arrived, and we all settled down around Jo's ginormous dining table and dug in while discussing ways in which to put off the press if they continued to call the office.

As the evening wore on, I was pleased the conversation gradually moved on from my awkward circumstances to current affairs and the latest reality TV shows. All in all, we had a lovely night.

Tony and Zara were the last to leave. It was clear Zara had wanted to say something to me but, every time she approached me, Tony would suddenly appear, smiling, as if not wanting his lovely lady to leave his side. He hadn't stopped holding her hand almost all night.

I went to bed confident my friends would protect me at all costs and I eventually drifted off into the land of sleep, my last thought being Fred (naturally).

CHAPTER 19

I called Liz the following morning.

'Kate! Jorge, it's Kate!' she yelled so loud I'd had to hold the phone away from my ear.

"Hi, Liz!' How are things?' I asked, thrilled to hear her so happy. It was so long overdue.

'Fantastic, really fantastic. Jorge and I are so happy over here. I could do with a proper job, though, but I'm sure something will come up eventually. But its soooooo good to hear from you. How are things with you? When are you coming over? Found a man yet? How's the gang?' she asked, giggling.

'Fine, fine. Everyone's great, thanks. However there's a bit of an odd situation developing, which is the main reason I'm calling, apart from finding out how you are, of course,' I laughed before continuing. 'You know that article I wrote for Liberty? Well, people are asking questions. Julianne has had the world and his brother ringing up asking for my true identity. For obvious reasons, I don't really want anyone to know. So I was just ringing to ask you not to tell anyone about me. I realise that there will be people on the island that will know me, but I doubt the press will go over there. But, just in case they do, can you keep my secret?' I babbled

'God, you really are worrying, aren't you? It all sounds like something out of a movie, doesn't it? It's quite exciting really, isn't it?' she laughed, before stopping herself abruptly. 'But of course I can keep a secret, Kate. I wouldn't dream of telling anyone. You're one of my best mates, and you need to be protected,' she said.

'It's funny,' I said. 'That's what the rest of the gang said. Thanks, Liz, I appreciate it. I really do. But now, enough about me, when are you two going to tie the knot?'

Liz promised me I would be the first to know, after her mum. We spoke for another ten minutes or so before promising to talk again soon, and I put the phone down and flopped on the sofa.

Seconds later, the phone rang. I didn't bother getting up, I just reached across and picked it up, still horizontal.

'Hello?'

'Hi sweetheart, it's Mum!' yelled a voice on the other end of the phone.

I jumped up immediately. 'Mum!' I shouted back.

I could hear her laughing. 'How are you, my angel? I felt the urge to call. There's nothing wrong, is there?'

How is it that, since she has lived in Africa, she always seems to know when to call?

'There's nothing seriously wrong, no,' I answered back, stifling a yawn. 'It's just that I've got myself into a bit of a situation here. Nothing to worry about really, Mum. It's just that the whole world seems to want to know who I am.'

I could virtually sense the confusion in her voice, so I explained everything.

I could tell she was shaking her head. 'Oh, dear. Oh, dear,' she said. 'It's money. It's the root of all evil. It really is.'

'Mum, that doesn't really help,' I said, trying not to laugh. She always had been a bit dramatic.

'What does your dad think of all this?' she asked, genuine concern creeping, unintentionally, into her voice.

'Errrrm.....'

'You still haven't told him, have you?'

It was like she was clairvoyant or something.

'You're worried what he'll think about Sam, aren't you?' as if she knew I was nodding, she continued, 'Kate, sweetheart, you're not Sam's daughter. You're Bob's daughter. Sam left you everything because he loved me so much. He knew I didn't want anything, and you were the closest thing to me. It was the most beautiful gift from a wonderful man. You need to enjoy it. But Bob has the right to know that his daughter has become a millionaire. Have you thought about donating anything to him and his other daughters?'

'It has crossed my mind. I was thinking more about a trust fund for the girls for when they're older?' I said.

'Sweetheart, that's a lovely idea, and I think your dad will be really chuffed with that. Honestly, though, I think he will be chuffed for you. Sam was a very long time ago. Your dad's moved on. I've moved on. You've moved on. Tell him. You'll be surprised by his reaction, I'm sure. When you do speak to him, give him my best wishes,' she waited a second, hearing my gasp.

'Like I said, Katie, I've moved on as well.'

'How's Nick and life in Africa?' I asked.

'Wonderful. Absolutely wonderful. You should come and see us, you know. I bet you'd fall in love with the place and its people. It's fabulous. You did promise me you'd come soon.'

'One of these days, Mum, I promise I'll come and visit. Although I'm not sure about all those bugs and stuff over there,' I answered honestly. 'But when are you going to come and visit me, Mum?' I asked smirking.

'I think you know the answer to that, sweetheart. Africa is our home now. We don't really want anything to do with England anymore.' I knew that's what she would say.

'Well, I have another idea. Why don't you come and visit me in the Azores? That place out there is incredible. I'll pay for your flights. I'd love to see you, Mum.'

For a moment, she was silent, chewing it over in her mind.

'At some point, I need to go and check out the apartments in New York and Toronto – I could meet you there instead?' I asked, hoping that she would say yes to at least something.

'It's a lovely idea, sweetheart but I'll have to decline. You know how I feel about the western world. I'd love to see you, though. But for now, I need to get back. I'll speak to you soon. Don't worry about the magazine thing. Something will happen in the news, and then your story won't be as interesting to them. Just give it a bit of time, and it'll die down. And don't forget to talk to your dad. I love you, Katie.'

'I love you too, Mum. Bye. Love to Nick, too. Bye.'

I flopped back down on the sofa, thinking about what Mum had said. She was right about the news. There obviously wasn't anything significant happening at the moment, which was why everyone was trying to find out 'Who's That Girl'. I laughed to myself, thinking about how ridiculous this whole thing had become. It would die down. It would just take time.

I thought about ringing Dad but decided against it. Maybe it would be better to just go to his house and talk to him? Yes, that's what I would do. I'd give it a few days and do that.

Since the magazine article had been published, Julianne had insisted I take a break from the office, at least until things, hope-fully, quietened down a bit. She told me if I wanted to work, I should do it from home, so I hopped up and went and made myself a cup of tea and grabbed my laptop. Before starting work on my latest column, I checked my emails, but there was nothing of great interest, except a short email from Mini confirming my little pink and cream car should be ready for delivery in about another three months. It seemed like ages. I sighed, wishing I could speed it up. Patience was all I needed.

CHAPTER 20

$\mathcal{A}$ few days later, I finally found the courage to go to Newcastle to see Dad. I rang first to make sure he and Julie would be there. She needed to be there too. After all, it did concern her and the kids.

Clearly, Dad was concerned when he heard my voice. It had been a few months since I'd spoken to him, so he automatically assumed something must be wrong, especially when I asked if it was okay I visit them.

I was so nervous and had no idea how he was going to react. It's not every day your eldest daughter tells you she's inherited a fortune.

The train journey was uneventful. And, even though I'd taken a novel with me, I just couldn't concentrate. My mind was all over the place. Just thinking about telling Dad about Sam made me break out in a cold sweat.

I thought about why I still hadn't done anything wild with the money. Why I didn't want everybody to know. Why was I still living in a little flat that belonged to someone else?

There was so much to think about, yet I just felt incapable of making decisions until I was in the right frame of mind.

Perhaps once I'd spoken to Dad? Maybe then I would feel ready to go a little bit mad.

Is that what I wanted? Did I want to go a bit mad? Maybe I needed to go a bit mad?

Maybe I just needed a psychiatrist.

Dad's place was a short walk from the train station, so a bit of fresh air would probably help clear my head in preparation for his reaction. Whatever that might be.

'Hi, Dad,' I said sheepishly as he opened the front door.

"Hello Petal,' he said, giving me one of his lovely bear hugs. I'd forgotten how great it felt to get one of those.

'Let me get a good look at you,' he said as he pulled me away and looked at me at arms' length. 'You look lovely, love. A bit thin, mind, but lovely all the same.'

As he took my coat, Julie bounded down the stair's carrying the latest little one on her hip.

'Kate! It's so great to see you,' she said with genuine pleasure in her voice.

I had always known Julie liked me and enjoyed my company, and this time it seemed the old guilt had finally faded away.

'It's been ages, you shouldn't leave it so long before you visit, you know? Your dad does miss you. And the kids love to see you too. And me,' she added with a smile, as we hugged as best we could with little Chloe in between us.

'Chloe! You're so big,' I said, taking the little toddler out of her arms for a few minutes, playing with her tiny hands.

'You've got another beauty, here, you two. I guess the girls are all at school?'

They nodded.

'They were sad they weren't going to see you,' Dad said. 'Unless you wanted to stay over, of course. You're more than welcome.'

'That's nice of you, Dad, but I can't. I've got a mountain of things to do, which is what I've come to talk to you about.'

As we headed into the living room, Julie put Chloe down in her sleeper and then popped into the kitchen to fetch a pot of tea and biscuits, before we sat on the old faded leather sofa they'd had for years.

They could use a new suite, I thought to myself as I waited for Julie to finish pouring before I began.

'So what brings you up to Newcastle, love, if it's not just to see your old man?' he smiled.

'Well, Dad, Julie. I've got something really important to tell you. Please don't say anything until I've finished. It's probably going to be a bit of a shock, so just sit and listen.'

Their faces belied their calmness; I could tell they were worried.

'Dad, do you remember Uncle Sam, from when we used to go to the caravan park in Skegness?'

I noticed him tense up, just a little bit, before nodding apprehensively.

'I'm sorry to say that he died recently, after a really long and horrible battle with cancer.'

Dad's eyes turned downwards, and his smile dropped, but he said nothing.

'He was a very, very rich man. He owned that caravan site, he had a beautiful mansion in the Azores, an apartment in New York and Canada and.... millions and millions of pounds,' I stopped to take a breath. 'And he's left it all to... me.'

Dad stood up and sat back down again. Julie's mouth opened and closed like a fish.

'But... why you, Kate? Why would he leave it all to you?' asked Julie, looking confused.

Dad looked at me knowingly, and I nodded sadly, answering his unspoken question.

'You knew about him and Mum, didn't you?'

With a sad smile, he nodded. 'Of course I did, Kate. It was obvious, although I never caught them together, I just knew something was going on.'

'Yet you took us back, year after year. Why would you do that if you knew?' I asked.

'I couldn't put a stop to it, Kate. She was my wife, and I loved her very much, back then. I could tell that Sam made her happy, and when she was happy, we were happy as a family. I chose to ignore it. I would rather have had a happy wife than no wife. I was always prepared for her to leave me for him, but she always came back to me. It was just a few weeks a year, so I decided to accept it for what it was. A holiday fling.'

Wow... I was so shocked. To love someone that much, you're willing to let them see someone else, once a year. That must have been torture. I couldn't make my mind up if that made him a strong man or just an incredibly weak one.

Whatever he was, he was still my dad, and he was willing to accept it so that we could be happy as a family. I was choked up.

'But then why did you leave her in the end, Dad?'

'Honestly, Katie? I just fell out of love with her and in love with Julie. It's as simple as that. I'm sorry, love. This must be quite hard for you to understand.'

'Actually, it's not as hard as I thought it would be. I'm beginning to understand that love doesn't make any sense anyway, so why try understanding it?' I laughed, keen to relax the situation a little.

'I just can't believe you're rich, like so incredibly rich, that's what I can't understand,' said Julie quietly.

'Well, that's another reason why I wanted to come and talk to you. I'd like to open trust funds for the girls so that when they turn, I don't know, twenty-one or thirty or whatever, they'll have plenty of money to do whatever they want with.'

'Oh my god, Katie, thank you. Thank you so much! That is the kindest thing ever,' yelped Julie as she jumped up and wrapped her arms around me, narrowly missing the teapot that balanced precariously on the edge of the rickety little coffee table.

'Sweetheart, that's wonderful. Thank you so much,' said Dad as he swiftly wiped a tear from his eye.

'There's just one other thing, too. I'd like you to have this,' I said, taking a small folder out of my handbag and giving them a cheque for £1,500,000.

'I want you to pay off your mortgage and use some of it to refurnish your house! You could use a new sofa, for starters,' I laughed. 'And then use whatever is left for whatever else you need. Or buy a new house, of course.'

'Holy shit, Kate, we can't accept this,' they said together.

'Katie, darling, this is one and a half million pounds,' said Dad in shock.

'You can, and you will. Please take it. I know it will make your lives a lot easier. Dad, you could even change your job and stop working nights. If you pay off your mortgage, you could even pack your job in altogether! Please, take it and be happy.'

A couple of hours later, after I'd managed to calm them both down, we stood in the porch, while I put my coat back on to go home.

'Bye, Katie, and thank you so much. It's unbelievable,' said Julie as she kissed me on the cheek before rushing back indoors. 'I've got to go and change Chloe's nappy, it stinks.'

I laughed and waved goodbye.

'Katie, I don't tell you this enough, but I'm really proud of you. I should have told you that before any of this money came along. I am. I really am. You've always been such an amazing young woman, and I am so proud to be your dad. I'm sorry I haven't been around much over the past few years, but we will make an effort to come and see you soon, I promise,' he said as he tried to hide his tears.

'Thanks, Dad. That really means a lot to me, you know. I love you,' I said, giving him a hug. 'Oh, and Mum sends her best wishes too'.

He smiled. 'She's great, your mum. I'm so happy she met a nice man too, you know. Send our love back when you next speak to her.'

'I will, Dad, I promise.'

'You know, all I want now is for you to meet the man of your dreams and for you to settle down and have a family of your own,' he said as I kissed him again and skipped down the steps, waving.

'I've already met him, Dad,' I said.

I laughed at Dad's quizzical expression as I walked away with a grin, avoiding any questions.

On my way back to the train station I smiled to myself. I knew the whole truth about Mum, Dad and Uncle Sam. It was like something out of a movie. The tale of a tragic love triangle. At least both Mum and Dad were both happy. That's the most important thing.

CHAPTER 21

The following weekend, Tony and Zara invited me to their apartment in Wimbledon for dinner.

'And you ought to stay the night, too,' Zara had insisted, on the phone, earlier in the week.

'Then the three of us can completely chill out and not worry about getting you home.'

I arrived at Wimbledon Station just after 3pm on Friday afternoon and was met by Zara in her black Audi TT.

'Katie!' yelled Zara from the distance as I walked out of the station into the fresh air. She rushed over and kissed me on both cheeks. 'It's wonderful to see you. I'm so pleased you're staying over tonight,' she gushed.

'It's great to see you too, Zara. Thanks for inviting me. It's so kind of you,' I said as she took my overnight bag before I could stop her.

'I might be little, but I'm strong,' she laughed.

As we climbed into her car, I was almost sorry for ordering a Mini.

'I love your car, Zara.'

'Me too. We bought it last year. It's my pride and joy,' she laughed as we sped away from the hustle and bustle of the town centre.

'Tony is still at work, but he should be home around six-ish,' she said as if reading my mind.

I nodded as I looked across to Wimbledon Common on my left.

'Can you believe that I've never been to Wimbledon?' I said.

'Never? Oh my god! Well then, you should stay for longer so I can take you shopping. There are some lovely little chic boutiques down in Wimbledon Village,' she laughed as she put her foot to the floor, before slowing to turn off the main road, opposite the Common.

'Julianne is trying to keep me away from the office at the moment, so I would be delighted to stay a bit longer if you're sure?'

'Of course I'm sure,' she said as an automatic gate began to open into a large park surrounded by beautiful Victorian-styled houses and apartments.

'Why don't you stay until Monday?'

I nodded and grinned back at her.

'Here we are. Home sweet home. It's so nice to have you here, Kate,' Zara said as she reversed the Audi perfectly into the parking spot.

'Come on. It's this way,' she said as she refused to let me carry my bag again. I pushed my handbag onto my shoulder and looked around in awe. It was a beautiful location, with elegant apartment blocks overlooking a grand central garden where a small orna-mental fountain sprouted water high into the air.

Their home turned out to the most stunning two-bedroom apartment I'd ever seen.

'Wow, this place is amazing. Maybe I should buy myself one of these,' I laughed as she showed me around.

'You must make yourself completely at home. While you are here, this is your home, you understand. And don't worry, I'll let you know when any of them come onto the market. I'd love to have you as a neighbour,' she giggled as I followed her into a large white bedroom with dark wooden floors and white bedding.

'I'm dying for the loo,' she said. 'Take your time, and I'll see you in the kitchen in a minute.'

I smiled and sat on the bed with a sigh, looking through the window at the beautiful view of the Common beyond. I was in heaven.

After unpacking my clothes and slipping off my shoes, replacing them with my newest pair of comfortable slippers, I walked into the small but perfectly formed kitchen, where Zara was pouring us both a glass of chilled white wine.

As she handed it to me, she said, 'Before Tony comes home, Kate, I just want you to know how grateful I am to you.'

I blushed, knowing that Tony must have told her about my little speech in the Azores.

'Please don't be embarrassed, he told me what you said, and it's just what he needed to hear. I credit you with saving our marriage. And I just want to say thank you. I owe you an awful lot. I really do. So thank you,' she said as we clinked glasses.

'All in a day's work,' I laughed.

'Now, you must tell me more about your Fred,' she said with a twinkle in her eye. 'Yes, yes, of course he told me about him. I think it's the most wonderful, romantic story I have ever heard. Beautiful.'

I blushed again.

A couple of hours later, Tony arrived home, bringing with him two bunches of flowers.

'One for my beautiful and adorable wife,' he said as he gently placed a loving kiss on her lips. 'And the other for my dear friend,' as he planted a smacker on my cheek.

"Wow, he's a romantic too,' I laughed, pretending to swoon. 'You're a very lucky girl, Zara,' I winked. And you're a very lucky man too, Tony.'

'So am I taking two lovely ladies out for a meal tonight or are we ordering in?'

We decided to order in, choosing instead to go out for dinner the following evening. That way we'd have more than enough time to get dolled up, we agreed, as Tony rolled his eyes.

'In that case, you two do the ordering while I go and have a quick shower and get out of this suit.'

With a vast choice of dining options, we eventually decided on Indian, ordering enough food to feed a small army. Having said that, Zara might be a little lady, but she could certainly pack away plenty of food.

Over dinner, I discovered Zara is half English which explained why she was at such ease with the language.

'I grew up in Portugal,' she said. 'In the Algarve, actually. I met Tony when he and his family moved into my neighbourhood. I think we were barely teenagers.'

'I was fourteen, you were twelve,' he added, knowingly. 'I remember it like it was yesterday. My family and I had moved from Lisbon to the Algarve – my father had been offered a job in a school there, he was a headmaster. And I remember the exact moment I first saw Zara. It was while I helped my parents carry all our belongings into our new house, I'd heard a girl singing quietly, and when I looked over, I saw this tiny girl sitting on a swing singing to herself. I thought she looked like an angel,' he said adoringly. 'I thought there and then, I will marry that girl.'

'That's the most romantic thing I've ever heard,' I said, with a tear in my eye. I guess it was very much like my story with Fred, only I didn't have a happy ending.

As if reading my mind, Zara said, 'That's like you and Fred, isn't it? Which is why you have to find him.'

The two of them nodded as I sighed, I'm sure they were thinking the same as me: how on Earth could we possibly find a boy without a name that hasn't been seen for nearly 20 years.

'I think Fred is becoming even more of a fantasy. I doubt I'll ever find him.'

'No, I don't believe in giving up. He's out there, somewhere. It's just a case of locating where he is. We will find him, Kate. We will,' said Zara as she squeezed my hand.

Smiling, Tony added, 'I forgot to tell you something about my wife, Kate. She's very stubborn, and once she's got something in her head, she won't forget about it. She'll keep on going and going until she's entirely satisfied with the outcome. If that means looking for Fred until she's old and decrepit, she will,' laughed Tony.

Oh, God, I hoped not. I hoped I'd find him way before then.

Watching Tony wander into the kitchen in his pyjamas, yawning, I fidgeted, eager to do something.

'Good morning!' I said, brightly, pouring him a cup of coffee.

'Morning,' he mumbled, still half asleep. 'Thanks.'

'I guess you're not quite awake yet?'

He shook his head with a partial grin while taking a long sip.

'Tell you what, I'll go and have a walk across the Common. Where's the nearest shop? I could stop and get some fresh bread or croissants for breakfast?'

Running across the road to the lush green Wimbledon Common, I was saddened not to see any Wombles, but I did see a lot of dog walkers and joggers doing a bit of exercise.

It was a bright and fresh morning, perfect for a short amble, and I felt thoroughly refreshed after half an hour's walk. It was strange that I was out walking in an area I'd never visited and yet I felt so happy and independent. So... at home.

As my mind wondered what it would be like to live in that lovely little enclave in Wimbledon, I crossed back and headed down to the local shop to buy some goodies for breakfast.

On my return to the apartment complex, I was in for a surprise. As I waited for the elevator to reach the ground floor, the doors finally opened and I found myself face to face with singer and actress Tiffany Chantelle.

'Oh, excuse me,' I stuttered as I very nearly walked straight into her, as she tried to hide behind her rather large sunglasses.

She smiled but said nothing. Instead, she made as quick an exit as she could out into the car park and, I noted, into her brand spanking new red Mini Cooper S.

As the elevator reached the top floor and I virtually ran into Tony and Zara's place, I yelled out, 'Oh. My. God! You'll never guess who I've just seen!'

Laughing, the couple appeared from the bedroom at the same time, Zara brushing her long hair and Tony trying to put a pair of socks on.

'That wouldn't be Tiffany Chantelle, by any chance?'

'How do you do that? You always know what I'm thinking?' I gasped.

'Erm, Tiffany is our neighbour, Kate. She moved in last year. She's really quite pleasant. Pretty much keeps herself to herself, though.'

'You have a celebrity neighbour, and you just neglected to tell me?! I work for a magazine, you know? We have to know these things. I could have taken some photos. Oh my god. I can't believe it.'

'Kate, I think you should just breathe for a moment.'

I did as I was told and went and sat down at the dining table. Zara took the food from me, and I left it to her to prepare breakfast.

Eventually, the three of us sat down to a lovely meal of fresh coffee, croissants, American bagels with jam and Portuguese honey, and orange juice.

'I still can't get over the fact that Tiffany lives here!' I said for about the third time in ten minutes.

'Kate, I think you ought to see this from Tiffany's point of view. Actually, let me re-phrase this. You are on the verge of becoming a celebrity yourself. As much as we are trying to stop people from knowing your true identity, it will probably be revealed at some stage, and the world will want to know everything about you. Can you imagine then, if you lived here in this apartment complex and someone appears with a camera to take photos of you? You would be very upset, wouldn't you? Tiffany probably chose to live here to avoid people and paparazzi. Think about it,' said Tony.

'Oh my god, Tony, you're so right; how stupid of me not to see it like that. Oh, I'm such a moron. I keep forgetting about my 'celebrity status.' You're right. Oh, God, what am I going to do? Maybe I could try and have a chat with Tiffany and find out if this is a good place to live if you're in hiding'.

By this time, both Tony and Zara were in stitches.

'Oh, Kate. You're a bit melodramatic, aren't you,' said Zara as they both giggled.

Seeing their faces, I soon realised that I too often took myself far too seriously and so I began to laugh.

'Oh, guys, what are you going to do with me?'

That morning's events had cemented a seed in my mind, though. At some stage or other, it would probably come to light about Who That Girl really was, and I may well need my own bolt hole. Somewhere to live with a certain amount of security – a gated community, at least. I guess it would all depend on whether people would still be interested after finding out the truth about me.

Whatever happened, I realised that I did need to buy myself a home. My own home.

As much as I loved it there, I couldn't stay at Jo's flat forever. If I was going to be hounded by the press, or by anybody, it would be totally unfair and selfish of me to let it happen anywhere near Carly. She was only thirteen. No, I had to find a place of my own. Not Uncle Sam's homes either, somewhere that belonged entirely to me.

And now that I could afford to have a place practically anywhere, the feeling I'd had that morning in Wimbledon was like fate telling me that's where I should be. So Wimbledon it would be.

CHAPTER 23

*E*ven though I'd been enjoying sushi for a few years, I still hadn't quite mastered the art of chopsticks. As we sat in Zara and Tony's local Japanese restaurant, I struggled with a cute little spring roll, before I followed Zara's lead and picked it up with my fingers, dunked it in the sweet sauce and popped it in my mouth.

Tony shook his head and laughed as he expertly lifted the remaining roll deftly in between his two chopsticks, covered it in sauce and placed it expertly in his mouth.

'He's just showing off,' said Zara, as she took a sip of white wine and watched the wide variety of dishes slowly make their way around the conveyor belt in front of us before choosing a small bowl of edamame beans.

'Ooh, I love those,' I quipped as she handed me a few to go with the sushi rolls and sashimi I'd taken for myself.

'Thanks. You know, Tony, I've never actually asked you what it is that Samuel did for a living?'

'He actually built up a bit of a hotel empire, back in the late seventies and early eighties. He sold them all in the mid-eighties and made a fortune,' replied Tony just as he dropped a piece of slippery sashimi into his wine.

'Shit,' he uttered seconds before the waitress appeared out of nowhere with a clean glass and a smirk.

'Thanks,' he said with a slight blush to his cheeks.

'No problem, sir. It happens all the time,' she giggled while pouring him a fresh glass of wine.

'So, not that much of an expert with the chopsticks then,' I laughed, relieved that it wasn't just me that had made a fool of myself.

'Haha,' he said, continuing. 'Samuel was very well known in the hotel industry back in his day. His first hotel was just a small place in the Algarve, but it proved to be such a huge success that he opened two more in the region, another in Madeira and one in the Azores. That was when he went Stateside and opened a couple in New York and Boston, and one in Toronto too.'

'I had no idea he was such an accomplished businessman. To be honest, I'd just assumed that it was old money, you know? I should have known.'

'Not at all,' said Tony as he leaned forward to take a plate of vegetable tempura.

'You wouldn't have known. He'd sold most of them by the time he bought the resort at Skegness.'

'That's the weird thing,' I interrupted. 'If he was such a high flying businessman, with hotels all over the world, why on Earth would he buy a little caravan park in the East of England? I don't get it.'

'Why not?' answered Zara as she tucked into her second helping of tuna sashimi. 'I've been to Skegness, and it does have a certain charm.'

'Do you really think so?' I asked as I pinched a slice of her sashimi.

'Of course,' she answered, pinching one of my salmon rolls as I shrugged my shoulders and sat back to ponder it for a while, in silence.

When Tony laughed at my expression, I realised I was being silly, and so I changed the subject.

'So did Tony tell you about my new car, Zara?'

Spluttering into her wine, she laughed.

'Yes!' she cried. 'I love it! A pink Mini. You're a woman after my own heart, Kate.'

'What? You'd like a pink Mini too?' asked Tony in astonishment.

'Every woman has to have a bit of pink in her life,' his wife laughed.

'Really? Women,' he said, shaking his head in amusement.

'But don't get me wrong, I still adore my little Audi too.'

oOo

The next morning, the three of us spent a few hours searching online for local property for sale. Although a few houses looked appealing, none of them was situated within a gated community, something I'd convinced myself that I needed.

So we took to the road in Tony's 4x4, to see if we could find anything suitable with those elusive 'For Sale' signs outside. Sadly, we came back empty handed, not spotting a single property that would suit my needs. Feeling rather sorry for myself as we parked next to Zara's Audi, Tony's mobile rang. As we climbed out and waited for him to finish his conversation with a client, Zara and I wandered around the grounds. As if fate had intervened, a stylish middle-aged woman with a toddler on her hip, appeared from within her townhouse next to a man carrying a sign which he promptly hammered into her front garden (which could easily be seen from the main road). It was a For Sale sign!

The man shook her hand and then climbed into his car and drove away.

With excitement pulsing through my veins, I called out to her.

'Excuse me. Excuse me!' I yelled as I ran to her side.

Her little boy had already scrambled back indoors when she turned to me with a warm smile.

'I just spotted your sign,' I said, almost out of breath. 'I'm looking for a property around here. Would it be possible to arrange a viewing?'

'Of course,' she said. 'In fact, why don't you come and have a look now, if you have time, that is? My cleaner has been in this morning, so it's pretty spotless. It won't be in a couple of hours, though. Harry can create rather a lot of mess,' she replied as she held out her hand. 'I'm Amy, by the way.'

'Kate,' I answered, immediately warming to her as we shook hands. 'And this is Zara.'

'Oh hi, I've seen you around,' Zara said with a grin. 'But we've never met many of our neighbours.'

'I know. We're actually heading out of London. We just bought a place on the outskirts of Bath. Figured it would be beneficial to Harry, to grow up away from all the hustle and bustle, if you know what I mean?' she smiled.

'Absolutely,' I replied as we walked through the front door.

I was immediately impressed by their stylish colour scheme of taupes, browns, greens and beiges. Their oversized leather sofas just seemed to fit perfectly into the slightly cosier sunken lounge. On the upper level was a large open-plan kitchen diner, which would be absolutely ideal for me.

'There's a downstairs cloakroom over there,' said Amy as she opened the door to reveal a little toilet and sink, cleverly hidden from view. 'And a small room which Jack, my husband, has been using as an office, just here. This is one of my favourite rooms,' she said as she pushed open another door just off the kitchen to reveal a large pantry and utility room.

We followed her up a flight of stairs where there were three good sized bedrooms, one en-suite and a family bathroom. And then an additional room in the converted loft space.

'Which we haven't really used, to be honest, other than for storage.'

As we walked back downstairs, I couldn't wipe the grin from my face.

'I don't know if this is the kind of thing you're looking for or not, but I'm sure you'll need some time to have a think about it...'

'No, there's no need. I'll take it,' I said without even giving it a moment's thought. I knew I wanted to live there. It was perfect. It just needed a few tweaks to make it more me, but I loved it.

Zara gasped at my enthusiasm. 'But, but you don't even know how much it is?'

'It doesn't matter. I'll take it,' I repeated, almost like I was buying a used car.

'Really?' asked Amy in shock.

Nodding avidly, I smiled. 'How much is it? I have the cash available whenever you need it. How long will you need to move out?'

'Gosh, erm, I don't know. I need to speak to Jack. He's gone out for a run, this morning. But the price we'd already discussed. We were going to put it on the market for £895,000.'

'Furnished or unfurnished?' I asked.

'Erm, unfurnished, unless you want to buy the furniture too?'

'I'll offer you 900,000 for the property, the sofas and the dining suite?' I said confidently. 'But I understand if you'd rather speak to your husband first.'

'Erm, yes, I should really. But that sounds good. Can I give you a call when he gets back?'

'Of course,' I said as she scribbled down my phone number on a piece of paper, which she stuck to the fridge with a child's magnet.

'I can't believe you've practically just bought a house,' said Tony a little while later, as we sat having a cup of coffee in Starbucks, not far from their apartment and my soon to be home.

'I know, it all happened so fast,' I said, taking a sip of my soy caramel latte. 'I just didn't want to lose that place. I hope her husband agrees.'

'He will. They were probably expecting to get around 860 or 870, so for you to offer more than the full asking price... Well, you've probably just made their day,' Tony said with a smile.

'But they haven't called yet, so maybe not.'

'I'm sure he's just out taking an extra long run, that's all,' suggested Zara.

Sure enough, an hour later, my mobile rang. It was Amy. They agreed to my offer. We arranged to meet with our lawyers the following day in the city.

That was it. I was almost a house owner! My very own home!

Sadly, my good mood was spoiled rather dramatically the following morning with the arrival of the day's newspapers.

My face was plastered all over the front page.

CHAPTER 24

'What am I going to do now?' I groaned miserably as my mobile phone began ringing non-stop. Tony had taken to answering it whenever the number was unfamiliar. Somehow, members of the press had managed to get my number and were ringing me for comments.

'It's okay,' he said after the twelfth time. 'It's just Julianne. She picked up Syd's mobile this morning by accident.'

'Julianne?' I said unhappily. 'What happened? How did they know? Who told them? What am I going to do? I'm just glad I'm still at Tony and Zara's place. I don't want to go home in case they're there.'

'Honey, I'm so sorry. We've no idea who told them. I've been reassured by all the staff here that they had nothing to do with it. Somebody must be telling porkies, though. I'm so sorry. Look, lie low for a few days, and we'll try and keep them off your back. Perhaps you ought to stay in Wimbledon a little while longer?' she asked.

But I shook my head, not wanting to cause problems for Zara and Tony.

'No, I should go home. I doubt it's that much of a big story. I'm sure they won't be there.'

How wrong could I have been?

As we turned into the road where Jo's house was located, I was shocked by the sight ahead of me. Crowds and crowds of reporters stood waiting for my arrival.

'Duck down, Kate,' said Tony. 'I'll turn around. We'll go back to our place.'

'No,' I said firmly. 'I can't run away from this lot. They'll track me down wherever I go. I just want to get indoors. Even if I do run away, there are things I need from home,' I sulked.

'If you're sure?'

I nodded as we slowly made our way down the road, eventually pulling up outside my little apartment. Curtains all along the street were twitching, with neighbours eager to find out what was going on.

Carly and Jo suddenly appeared from their home next door to mine, opening the car door for me and protecting me from the over-zealous reporters, all shouting at me, asking questions about my newly acquired fortune, and the boy I'd lost as a child. I could barely breathe as we eventually made our way through the throng and down to my front door. My fingers shook as I tried to unlock it, but I failed, dropping the keys on the floor, fully aware of the camera flashes that continued to click behind us.

Carly picked up the keys and unlocked the door, pushing me in before she and Jo, Zara and Tony followed, closing the door behind them and then rushing to close the curtains in the lounge.

'What the hell?' I cried. 'Why are they so interested in me? I'm not like… Madonna or something, Jeeze…'

'Well, you're the news today, kiddo, whether you like it or not,' said Jo with a smile.

'Inheriting close to 150 million pounds is going to get you noticed - and that magazine article? Well, I think it made everyone just fall in love with you a little bit. You're going to have to get used to this, I'm afraid. At least until, I dunno, Madonna has another baby or something,' she laughed.

I cringed but saw the funny side. Jo could always make me smile, even when I didn't want to.

'I feel for all those celebrities out there who have to deal with this every day. I used to think they deserved it, that it was just part and parcel of their jobs and lives, but now I understand, nobody deserves this,' I said throwing myself on to the sofa as the doorbell rang. Pulling a face, I went to stand up, but Tony stopped me.

'I'll deal with this.'

After a few moments, he returned, handing me a business card.

'Greg Malone would like to organise an interview with you for next week's edition of State of Life Magazine,' he smiled.

'State of Life Magazine?'

'Oh, that reminds me,' Jo said as she pulled out a huge bunch of cards from both her back pockets and her front ones. 'These are all cards from other reporters out there, all wanting exclusives with you.'

'No way?' I said, shaking my head. 'Were they banging on your door this morning?'

'Afraid so. It started at 6am.'

I felt sick. 'Jo, I'm so sorry. 6am? Jeeze,' I said, putting my head in my hands.

'It's not your fault, my love.'

'Of course it's my fault. Tony, can you contact Amy and Jack and see if they can speed up the moving process. I need to move out of here as quickly as possible.'

He nodded, 'Our meeting was scheduled for this afternoon, though. Let's just go to it as planned and then we can talk to them there, okay?'

My head was all over the place as I nodded.

'I don't know what I should do now. Anybody have any ideas?'

'How about going and talking to them?' suggested Carly.

'No darling, she's not going to do that. But maybe Tony could just go out and tell them she's not ready to talk to the press just yet. Maybe tell them that she will speak to them in her own time?'

'Sure, I can do that,' he answered.

I held out my hand to him. 'Thank you,' I whispered as Zara sat beside me and made me drink a cup of hot, sweet tea.

CHAPTER 25

Thank God for antiperspirant, I thought as I sat on the couch and waited for the countdown to begin. I clutched at my hands until they were white and looked across at the two people sitting opposite, both completely at ease in front of the cameras.

Five, four, three, two, one...

'Welcome back to today's edition of Good Morning GB,' announced Ireland Rothschild, the blonde-haired, blue-eyed darling of morning TV.

'I'm here with Fergus O'Reilly, and we've a special guest with us this morning. None other than Britain's love-struck multi-millionaire, Kate Robinson. Welcome, Kate,' she said with a dazzling smile aimed more towards the camera than at me.

As my cheeks began to heat up, I was so grateful to the make-up artist, who had insisted on caking on the foundation before the show had started. In fact, I had so much make-up on that I was hoping once I'd removed it, nobody would recognise me when I headed to the airport in my now rather stupidly chosen car. I couldn't exactly blend in driving a pink Mini, could I?

'Good morning,' I whispered shyly.

Fergus grinned back at me, tilting his head as if he was about to speak to a child. 'Now, tell us, Kate dear, how does it feel to never have to worry about money ever again?' he asked, his toothpaste advert teeth twinkling beneath the heat of the studio lights.

'Erm, well, I guess it's... erm, kind of... erm,' I felt so bloody stupid. Great time for my brain to stop working. 'I - erm. Great,' I nodded. 'Great, really great.' Idiot.

Ireland glanced across at her grey-haired colleague and pouted before nodding. 'Tell us how you knew this man. This,' she glanced down at the iPad on her lap and continued, 'Samuel?'

I cleared my throat and lifted my head, feeling like my brain was back in action. 'He was a very good friend of the family, some years ago,' I answered.

'Just a friend? Why did he leave you all his money and his property?' asked Fergus.

'He didn't have any family, and I guess you could say that my mother and I were the closest he ever had to a family.'

'Isn't that lovely?' pouted Ireland. 'You certainly are a lucky woman. But what about your mother? Didn't she receive any of his inheritance?'

'No,' I said before swallowing hard. 'My mother lives a rather... nomadic lifestyle in Africa. She doesn't want any of it. All she asked of me was to donate a sum to charity which, of course, I have done.'

'She lives in Africa? A nomadic lifestyle? That sounds intriguing. Perhaps we should interview her one of these days,' laughed Ireland and Fergus together.

'Have you splashed out on anything since receiving your inheritance back in June?' they asked, leaning forward eagerly awaiting my answer.

'Yes, I have actually. I bought a car and a new house.'

'Well, good for you, Kate. But now, most of us are curious about this boy you lost. Tell us about him?'

Oh no. Why did I agree to this?

Taking a deep breath, I knew I had no choice. Several articles had been printed since the one in Liberty; everyone wanted to know more, and nobody was going to leave me alone until I told them everything.

'He was just a boy who I had a connection with when I was

much, much younger. It was at Skegness. At an afternoon disco for kids. I was dancing, and I felt someone touch my back, and when I turned around there he was. The most beautiful boy I'd ever seen,' I said, stopping and smiling as I reminisced. 'It was one of the happiest memories of my life.'

Sighing, I continued, 'We just looked at each other, and it was like everything else just disappeared into the background. We stood staring, for what seemed like ages. I could barely move. And then, almost as soon as it had begun, my dad appeared and took me away. I couldn't do anything as we walked to the car. I looked around for the boy, but he was gone. And then, just as we were driving away, I turned around in my seat and there he was. He had a daffodil in his hand. I always assumed he'd gone to pick it for me, but that's just a childish fantasy, I guess. The whole thing is probably nothing but a childish fantasy, really.'

Ireland was very carefully dabbing at her eyes with a tissue, pretending to be moved, while Fergus smiled sadly.

'What a beautiful story, Kate. I don't believe for one second that this is a childish fantasy. It's romantic and beautiful,' Ireland said.

'Now, tell us, Kate. Why did you call him Fred?' asked Fergus.

Smiling, I explained about the Right Said Fred song, just as the music began in the background.

'What a wonderful tale. Thank you, Kate, for joining us today. It's been a pleasure having you with us to share your story,' said Fergus.

'Thank you,' I whispered before the camera moved back to Ireland as she straightened her skirt and looked alluring. 'Do you remember this moment in time?' she asked. 'Are you the elusive Fred? We'd love to hear from you. You can contact us at...'

Before I could hear anything else, I was ushered off the couch and back behind the scenes where Jo stood, waiting patiently for me, with open arms.

'You were great,' she whispered as the team directed us out of the studio.

'You think? I was terrible...' I groaned.

'No, you weren't. Seriously. Did you see everyone in there? You almost brought them all to tears, Kate. You were great. I wouldn't lie to you.'

Before we got into my car, I dropped my head on to her shoulder as she gently rubbed my arm. 'There, you've done it now. You promised you'd speak to the press and you've done it. You gave your exclusive. Hopefully, they'll leave you alone now,' she said as we climbed into the little car and sped off, away from the TV studio, towards the airport.

'Thanks for coming to the airport, Jo, and for taking my car back home.'

'No problem. I wouldn't want you to drive all that way on your own, although you could have taken a chauffeur driven limo,' she said with a wink before continuing. 'Seriously, though, I've been dying to drive this little thing,' she giggled as she put her foot down on the accelerator.

CHAPTER 26

*D*inner was at a cosy Portuguese restaurant that just happened to be owned by Jorge's brother, Miguel, and his sister-in-law, Isabel, who had made me feel very welcome from the moment I'd been introduced. Jorge and his family were down to Earth, honest and kind, like most Portuguese people I'd met, and they didn't seem to care about my newfound wealth or 'celebrity' status.

After we'd ordered our dinner, Jorge poured the two of us a glass of red wine before disappearing to speak to his brother.

Shifting excitedly in my seat, I leaned forward and took Liz's hand in mine.

'Liz, I've got something I'd like to discuss with you.'

She leaned forward and smiled. 'Yes?'

'I've finally decided what I'm going to do with Casa Linda...'

'You have? Oh, are you going to sell it?'

'Hang on, I'm getting there. I've decided to transform it into a retreat: a health and beauty spa and... I want you to run it for me.'

Liz's eyes widened, and she dropped my hand in shock before moving her hands to her face.

'I...I...I don't know what to say,' she whispered.

'Just say yes. Say you'll do it.'

Swallowing hard she turned to look for Jorge. When he spotted her looking for him, he smiled warmly before rushing to her side.

'What is problem?'

A grin began to spread across her face.

'Kate wants me to run a health and beauty spa at Casa Linda. Jorge, she wants me to run a spa... here... on the island!' she squealed.

Jorge looked from his fiancée to me and back again, confusion clouding his eyes.

'I... I do not understand.'

'I want to make Casa Linda into a spa, Jorge, and I want Liz and you to run it for me. Would you like that?' I asked slowly, hoping he'd understand.

When he realised what we meant, he smiled proudly at Liz.

'Business? You want us run a business here in the Açores? A spa?' he asked as we nodded.

'Yes.'

Liz stood up and came round to my side of the table, hugging me tightly.

'Of course we'll do it. There's nothing more I'd love to do in the whole world, Kate. Thank you, thank you so much.'

After Jorge kissed me on both cheeks and all three of us sat back down, he poured himself a glass of wine.

'I know you've never run a business before, Liz, but Tony has said that he's just at the end of the phone if you need help with anything. And I am too, obviously. I couldn't think of anyone I'd rather have running the retreat than you. You're perfect for the job, and you can also continue to carry out treatments - if you want to, of course.'

I sat back down and relaxed my shoulders into the comfy, high-backed hair.

'Ooh yes, I'd love to carry on. I can't believe that's your decision. Casa Linda is going to make the most beautiful spa. I can't wait!' she said. 'Have you decided exactly what you'd like to do with the place?'

'I've got some ideas, but I want your input first. If it's okay with you, I thought we could make some plans tomorrow?'

'That would be perfect,' Liz said as we clinked glasses just as our presunto and melon arrived.

. . .

oOo

I leaned over the balcony of the bedroom I'd initially chosen as my own and watched the waves slowly make their way across the Atlantic Ocean. Although I couldn't see them crashing against the rocks below, I could hear them gently pounding the cliffs.

The curtains began to sway in the soft, gentle breeze as I took a sip of my tea, watching a seagull circle up above. Shivering, I closed the window and looked at the view from the warmth of my room.

It was such a spectacular spot. I smiled as I thought about the plans Liz and I had sketched a few days earlier. The retreat was going to be stunning, and I couldn't wait until it was finished and ready for business.

Julianne had already informed me that she planned to do a special feature on the spa, in an upcoming edition, which was fantastic.

I'd spoken to some local builders and had been in touch with several specialist spa equipment companies in the UK and the US. I had given them all Liz's contact details, as she was happy to take over, allowing me to 'get on with my life back home.'

She was such a gem, and it was absolutely fantastic she'd finally met her soul mate. And to think, it all happened because of Samuel. I looked up at the sky, and whispered silent thanks to him, as if he were up there somewhere, watching from above.

The sound of a bell almost caused me to drop my tea, and I cursed, spilling a drop on my fluffy white nightgown.

Rushing downstairs to the front door, I lifted the phone connected to the front gate.

'Hello?'

'Kate Robinson?' asked a deep voice.

I sighed, knowing what was coming next.

'Miss Robinson, my name is Greg Malone. I'm a reporter for the......'

Looking up at the ceiling, I cursed silently. How was it possible for the press to follow me halfway across the Atlantic, for good-ness sake?

I would have loved to tell him to bugger off, but I felt sorry for the guy. After all, I worked as a feature writer for Liberty maga-zine, so I knew how it felt to get the brush off.

'Mr Malone, please come on up,' I said slowly, pressing the automatic buzzer that allowed the gate to open.

Rushing back up to my bedroom, I threw on a pair of skinny jeans, a warm sweater and a pair of knee high boots before opening the front door just as he was climbing out of his hire car.

'Miss Robinson, thank you so much for agreeing to speak to me,' he said, his hand outstretched.

'I couldn't exactly turn you away now, could I? You've travelled miles to see me,' there was just a hint of irritation in my voice.

'I'm so sorry. It's my boss, well, she insisted, you see... Well, she's a little...erm...'

'Pushy?' I suggested with a smile. 'It's alright. I understand. I work for a magazine, so I know what the business is like. Please, come in,' I offered, holding the front door open for the tall dark-haired reporter.

'Wow,' he whispered, stepping through the living room and out onto the terrace.

'Impressive, isn't it?'

Greg nodded speechlessly.

'Can I get you something to drink, Mr Malone?'

'Greg, please,' he smiled, revealing a chipped front tooth as he took out a large notepad and pen, as well as a dictaphone. 'A glass of water would be great, thanks.'

I walked back indoors and poured us both a tall glass before heading back outside, where I sat opposite him.

'Thank you,' he downed it in one go.

'You were obviously thirsty.'

'I've been driving around for ages trying to find the house,' he admitted.

'Well, here you are.'

'Yes, and it's absolutely stunning. What a fabulous holiday home you have now.'

'We're actually going to be turning it into a spa. We've just been working on the plans over the past few days.'

Greg nodded and switched on the dictaphone.

'Congratulations on your recent inheritance. You must be delighted?' he asked.

'Thank you. It is quite life-changing.'

'Can you tell me what you plan to do with the money?'

I raised my eyebrows.

'Well, I donated some to charity, and then I bought myself a house and a new car. And, as I mentioned earlier, I'm transforming Casa Linda into a health and beauty spa.'

Greg nodded with a smile.

'Tell me a little more about the spa?' he asked.

'Erm, it will simply be called 'Spa Casa Linda Azores'. There will be at least ten bedrooms, for staying guests, and we will offer the usual spa treatments, although the manager, Liz Stilwell, is currently looking into some more unusual alternative therapies as well. But I can't tell you much more about it, at the moment. It's still early days.'

'When do you intend the spa to open to the public?'

'It will be open for business on New Year's Day, but we won't be doing a launch until the summer when we'll have more equipment and treatments available.'

Greg waited for a moment, holding his pen to his mouth deep in thought before asking, 'What can you tell me about the man who left you all of this, Mr Samuel Simoes?'

'Just that he was a very gentle and friendly person.'

'Why was he such a good friend to you and your mother?'

'Oh, I, erm...Well, we spent many summers with him. I guess we just clicked.'

'Is it true that he and your mother, were in fact... lovers?'

Blood rushed to my head, and I felt myself sway slightly to one side as I stood up so briskly that I needed to lean on the chair.

'I'm sorry, Mr Malone, but I refuse to answer such terrible questions. I gave you the benefit of the doubt by letting you into my house. I would like it if you would please leave now,' I said shakily.

'I'm sorry, Miss Robinson. I didn't mean to offend you. My boss insisted I ask you that question. Please allow me to continue. I promise not to bring it up again,' he said, nervously remaining seated.

Breathing heavily for a moment, I calmed myself down and returned to my seat, looking at him, waiting.

'How has your father taken the news about your inheritance?'

I gulped and answered. 'Very well. Naturally, he was a bit shocked, but he's very happy for me.'

'And his wife? I believe she used to be a friend of yours?'

I rolled my eyes. 'She still is a friend of mine, and yes, we did go to school together. She's delighted for me, of course she is.'

Nodding, Greg continued, 'You stated in the Liberty article that you've returned to Skegness on numerous occasions hoping to find...' he stopped, checking some of his notes before continuing. 'Fred. Did you honestly think he would ever really be there?' he asked, smirking.

I chuckled. 'Honestly? Deep down, I probably knew I'd never see him again, but I hoped. I always had hope.'

'Why haven't you ever settled down?'

'I've never met the right guy, I guess.'

'Is that because of Fred?'

I raised my eyebrows. 'Partly, I suppose it is.'

'So Julian Smith was not a serious boyfriend then?'

'How did you find out about Julian?' I asked through gritted teeth.

'I'm a reporter, Miss Robinson, it's my job to find out these things.'

'Julian Smith was my boyfriend when I was about seventeen years old. He was a great guy. I was very fond of him.'

'But it wasn't serious?' asked Greg.

I shook my head. 'Of course it wasn't serious. We were seventeen, for goodness' sake!'

'So you didn't split up because of Fred?'

I didn't like where this was going.

'No, not really. We just... grew apart,' I whispered.

'Not because you compared him to Fred?'

'Oh, maybe I did, what does that matter?' I answered, exasperated.

Greg nodded and wrote down more notes.

'Would you say you were... obsessed with this Fred character?' he asked.

The question actually made me laugh, and I couldn't help but nod. 'I suppose I have been a bit obsessed in the past. But not anymore. It's just a childhood fantasy, now. I know I'll never see him again. I think everybody's taking it way out of proportion. I was just a kid.'

Greg smiled, genuinely this time.

'I understand,' he jotted down a few more notes before leaning sideways and placing his satchel on the table. He pulled out a number of newspapers and handed them to me.

'So, if it's just a fantasy and you don't believe you'll ever see him again, what do you think about these?' he said as I unfolded them to find pictures of me all over the front pages, me in my dressing gown opening the front door of my old home, me heading to the office, me and Jo leaving the TV studio and even more shocking of all, me sitting all alone at the beach just down the road from Casa Linda.

I sat, mouth agape, flicking through them all. Each article pointed to a more substantial article within, and when I opened the pages, there were small pictures of hundreds of men... all claiming to be Fred.

CHAPTER 27

'Hello, Miss Robinson? Hi. I'm calling from the Good Morning GB Studios. We've got rather a lot of mail for you here, and we'd like to arrange for it to be delivered to you. Would it be possible for you to give me your address? Alternatively, if you'd rather not do that, can you tell us where else we can deliver it to?' asked the woman sweetly.

'Erm, of course,' I said not quite sure what to tell her. 'Please, can you hold for a moment?' I asked as I covered the phone and looked across at Julianne while we sat in her office. Explaining the situation, Julianne insisted I tell them to have it delivered to Liberty.

'Erm, hello? Can you deliver it to the office of Liberty magazine in London, please? Thank you so much,' I said before putting my mobile back in my handbag.

'Thanks, Julianne, you're a star. I've no idea what that mail is, though.'

'You're kidding, right?' she said as Beckham jumped onto my lap and began purring, begging for me to stroke his belly (if only it were the real Beckham). 'It'll be mail from potential Freds. No doubt about it.'

'Urgh,' I sighed. 'If I'd realised that I would have told her to throw it all in the bin.'

Julianne put down Clooney, who had been rubbing himself against her chest, and stood up.

'You're joking? Fred might actually be among that lot,' she leaned forward on her desk. 'I think we need to go through all the letters and then do a follow-up article about all your 'fan mail'. It would make for some hilarious reading.'

I raised my eyebrows.

'Didn't you look at some of those guys the newspapers featured?'

Julianne pouted, her eyebrows knitted together.

I shook my head for a moment before giving in. She clapped her hands together and squealed. 'Thanks, honey, you won't regret it. Even if Fred isn't there, you might just find the man of your dreams. Well, you know what I mean.'

'Yeah, yeah,' I said as Beckham hopped down, clearly having had enough of me for one day. Sigh.

'Sales have continued to go up, you know. Since your article,' she said, sitting back down across from me.

'I figured as much. I know, I know. I'm happy to do anything to help you, Julianne. You know that.'

'Thanks, honey. I'll get a few members of staff to start sifting through the mail as soon as it arrives. Perhaps you could just tell them what, or who rather, they should be looking out for?'

I nodded, unsure what to tell them really. The guy I knew, okay I didn't know him. The guy I saw wasn't even a guy, he was just a kid. Not a lot to go on.

After lunch, Julianne, Charlie, Jasper, Chloe and I sat in the meeting room while I told them what Fred had looked like. Piercing blue eyes, dark hair, high cheekbones. And that was it. I couldn't tell them any more.

Jasper clasped his hands together under his chin and squealed like a girl. 'I'm so excited, Katie,' he said, his body shaking in excitement from head to toe. 'We might actually find your true love for you. I can't wait to get started. When did they say they would deliver the mail?'

'They just said as soon as possible.'

As if on cue, there was a knock on the door and in walked Jasmine carrying a huge sack.

'It's arrived,' she dragged it across the floor and with Jasper's help, heaved it up on to the table.

'Oh, m..my g..god,' I stuttered. 'There's loads!'

'What?' said Jasmine. 'You ain't seen nothing yet. There are another two sacks the same size as this out in reception.'

'Holy crap!' announced Chloe as she rushed outside to have a look, dragging one of them back in with her just as Jasmine nipped out to get the other one.

'Erm... I think we're going to need some more assistance,' Julianne said with a grin on her face. 'But first, I'm going to go get my camera and take a photo of them!' she said before rushing out towards her office.

'Thanks so much for coming to help out, Jo,' Julianne said later on, as my best friend arrived with Carly after school.

'I'm happy to help.' She and her daughter got stuck in, sorting through the letters, adding the majority to the DEFINITELY NOT pile, some to the POSSIBILITIES and a few to the YES pile. The YES pile were the ones I'd reluctantly agreed to meet. Crazy, I know.

'Ooh, check this one out,' swooned Jasper as he revealed a photo of a particularly good looking guy built like a rugby player wearing nothing but a smile.

'OMG!' squealed Carly. 'Let me have a look,' but Jo snatched the picture out of her hands before she even got the chance. 'I knew I shouldn't have brought you with me.'

Carly stuck out her tongue and carried on sifting through the letters as Jasper discreetly stole the picture and placed it in his back pocket with a wink to Jo, who burst out laughing.

'Jasper, you're just so... so gay,' she laughed.

'I know. Fabulous, isn't it?'

'Oh, I think I found one,' said Charlie as she handed a photo across the table towards me. Looking down, a breath caught in the back of my throat and I coughed. The most gorgeous guy, with long black hair, stared back at me and his eyes I could have just melted into them. I smiled and sat down staring at the picture while Charlie read out some of the information on the letter.

'Says his name is Luigi. Italian.? Interesting. I take it I should put that in the YES pile then?' she smiled as Julianne took both the letter and the photo out of our hands, clipped them together and placed them firmly in the right pile.

'I never would have thought Fred was Italian, but I guess it's a possibility. Wait a minute... does he live here or in Italy?'

Julianne picked the letter back up and looked at the postmark. 'Rome.'

I gulped, 'You mean... you mean... I'm now in the European news, too? Jeeze, when will it ever end?'

CHAPTER 28

$\mathcal{E}$very time I switched on the morning TV, someone was talking about, well, erm… me, actually. It was the weirdest thing. I'm just so relieved I moved into my new house when I did. At least the gates kept out those wretched members of the press. Wait a minute, I was a member of the media too! Okay, so perhaps they weren't wretched. They have a job to do, I understand that. I just wish they'd hound someone else, for a change. Unfortunately, they soon realised that the owner of the pink Mini was me. Even hiding under a large floppy hat and massive sunglasses didn't help. Why, oh why, did I buy such a highly visible car?

So I'd been borrowing Zara's car lately, or Tony's. Occasionally, I even hired the services of a chauffeur driven alternative. Anything to allow me to get out of the house without being followed. It wasn't easy. I'd been toying with the idea of going over to stay in New York, just for a bit of peace and quiet and to do the kind of stuff I hadn't been able to do for a while. You know, like pop down to the local coffee shop, browse my favourite shops or even go to the movies. I'd have loved to go and see the latest Johnny Depp flick, but how could I, like this?

'Right, we've got the first five set up for you, which will take place next Monday. Kate, Kate - are you listening?'

'Hmm?' I said, turning from Julianne's window, overlooking the Thames. 'Sorry, what were you saying?'

Julianne stood up and walked over to me, looking at me like a mother might look at her adorable child. 'I was just saying that the first meeting has been set up. They're all coming here, on Monday morning, to see you and I thought th...'

'Sorry, who's coming to see me?' I asked, confused.

'The potentials.'

'Oh,' I sighed and sat down on the little sofa that was tucked away in the corner of her office.

'You're really not here with me today, are you?' she asked as she sat back down at her desk.

'Sorry, Julianne... there's just so much going on at the moment. It's difficult to keep up.'

'I understand, I really do. But the sooner you find Fred, the better your life will be. Don't you agree?'

I kind of nodded and shook my head at the same time, before chuckling quietly. Deep down, I knew I wasn't going to find Fred, but I'd agreed to try. I'd decided to meet them, and so that's what I would do. But I didn't have to look forward to it.

'We're bringing in Carluccio to take the photos, and we thought we might use the roof, provided it's not wet or snowing. Although, it'd look great in the snow. But, if not, we're stuck with the studio.'

I nodded, semi listening, just as Jasper burst through the door, with barely a knock.

'Oh, I'm sorry. I hope I'm not interrupting anything,' he said before continuing, 'it's just that there's a man here to see you, Kate. A rather nice looking man,' he winked.

Not expecting anyone, I sighed heavily again. Another reporter.

'Oh, Jasper, you know she'd rather not have to talk to any more members of the press. And besides, Kate isn't working at the moment, at least not officially, anyway. Nobody should know she's here,' scolded Julianne, while he looked a little upset.

'No, it's okay. I'll go,' I said as I reluctantly stood up and straightened my long black skirt. 'Where is he?' I asked.

'I asked him to wait in the meeting room,' Jasper giggled as I followed him.

'Thanks, Jasper.'

He smiled cheekily at me before going back to his cubicle.

As I pushed open the door, I was surprised to see a vaguely familiar face. I suddenly had a quick flashback. It was the guy I'd tripped over on the tube almost a year ago. What was his name? I couldn't, for the life of me, remember.

As soon as he spotted me, he stood up and grinned. 'Miss Robinson,' he said, with such warmth that I felt immediately at ease.

'Oh, hello,' I said, blushing slightly.

'It's good to see you looking so well, and not covered in blood,' he joked.

As he held out his hand, a memory flashed in my mind, and I remembered his name.

Shaking hands, I said, 'It's good to see you, Mr Walker. Thank you so much for coming to my rescue back then. I don't know what I would have done, had you not been there.'

Paul Walker smiled, his cheeks pinking slightly. 'I'm afraid to say that had I not been there, you wouldn't have fallen over in the first place. It was my fault if you remember?'

'Not at all.' I replied. 'It was completely my fault.'

I suddenly realised we were still shaking hands, so I pulled mine away quickly, embarrassed as neither of us uttered a word while he just looked at me.

'What can I do for you, Mr Walker?'

'Paul, please. I was actually just passing the building, and I remembered reading that you worked here, so I thought I'd pop in on the off chance that you might be here. I just wanted to make sure you were well.'

Clearly, he knew I was well if he'd read about me in the newspapers. But I just smiled and nodded. 'I'm very well, thank you. After all, it was about twelve months since my concussion,' I laughed. 'You really needn't have come, but I'm very pleased that you did, of course. Can I offer you a drink?'

'Well, actually, I was wondering if you might have time to join me for a coffee... elsewhere?'

I don't know why I did it, but I looked at my watch.

'But if you don't have time, that's okay. No problem,' he smiled.

'No, I mean yes. I have time. There's a Starbucks just down the street. We could pop in there although...'

Paul lifted his eyebrows, waiting for me to finish. I was going to say if he didn't mind being photographed by the press, but I thought better of it.

'Never mind. Let me grab my coat.'

Paul kindly got the coffees while I found a table, hidden in a corner, away from the entrance and the windows. When he approached, carrying my cinnamon soy latte and his own cappuccino, he sat down and smiled.

'I hope you don't think I was too forward, asking you out for coffee,' he said.

'Of course not.'

'But I've been trying to get up the nerve to contact you ever since the accident. Well, ever since the hospital. You see, I was...' he stopped and blushed again, looking to the floor before continuing. 'I was hoping you might put me in touch with your friend who was with you at the hospital,' he said, finally.

My mouth fell open.

'Oh. Have I gone about this the wrong way? I'm so terrible at these sorts of things. I'm sorry. I hope I haven't offended you?'

I burst out laughing. Paul was interested in Jo and, for some reason, I was actually quite relieved - and delighted.

I put my hand across the table and placed it over Paul's; he was looking somewhat downtrodden.

'I'm sorry, Paul,' I said between giggles. 'I'm not usually like this...'

After a couple more minutes, my giggling spread across the table, and he began to laugh too. The ice was well and truly broken.

I let my head fall to one side, and I looked at him. I mean, really looked at him. He was classically handsome, with a long nose, short blond hair, large brown eyes and full pink lips. I guessed he was about 35. I looked down at his hand and noticed there was no wedding ring, and no sign of there having been one, either. So he was single, and he fancied Jo.

'I understand if you feel the need to scrutinise me,' he said, smiling. 'I could tell when she arrived that she is a very close friend.'

'Why didn't you speak to her?' I asked.

He looked away sheepishly. 'Honestly?'

I nodded.

'I was terrified.'

'Really?' I asked, wondering how Jo could terrify anyone.

'Have you ever had one of those moments? You know, when you see someone and feel like you should be with them? I guess some people could call it love at first sight? Oh gosh... of course you have. I almost forgot about your whole lost love thing. I'm sorry,' he said, but before I could answer, he put his hand over his mouth. 'I'm so sorry. It must be awful that everyone knows so much about you, and then here I go just blurting it out. Very insensitive of me.'

He was a gentleman, and he was in love with Jo. Now I knew I could introduce him to her.

'Please stop saying you're sorry,' I laughed. 'Everyone knows the truth about me. So? It doesn't matter. I hadn't really noticed you'd mentioned it, to be honest. I was still hanging on your previous words,' I smiled. 'I'm very touched that Jo had such an effect on you. Just from seeing her at the hospital. It's lovely. And yes, it is like my experience as a child, but completely different in that you could have spoken to her. That you're both adults,' I said, before taking a long sip of coffee.

'I thought I'd never see her again, or you, and then when I saw that first newspaper article about you, I was speechless. I've been trying to drum up the nerve to come and see you ever since.'

'Paul, you are very sweet, and I would be delighted to introduce you to her.'

'Thank you,' he said beaming.

CHAPTER 29

The gossip magazines were filled with the same photo of Paul and me in Starbucks. Me smiling at him with my hand placed over his. The headlines read, 'Is this Kate's new love?'

I groaned. Poor Paul.

Jo, on the other hand, seemed to think it was hilarious.

'So, you're having a thing with my man?' she asked with her hands on her hips.

'You haven't even met him yet.'

She laughed again while pouring two glasses of wine and sat down.

'Well, at least I get to see what he looks like before our big date,' she smiled. 'He is quite handsome.'

'Quite handsome? He's gorgeous, Jo, and he's got a massive thing for you.'

'Yeah, I know, you already told me all that,' she said nervously. 'I still can't quite believe you've organised for us to go out on a date. I mean, I haven't been on a date for years.'

'I know, and it's time that changed. You're young, and you're beautiful. Charles would hate for you not to carry on, you know that?'

She smiled. 'I know. I'm just scared, that's all.'

'There's really no need to be. Paul is such a gentleman. I have a feeling you're going to get on brilliantly. And besides, I'm just a

151

phone call away if you want to leave. I could even call you, mid-date, with a 'family emergency', if you like?'

She picked up the magazine and gazed at his picture for a long moment before she shrugged. 'Nah,' she said, 'I don't think that will be necessary.'

Smiling, I stood up when my mobile began to ring. 'Hello?'

'Kate?'

'Speaking.'

'It's Paul, Paul Walker.'

'Oh, hi, Paul!' I said, turning to pull a face at Jo, whose face reddened.

'I was just phoning to make sure you were okay. I presume you've seen the gossip mags today?'

'Yes, Jo just showed them to me, and I'm fine. I'm so sorry. I really am. I should have warned you that it could have happened.'

'Oh, don't apologise. My friends and colleagues are grilling me about it, but other than that, it's been no bother. I just thought I should call you, you know.'

I grinned. 'Thank you. I really appreciate it. I'm, erm, actually here with Jo at the moment.'

I could almost hear him blush over the phone.

'Oh... I'm sorry for the intrusion...'

'Oh, stop being sorry. She's actually wondering if she might just say hello...'

Jo's eyes widened, and she almost spat out the wine in her mouth as I handed her the phone with a wicked grin, giving neither of them a chance to get out of it.

As she said hello, I tiptoed out of the room, taking my wine with me. I figured once they started talking, they'd be a while.

Satisfied that I'd done my bit for the day, I moved into the lounge and switched on the TV.

oOo

I couldn't decide what to wear. I mean, what do you wear when you're about to meet a selection of potential dream guys? A trouser suit? A skirt suit? Jeans? A dress? It was clear I needed help so I called Zara, hoping she'd be home.

'Give me five minutes, and I'll be right there.'

Sure enough, precisely five minutes later on the dot, Zara stood on the doorstep with a smile.

'I'm a mess. I haven't a clue what I should wear for this... this... meeting thing. Please help,' I dragged her through the house and up the stairs to the smallest bedroom that I'd made into a walk-in-wardrobe.

She stood for a moment and took in the clothes strewn all over the floor. Turning to look at me, she shook her head with a sweet smile before picking things up and putting them back on hangers.

'How long have we got?' she asked.

'The driver's picking me up in precisely one hour.'

'Right, you go back into your bedroom and finish doing your hair. Leave the clothes to me,' she said as I placed my hands on top of my head and suddenly realised I still had the giant curlers in.

'Doh,' I cried as I ran back to my dressing table, desperately trying to pull them out without making too much of a mess of my newly-highlighted locks.

Sitting in front of the mirror, I managed to retrieve two rollers, but the other wouldn't budge, and the more I tried to pull it out, the more entangled it became.

'Oh, for God's sake,' I shouted.

'Goodness,' Zara walked into the bedroom only to find me hunched over the dressing table, sobbing.

'What is it? What's the matter?' she asked as I revealed mascara running halfway down my face.

'It's, it's just one of those days. Everything is going wrong. I even blew up the toaster this morning.'

Zara couldn't help but laugh. 'I wondered what the burnt smell was. Now, calm down. We have just under an hour to sort you out and if it takes longer, then so be it. Those guys will wait all day if they have to. Stop worrying and let me have a look at your hair.'

I gave in and slumped back in the chair, letting her take control. Within seconds, she'd untangled the curler from my hair, and it looked a mess.

But before I could get even more hyped up about it, she removed the brush from my fingers and began to calmly and gently brush it through my shoulder-length brown and copper locks, instantly relaxing me.

I sighed and smiled as she removed the eye make-up from my cheeks with a cotton wool pad and my favourite cleanser.

'Now,' she said. 'Do you want to reapply it or would you rather I did it?'

I was so relaxed I asked her to do it. I just sat there and let the stress of the early morning wither away.

After fifty-eight minutes exactly, I stood by the front door, waving her back to her own apartment across the garden.

'Thank you so much, Zara, you're a star,' I waved, watching her disappear indoors just as my driver arrived.

'What do you mean, you can't come and pick me up? My audition's in thirty minutes. Now, what am I supposed to do? I can't drive. My car's being re-sprayed... that's why you were going to pick me up!' shrieked a voice from the main entrance of the apartments.

I was shocked to see a rather distraught looking Tiffany Chantelle. She shoved her mobile phone into her pocket. She looked like she was about to burst into tears.

'Excuse me,' I walked over to her. 'I couldn't help but overhear. Are you alright?'

Sniffing, Tiffany took out a tissue and blew her nose loudly.

'Oh... you're Kate Robinson,' she said matter of factly, making me feel a little silly considering she was the real star.

'And you're Tiffany Chantelle,' I smiled.

She looked at me and smiled apologetically. 'I'm sorry. I've just got a crucial audition to get to and my ride, who was supposed to be here ten minutes ago, has decided he's not coming. My car is being re-sprayed at the moment, and I'm stuck. I could take the Tube but...'

'Why don't you come with me? I'm heading into Central London.'

Tiffany's eyes lit up. 'Me too,' she said. 'Thank you. Thank you so much.'

'Come on, let's go before we're both late,' I offered as the driver got out to open the doors.

'Oh, it's okay, we can do it,' I said as he nodded curtly and returned to the driver's seat before we set off together.

'I'm so grateful, Kate. Thank you so much,' Tiffany said quietly as we sat in the back of the hired 4x4.

'It's no problem at all. I'm just glad I could help. I must admit, I feel quite honoured,' I smiled.

'You feel honoured? You're the superstar now,' she smiled.

I laughed. 'A superstar for having done nothing but inherit some money. It's not quite the same, is it?'

'It's not just the money... it's the romance that's making the papers, isn't it?'

'The non-existent romance,' I added. 'I'm actually on my way to meet some of the men who got in touch after my first appearance on Good Morning GB.'

Tiffany cringed. 'Oh... poor you.'

I was relieved that finally, someone saw it the same way as me: cringe-worthy.

'I know, right?'

'God knows what they're going to be like. I bet they sent in other people's photos,' she said cheekily.

'I hope not, but you're probably right.'

We both laughed and got to know each other over the next twenty minutes, and when the car finally pulled up outside Tiffany's audition, she turned and handed me her card. 'I'm so glad we got to meet, Kate. I feel like we'll be firm friends from now on. It's nice to have finally met a neighbour I can relate to. I'd love to hear all about your meeting, give me a call if you're free for dinner. Thanks again for the ride. I really appreciate it. See you later.'

'Thank you, Tiffany. Break a leg,' I shouted out the window as we drove away.

oOo

Jasper grabbed me the moment I stepped through the revolving door.

'Jasper, what's going o...' I shrieked as he pulled me away from the lift doors and around the corner.

'Shhh,' he whispered as he sneakily peered around the corner, keeping me pressed against his side.

'What on Earth are you doing?'

'It's the men, they're over there. I didn't want them to see you before the... big meet.'

I shook my head in disbelief as Jasper proceeded to act like James Bond. A very, very camp, James Bond.

'How long have you been waiting down here?'

'Only... forty-five minutes,' he whispered, peering around the wall again.

'Forty-five minutes? Does Julianne know?'

He glanced momentarily at me with a cheeky grin. 'She sent me down. She keeps ringing me to find out what they're all like.'

I tried hard not to laugh while he rushed past me, yanking my arm, so I followed him, toward the other set of lifts in the far corner of the lobby.

'Okay, okay, I'm coming.'

Once the lift door opened, I stepped inside as Jasper continued to act like some kind of weird alternate reality international spy, peering from left to right, making sure nobody was behind us. When the door finally shut, he let out a deep sigh.

'I could get used to this,' he said, seriously.

'Jasper, you don't half crack me up.'

Unusually, for a cold winter's day, the sun was shining brightly in the sky as I tiptoed onto the roof, eyes squinting as I searched for Julianne. Some of the magazine's assistant fashion editors were busying themselves rifling through rails of clothes, two hairdressers were preparing their gear in a corner while the beauty editor stood scouring the proceedings.

'Kate,' she yelled as she spotted me. 'Are you all set for make-up?'

'Erm...'

'There you are,' yelled another voice from around the corner.

'What's going on, Julianne?'

'What on Earth do you mean? We're prepping for the shoot.'

'Shoot?'

'We want to capture every moment on camera, my dear. And so we're combining it with next month's fashion spread. You are the star of the edition.'

I groaned and leaned back onto the cold bricks.

'I am?'

'We talked about it. Have you forgotten already?'

I shook my head. No, I hadn't forgotten. I'd merely removed all thoughts of such a horrendous nature from my consciousness.

'Right then, let's get you to hair and make-up,' she practically dragged me along.

'Jasper!'

He skipped through the throngs of people, relishing the day's activities.

'Yes, boss?'

'I want you to go back downstairs and start prepping the boys. I want them all up here in precisely,' she glanced down at her Gucci watch, 'twenty-three minutes.'

He grinned and nodded before skipping away.

An involuntary sigh escaped my lips. Julianne scolded me with her eyes alone before I sat down and let make-up and hairdo their worst.

Closing my eyes, I let myself drift away to a far off place. Recalling the deep blue of the sea and the whitewashed walls of the villa, I tried to remember the smells from the garden, all those beautiful wildflowers and overgrown lawns. But my mind refused to cooperate and I found myself instead remembering the words to I'm Too Sexy.

A flash memory invaded my mind. One I'd been trying to forget. What with everything that had been going on, I didn't want to think about him. About the possibility that he might actually be downstairs, right now. I just didn't know what to think. I didn't know how to handle it. To be honest, I was scared.

'Oh, wow, you look a million dollars,' said a familiar voice as it approached.

'Jo?'

I opened my eyes wide and saw her standing there, grinning.

'What are you doing here?' I hopped off the stool and gave her a hug.

'I couldn't let you go through all this on your own. I figured you'd need some support.'

'Thanks. You're so right,' I looked around and pulled her towards the door.

Laughing, Jo linked arms with me and walked me backwards until I was at the make-up stool again.

'No matter how hard you try, you're not going to get out of it, so you may as well just enjoy the moment. I was serious, by the way. You do look amazing. Like a supermodel, just a short one,' she grinned.

Relaxing a little, I nodded to Michelle, the girl doing my make-up, and let her carry on as her colleague, Annabelle, continued messing with my hair.

'So, how are you feeling?'

'Honestly?'

Jo nodded.

'Terrified.'

Jo dropped her head to the side and pouted before she squeezed my arm.

'Well, I'm here now. There's no need to be scared. I got your back.'

oOo

Taking some deep breaths, I looked down at London below, wishing I was down there with all those little people, rushing around getting on with their lives. Yes, that's what I wanted to do. I wanted to get on with my life.

I looked towards the London Eye and smiled. How nice it must be to stand in one of those pods and have nothing to worry about. Just stand and watch the world go by. Glancing across at the Gherkin, I frowned as Julianne suddenly took me out of my daydreams.

'Earth to Kate,' she said loudly. 'All set?'

'Nope, not at all,' I whispered under my breath. 'Yes, absolutely,' I forced a smile.

'That's more like it. Right, time to bring in the boys.'

My heart suddenly leapt right out of my chest. Seriously, I could swear I saw it hop over the edge of the building, with me right behind it.

Palpitations. That's what they were called. Severe palpitations. These photos are going to be disastrous. I'm going to look like a corpse. Taking a gulp, I forced myself to smile as five men were slowly brought outside and paraded towards me. I could hear the camera clicking away as Julianne looked on like a proud momma.

Glancing away from them for just a moment, I saw Jo give me the thumbs up. My body responded by relaxing - just a little bit - as I caught my first glance of the Freds.

'Oh.'

I couldn't help it, the word slipped out of my lips as I watched him strut towards me. He was cute. Very cute and he had dark hair and blue eyes. Forcing my eyes to look away from him, I glanced behind him, and my smile dropped a tad as a receding man in his erm, late fifties gave me a wink. And then another, who was clearly wearing a black wig, grinned across at me, giving me a Dr Spock hand gesture. Erm, okay, right then. An ordinary yet nice looking guy my age gingerly smiled and nodded before the final one appeared. He was the right age, I'd give him that, but his fake bronzed and buffed muscular appearance and bright blond hair made him a definite no-Fred contender. So, back to Fred One then.

They were all positioned around me for a few photos before the introductions actually began. I could feel myself reddening as Mr Universe's muscles rubbed against my arm and gave me goosebumps - the cringe-worthy ones, that is. I gulped back and tried to look happy for the camera, but it was a struggle.

I wondered if the first guy was Fred. He could be. He certainly looked like him, with his slightly high cheekbones and deep blue eyes. The butterflies in my stomach did a quick flight upwards, towards my heart, as we were re-arranged so that Number One and Number Four were standing beside me. They were both cute, for sure. But I doubted Number Four was a real contender. As much as I liked the look of his face - and his physique - he didn't look like my Fred.

Finally, the camera stopped rolling for a moment; Jasper rushed forward and introduced us all. Mr Universe was actually Austrian, had been living in England for several years and apparently, he used to visit Skegness when he was a kid. Yeah, right. If I lived in Austria, I doubted very much that I'd ever nip across the pond and check out a caravan park, would you? Clearly, he was after some coverage in a national magazine. Fair play to him. His body probably deserved some magazine coverage, just not at Liberty.

Number Two, the ageing Fred, admitted to having sent in a picture he'd scanned from a magazine - for a laugh. I smiled as Jo shook her head with a snigger.

Number Three, the Star Trekker, was indeed an Englishman who grew up in Skegness. But Fred he certainly was not. Removing the Dr Spock wig to reveal a shiny bald head, he smiled shyly and shrugged his shoulders.

'I had many a fling with tourist lasses when I was a kid, so I thought I may as well write in. It could have been me,' he shrugged again. 'But I can see from your face that it isn't.'

I smiled. 'Thanks for writing in...'

'Jim.'

'Thanks for writing in, Jim.'

'Maybe we could get together for a drink later,' he suggested.

I shook my head. 'Thanks but, erm. I'm not much of a Star Trek fan.'

He looked outraged. So much so that I took a step backwards, where I was confronted by the other two possibles, Jack and Luigi.

Luigi? Italian? Huh?

Luigi was the one who looked the most like my Fred. He was simply gorgeous, and I almost melted at the mere sight of him. When Jack realised this, he put his hands in his pockets and relented with a nod, quietly walking away, making me feel pretty bad.

'Luigi?' I asked.

The dark-haired God nodded. 'That's right, love,' he said with a broad Yorkshire accent.

'Oh.'

Laughing, he combed his hair with his steady masculine hand, and I swooned.

'I get that a lot. I'm from Italian descent, but I actually grew up in Rotherham. We went to Skegness a few times when I was about twelve or thirteen. To be honest, though, I don't actually remember the story I read about you, but,' he shrugged, 'we don't remember everything that happens to us as kids, do we?'

'I guess not,' I replied, my heart sinking. All these years, I thought Fred must have felt the same as me. That 'our' moment was etched in his head for eternity, too.

'So we might have met,' he smiled, and my knees went weak.

'Do you have a picture? Of when you were younger?'

His face fell slightly, but he smiled warmly and shook his head.

'Afraid not, love. We had a fire when I was seventeen... everything was burned. We lost everything. Even my little brother.'

'Oh God, that's horrendous. I'm so sorry, Luigi.'

My insides squeezed, and my stomach suddenly felt like it was going to propel that morning's contents all over him. I turned away and noticed Jo smiling at us. She motioned me over. I excused myself from the great hunk of a man and rushed to her side. Julianne was scanning through some of the photos while Jasper handed out coffee.

'Ten minutes, people. Ten minutes,' Julianne shouted out without looking up.

'You like him, I can tell.'

'No,' I said utterly unconvincing.

'You ought to. He's cute, and he's got that whole Fred look down to a tee. Do you think it's him?'

I shrugged my shoulders as the redness crept up my neck and piqued on top of my cheeks.

'I'd like to think so, but he,' I took a breath before continuing, 'he doesn't remember.'

'Oh, honey,' Jo whispered. 'That's a bit of a shit.'

She totally got me.

'What about photographs?'

I shook my head. 'They burned in a fire - along with his little brother.'

She gasped, and we both looked across at him, watching him as he stood gazing out across London, occasionally taking a gulp of his coffee. Jasper stood reasonably close by, clearly eager to either chat to him or get his pants off.

'Go and talk to him some more, Kate. That guy could be the man of your dreams - in every way possible. Go.'

I was about to walk up to him when Annabelle appeared with

several combs, hairbrushes and a spray. I couldn't get away, so I stood, cursing under my breath.

'Okay, you're good to go,' she said a few minutes later.

I bounded across the rooftop and was promptly stopped by Michelle, with her powder, lip gloss and eyeliner on hand.

'Won't take a moment. You're just looking a little shiny, here and there. Right, that's better. Okay, off you go.'

Just as I approached Luigi, Julianne ended the break, and I was forced back with the other crazies… erm, Freds.

Screaming inside, I did exactly as I was told, posing in between them as Julianne and the photographer directed us - occasionally stopping so I could go and change into the latest fashions, some of which looked hideous on me. Well, I thought so, anyway.

'Right, just chat amongst yourselves, and we'll take some casual shots of you getting to know everyone a bit better, Kate.'

So, there I stood, like a complete melon, cherry, or whatever it is you call it these days, wondering what to do. I mean, I was surrounded by guys I didn't really know, and there was only one I really wanted to talk to. Could I just speak to Luigi? Was that rude? Yes, it was, really. So I put on a brave face and turned around and let them ask me questions. Occasionally, I'd interrupt and ask something back, so I looked at least a little bit interested. And then Julianne called time, and before I got the chance to do anything for myself, she'd sent them all away, and I was left wondering what the hell had just happened?

CHAPTER 31

I tossed my jacket onto the chair and flopped face down onto the bed, where I lay, dead still, for at least twenty minutes. My head was all over the place. I couldn't focus. I didn't know what to do. I just wanted the bed to suck me in and take me away from the world. Maybe it could spit me out into an alternate universe? One with no Freds.

The phone rang. I ignored it. Eventually, it rang off, and I sighed loudly as my mobile immediately began to buzz. Turning onto my back, I looked up at the ceiling and watched a little spider scuttle across it towards a web it had created in the corner. Maybe it was time I gave the place a spring clean. Or perhaps I should hire a cleaner?

A cleaner? What was I thinking? It was only a small house, I wasn't exactly working at the moment. Surely I could do a bit of cleaning myself.

Jumping up, I took off my nice clothes and swapped them for a pair of pyjamas. Armed with the hoover, I hopped back onto the bed and began stretching as high as I possibly could, trying to rid the room of the cobwebs. As the poor little spider was sucked up into the tube, I was racked by guilt. I'd killed it. Switching off the vacuum cleaner, I flopped back down onto the bed and looked around. What now?

Interrupted by the sound of my mobile, yet again, I shook my head and sighed. Several missed calls from Julianne.

Just as I was about to drop it back into my handbag, it rang again, making me jump.

'Oh, for goodness' sake, just answer it,' said a voice in my head.

Without thinking, I answered the phone.

'Finally! I've been worried sick about you. Why did you disappear like that? We needed to talk. Now, I know I put you through a bizarre experience this morning, and I feel terrible about it. I am truly sorry, Kate. You're my friend and I took complete advantage of you. Will you please forgive me?'

Her pout was audible over the phone. I chuckled.

'Are you laughing?'

The chuckle erupted, and soon I was lying on the bed, giggling my head off.

'Kate, Kate? Are you there? Are you alright? You sound rather... crazed.'

'I'm... I'm...fine. Julianne, I'm fine. I'll be fine. Honestly.'

'Erm, really?'

I nodded, even though she couldn't see me.

'Perhaps you ought to be with someone at the moment,' she suggested gingerly. 'Isn't Jo with you?'

I shook my head. 'It's her big date tonight, so she's off getting ready for that. I'm fine, honestly.'

'I'm not buying it, Kate. Something's wrong. Now, I can come over if you like, but...'

'Julianne, like I said. I'm okay. Besides, I have plans later. I'm going out with a friend. Don't worry about me.'

'Will I see you tomorrow?'

'I'm not sure. Can I call you in the morning?'

'Of course! I'll talk to you then. Are you sure you're alright?'

'I promise you, I'm fine.'

'Okay, then. Speak to you tomorrow. Have a great evening, Kate.'

'You too.'

I threw the phone on the bed just as I got a text message from her:

'4got 2 mention, Luigi wants a date with u xx'

oOo

'And then she told me he wants a date with me,' I placed my empty glass of white wine on the table as Tiffany filled it right back up again.

'Wow, he sounds absolutely gorge, Kate. Are you gonna go?'

'I really don't know.'

'What?! Are you insane? This could be THE guy. Fred. The one you've been dreaming about your entire life. Why the hell wouldn't you want to go on a date with him... and eventually have his babies,' she added with a giggle.

Shrugging, I leaned back into the booth.

'Because he didn't remember it. In my mind, the real Fred felt the same way as me. There should be fireworks, you know? Yes, there were some sparklers there, but fireworks? No.'

Tiffany put her glass down and stared at me before shaking her head.

'Girl, you're absolutely mad. Nobody ever shares the same experience. Ever. One person's ultimate dream is another person's nightmare...'

'Are you saying Fred meeting me was his nightmare?'

'I didn't mean that at all,' she laughed. 'You know what I mean, don't you?'

Reluctantly I nodded, as the waiter arrived with our pizzas. He blushed and placed them down in front of us before slowly backing away from the table.

'Oh, okay, that was weird.'

'Not really. You'll get used to it, eventually.'

'To what?' I asked.

'Being a celebrity, being stalked, being paparazzied, being plastered all over the papers,' she smiled sadly.

'I can't imagine ever getting used to it. I don't know how you manage it.'

'Well, for starters, that's why I live in the closed condominium with security. That place is a Godsend. I do love living there. I'm so glad we met, Kate. Most of my so-called friends are high profile celebs, who only care about how they are seen in the press. It does my head in, at times. You're so refreshing.'

'Aww, thanks. I must admit, I'm very surprised with you, to be honest.'

'You are? Why?' asked Tiffany as she took a huge bite of pizza.

I pointed at her plate and laughed. 'For starters, you're a famous actress with a stunning figure, and you eat pizza!'

Almost choking, she just managed to swallow the mouthful before giggling, 'I couldn't live without pizza. My secret? It's gluten-free, and I only have the smallest amount of goat's cheese on top. No dairy,' she winked.

'Really? Cool,' I said, feeling guilty as I tucked into my three-cheese pizza with extra salami, mushrooms and ham. Looking down at my slightly more substantial frame, I made a mental note to bin all the dairy in my fridge later.

'You'll get the hang of it. Besides, you're not on TV all the time, so you haven't really got to worry too much about it. You look great. Just ignore me. I'm paranoid,' she said as she pushed her plate away, leaving a quarter of it untouched.

'You not going to eat that?'

Tiffany smiled. 'Take-away,' she winked. 'It'll make a nice supper. So, what are you going to do about Fred, then?'

My shoulders shrugged, almost on their own.

'Oh, c'mon, Kate. You've got to at least go on one date with him. What if he is the one?'

Staring at the intricately painted ceiling, I nodded.

'What are you so afraid of?'

'That he won't be perfect, I guess.'

Tiffany almost choked into her wine.

'Honey, nobody is perfect. Especially a man.'

'Yeah, I guess not.'

'I know not,' she smiled.

'You've been hurt before, I can see that.'

'You and everybody else that reads the gossip columns.'

'Oh, sorry.'

'No problem. That's just another of the many wonderful advantages of being in the public eye. Everyone knows practically every-thing about me. And that includes all my previous relationships.'

'I read about Gerard. I thought you two were perfect together.'

'Yeah, I did too. He's an amazing guy, just not made for long term love. We're still buddies, though. I'll always love him,' Tiffany sighed as she poured the last of the wine into our glasses.

'Oh, that's tough.'

'Oh, not that kind of love. Not any more. I've moved on.'

'Are you seeing anyone at the moment?'

She looked at me oddly.

'I take it you haven't read the papers for the last few days?'

I shook my head. 'I'm avoiding them.'

'Ditto, the problem is my agent rings or texts me with all the latest gossip,' she laughed. 'Agents, gotta love em.'

'So what is the latest gossip, if you don't mind me asking?'

'That I'm responsible for a marriage break-up.'

'Oh, dear. What happened? And who?'

Tiffany shrugged her shoulders and slouched back in the seat. 'Well firstly, I didn't break up the marriage. They actually split up a year ago, but they cleverly did it on the sly, so the public didn't know. The paparazzi got a great picture of us in quite a passionate embrace on the beach in the Maldives recently. Now, I'm labelled a home wrecker.'

When tears started to fill her eyes, I put down my wine and placed my hand on hers. 'I'm so sorry, Tiffany. Isn't there anything you can do?'

'Hugh is planning on making a statement to the press tomorrow morning, so hopefully, things will die down after that.'

'Hugh... Blarney?' I scoffed as she closed her eyes and nodded.

'Wow, Tiffany.'

'Yeah, I know.'

'Do you love him? Oh, sorry, you don't have to answer that,' I cringed, realising perhaps I'd had a little too much wine.

But Tiffany shook her head. 'Nope. We were just having a bit of fun, that's all. He's a nice guy, but I realised in the Maldives that we're not meant to be together.'

'So you've already split up.'

She nodded and took a sip of her wine.

'You know what I'd love?'

I shook my head.

'To find someone to settle down with, maybe have a couple of kids. That's the dream.'

'Really?'

'You sound surprised.'

'Well, it just doesn't match your public persona,' I said, realising how awful that sounded as it came out of my mouth.

Tiffany laughed loudly. 'I know, right? Just goes to show how wrong the press really can be.'

'But don't you want the public to know the real you?'

'Why? Everybody has already made their minds up about me. Honestly, I don't really care what the world thinks any more.'

'You can't really mean that?'

She sighed and put her empty glass on the table as the waiter gingerly approached.

'May I clear the table?'

'Yes, please, Giorgio. I'll take the rest of the pizza to go please.'

He nodded shyly and disappeared with the plates balancing on his forearm.

'Maybe I don't mean it, but what can I do about it? Not much.'

'You could give an interview on morning TV,' I suggested.

'What, like you did? I bet it didn't do you any favours?'

'My situation is just a little bit different to yours, Tiffany,' I smiled.

'Yeah, I know. Maybe I will. You're good to talk to, you know that?'

'I am?'

She nodded.

'You're good to talk to, too.'

'You're a sweetie, Kate. I'm so pleased we've met. I'll tell you what, I'll do an interview if you go on a date with Luigi. Deal?'

I shook my head and chuckled. 'Okay, deal,' I replied as we shook hands.

a week later and my house was filled with my girlfriends, buzzing around helping me get dressed, doing my hair and make-up. Anybody would have thought it was my wedding day, certainly not just a simple date.

Okay, so perhaps it wasn't just a simple date. It was possibly THE date of my entire life. If Luigi was the real Fred, then... then... what? I cringed for about the 100,000th time that day and took a deep breath. What was I doing? Why had I let it get this far? Why couldn't I just have forgotten about him when I was a kid? Like he had forgotten about me?

'Breathe, Kate, just breathe,' said Zara calmly as she brushed my hair.

'I'm trying.'

Jo handed me a cup of sweet tea to calm my nerves and then sat down beside me, just as the phone rang. Leaning forward onto my dressing table, she picked up my mobile and handed it to me.

'It's Liz,' she smiled.

'Liz,' I squealed. 'How's the Azores?'

'Amazing!' she squealed back. 'But I'm not calling to talk about the islands, I'm calling to wish you luck, hon.'

She was such a sweetheart.

'So, what are you wearing?'

I rolled my eyes. 'She wants to know what I'm wearing,' I whispered to the girls.

'She can't make up her mind,' shouted Zara as she accidentally pulled my hair a little too hard.

'Ouch!'

'Sorry!'

'So what are the choices?' Liz asked.

'Well, we've got several outfits lying on the bed. Two are slightly more casual, and two are much more dressy.'

'How casual?'

'Black trousers and a green blouse, and a long floaty skirt and a tank top.'

I could almost hear her cringe over the phone. 'Lose the trousers. With your legs, you should be showing them off, which means you should lose the skirt too.'

'Oh, okay then,' I muttered.

'So what are the more dressy options? And do you know where you're going?'

I shook my head absent-mindedly, forgetting for a moment that she couldn't see me.

'Well?'

'Erm, no. Luigi is picking me up at seven. He said it's a surprise.'

'Don't you think that's a bit dangerous? You don't know the guy, he could be some sex-starved maniac.'

'I'm not worried about that, Liz. It's been ages since I had any,' I laughed along with the girls who were all ear-wigging.

'I'm serious, Kate. Can you at least get Tony and Zara to follow you to make sure he's taking you to a restaurant and not some dark alley to murder you?'

'Oh, Liz, you do make me laugh.'

'Right, put Zara on the phone,' she said, deadly serious. 'Please put Zara on the phone. Now, Kate.'

Pulling a face, I handed the phone to my Portuguese friend.

'Hey, Liz.'

She stood listening for a few minutes, occasionally nodding her head without saying a word. Eventually, she said, 'Okay, I will.

Promise. Take care, Liz. Love to the hunky fireman,' grinning, she handed it back.

'Okay, now tell me about the dressier options.'

I shook my head and rolled my eyes at the girls as Zara disappeared for a few moments. I could hear her on the phone; she was clearly talking to Tony.

oOo

Standing in the bedroom, in front of the full-length mirror, I must admit I felt like a million dollars. Or should I say, I felt like a hundred and forty-seven million pounds?

The deep blue belted pencil dress hugged me in all the right places and even the top part, with its lace midi sleeves and a pretty little bow in the middle, made my boobs look decidedly bigger than they actually were. I smiled at my reflection as the girls stood, waiting patiently for my reaction.

'Well?' asked Anna, who had turned up a little late to the party.

'It's great,' I whispered, twirling.

'I've no idea what you did to my hair, Zara, but it's perfect,' I said as I inspected the curls that she had somehow managed to pin up and let loose at the same time.

'Liz was right to choose this dress,' Jo said with a grin. 'That girl is always spot on where clothes are concerned.'

I nodded and turned to face them all.

'Thank you for doing this for me. I can't tell you how much I appreciate it.'

'You know we're always here for you, sweetie,' Jo stood up and gave me a gentle hug. The others followed suit, and before I knew it, I was ready to go. The doorbell rang and my cheeks flushed a deep pink.

'Are you ready?' Jo asked at the door.

Taking a very deep breath, I nodded and waited for them all to disappear before I opened it.

I bit on my bottom lip as Luigi stood admiring me before handing me a single yellow rose.

'This is for you, Kate,' he whispered and kissed me on the cheek. It tingled. I blushed.

But I couldn't help but think it wasn't a daffodil.

'Shall we?' he asked, holding out his arm like a proper gentleman.

Nodding, I took it, and we strolled to his car. I couldn't help but notice that he couldn't take his eyes off me. I squealed inside.

Just as we arrived at a brand new Mercedes CLS, he turned and said, 'I've never seen anyone so beautiful in all my life, Kate.'

Then he opened the door and waited as I climbed in, the butterflies in my stomach, making it difficult for me to breathe.

As we slowly drove towards the gate, waiting for it to open, I noticed Zara and Tony hop into her Audi. She winked at me as we passed, and I tried not to laugh at Liz's paranoia. They were seriously going to follow me to make sure I was okay. I guess it was sweet, really.

'So where are you taking me, Luigi?' I asked as I admired the Mercedes and its new car smell.

'To a romantic little Italian place I read about recently. I'm afraid I've never been, living up north, but the article impressed me.'

I nodded. 'Are you certain you'll be able to find it?'

Luigi gave me a cheeky grin. 'I spent most of the afternoon driving the route, several times, to make sure I wouldn't get lost!'

Chuckling, I relaxed back into the seat and breathed deeply as we drove through the city, occasionally spotting the little Audi TT in the rear-view mirror.

'So, tell me a little more about yourself, Luigi. Unfortunately, we didn't get the chance to talk at the photoshoot.'

I saw him cringe and I smiled. 'Was it as awful for you as it was for me?'

'I admit it was a little awkward and quite embarrassing. But it was worth it... to meet you.'

'I agree,' I smiled.

We eventually turned into a public car park and found a spot to leave the car.

'I'm afraid the restaurant doesn't have its own private car park, so we'll have to leave the car here.'

'That's okay, isn't it? This is London, after all. There aren't many private car parks around here.'

Smiling, Luigi got out of the car and went to open my door. As I climbed out, I spotted a car hire sticker on the inside.

'And there I thought you had a brand new car,' I said, absent-mindedly.

'It is a new car,' he answered. 'Shall we go?' he asked before I could ask more about it.

Perhaps it was hired for the evening. Yes, that was probably it. He was trying to impress me. I smiled.

oOo

The conversation had flowed, and so had the wine - albeit Luigi was a little more careful on account of him having to drive us home. He was a perfect gentleman, standing when I needed to head to the ladies room, laughing at all my jokes, keeping my water - and wine - glass topped up. He was incredibly attractive and had strong hands (I loved men with strong hands). The evening was a success, but there was something that bugged me - just a little bit. Never once did he mention Skegness.

I know he said he couldn't remember meeting me as a child, but he did go to the caravan park on numerous occasions. I expected him to at least talk about it, considering how important it was to me. But I didn't want to be the one who brought it up, I didn't want to appear too obsessed.

When I headed to the ladies room for the second time, I took my handbag with me and called Zara from the cubicle.

'Are you alright?' she breathed down the line.

'Yes, yes, I'm fine. Thank you for following me,' I smiled. 'What happened to you after we parked?'

Zara chuckled. 'Because we followed you into the car park, we figured we might as well stick around, so we followed you into the restaurant - just to make sure he was really taking you out to eat dinner - and then we headed down the road for a curry. We're still there now, so if you need a speedy exit, we can come and get you.'

I shook my head. 'No need. He's a perfect gentleman. I'll be fine. You guys can head home when you've finished your meal. But thanks again, for everything. You're absolute angels.'

'If you're sure?'

'I am. Thanks, Zara. Give Tony a kiss from me. I'll catch up with you tomorrow. Goodnight.'

Flicking through my messages, I saw that all the girls had texted me to make sure I was fine so I very quickly replied to reassure them, before checking my hair and putting on a little more lip gloss.

Luigi was waiting patiently for me. He stood as I approached and sat once I'd returned to my seat.

'I took the liberty of ordering some Tiramisu for us both. I hope you don't mind.'

'Not at all.'

'The article I read stated that it is the best Tiramisu out of Italy,' he laughed.

'Well then it would be a sin not to try it,' I smiled as I took a sip of my wine.

He sat watching me before leaning over and carefully moving a strand of hair behind my ear.

'You really are exquisite, Kate. And what's so wonderful is the fact that you don't see it. That's a rare quality to have.'

I could feel my cheeks blushing. Never before had anyone, let alone a gorgeous hunk of a man said such beautiful things to me.

'Thank you,' I whispered as I tried to hide behind my wine glass.

He chuckled. 'Don't hide from me.'

Smiling, I put the glass down.

'You know, you never did tell me anything about yourself. All evening, we've talked about me. I want to know Luigi. The real Luigi.'

Leaning back and relaxing into the seat, he very slightly shrugged his shoulders.

'I'm afraid there's not much to tell.'

'Okay then, I'll ask you some questions, and you must answer them.'

'And if I don't?' he smirked.

'Well then you have to do a dare,' I said cheekily.

'Truth or Dare?' he chuckled. 'It's been a long time since I played that. Okay then, but you have to play too.'

Sugar. I shouldn't have come up with the idea.

'Okay. I'll start. What do you do for a living?'

'Truthfully, I've had lots of jobs in my time - all in the financial industry. Currently, I'm a financial advisor.'

'Oh, what made you become a financial advisor?'

'With so much experience in the industry behind me and the fact that I love to help people make good with their investments, it seemed like the natural role for me to play. Now it's my turn.'

Oh, God.

'What's your middle name?' he smirked.

I laughed. 'Sorry to disappoint you, but I haven't got a middle name. I'm simply Kate Robinson.'

'Ah, but are you really a Kate and not a Kathryn or a Kathleen?'

I shook my head. 'Just Kate. My turn,' I grinned. 'What's your middle name?'

He laughed. 'I walked right into that one, didn't I?'

Nodding, I watched as the waiter arrived with two dishes of delicious-looking tiramisu.

'As you know, because my mother is English, she wanted me to have an English name too, so my full name is Luigi Ben De Santis.'

'That's a really nice name, Luigi Ben.'

'Thank you. My turn,' he said as he tucked into the dessert. 'Hmm. Not bad. Not as good as my grandmother's, though.'

I took a little spoonful and let it dance on my tongue. Boy, his grandmother's tiramisu must be amazing because it was divine. So divine, in fact, that I didn't say another word until I'd polished it off.

'I do love to see a woman with a good appetite,' he said as he watched me eat.

'It was so good.'

'Shall I order you another one?'

'Oh, God no, thank you! I couldn't eat another thing.'

'Where were we? Oh, yes, it was my turn. Tell me, how did you feel when you found out about your inheritance?'

Oh, I wasn't expecting that, but I shrugged my shoulders and told him. I sure as heck didn't want to have to do a dare in the middle of the restaurant.

'How did I feel?'

He nodded.

'Dumb-founded, completely shocked, over the moon, sad...'

'Sad? Why would you feel sad at inheriting a hundred and forty-seven million pounds?'

'Because it meant someone had died, and that someone was a really nice man.'

'Uncle Sam?'

I nodded. 'Yes.'

'But he wasn't really an uncle?'

I shook my head.

'Now it's my turn. What made you respond to the article about me?'

'That's easy, you're so beautiful, and I genuinely thought there was a chance I might be your, what was it? Fred.'

I smiled sadly.

'Tell me, Kate. What made you hold on to him, or me,' he smiled before continuing, 'for so long? It was such a brief moment in time, wasn't it? Do you really think he is your soul mate?'

'That's two questions,' I smiled sadly before I looked down at the floor. It wasn't him. Luigi wasn't Fred. I just knew, deep down, at that very moment, that I never met him as a child.

But did it matter? Did it really matter? Luigi was the most amazing, handsome, caring man. Could I see myself with him?

'Kate?'

'Sorry. Truthfully,' I shook my head. 'I don't really know. We just shared something so special, you know? I connected with him, even though it was just a tiny moment in time. It was...' I stopped and looked away. 'It was like it was destiny.'

'Destiny?'

I nodded.

'But perhaps so was this,' he suggested, as I looked up into his eyes.

'Perhaps every single moment of our lives has been leading up to this one. To us. To us, finally meeting. Perhaps this is our destiny, Kate. You and me. Kate and Luigi, not Kate and Fred.'

Tears welled in my eyes, and I didn't know what to say, or what to do. My glass was empty, I couldn't even hide behind that.

Luigi leaned forward and handed me a clean napkin to wipe my eyes, leaving his hand placed over mine.

Warmth enveloped me as I eventually looked back up into his eyes. Maybe he was right. Maybe all this Fred nonsense was merely fate's way of leading me to Luigi.

We'd been on five dates, three during the evening and two during the day, and not once had he asked to come back to my place - or suggested we go back to his, wherever that might be. Luigi was a total gentleman, but I was starting to feel there was something wrong with me. Didn't he want me?

I lay in bed with my eyes open, staring at the ceiling. Glancing across at the bedside alarm clock, I sighed when I saw it was only ten past six. But I couldn't lie still any longer. Throwing back the covers and climbing out of bed, I wrapped myself up in the lovely fluffy nightgown Jo bought me for Christmas and went and put the kettle on. Waiting for it to boil, I tapped my fingernails on the worktop. The sound of the phone scared me half to death.

'Hi, honey.'

'Mum!'

I could practically hear her smile.

'You do know it's barely after six in the morning, don't you?'

'Of course I do, my angel. But I felt I needed to talk to you and I wanted to speak to you before you headed off for work, or whatever it is you've been doing with yourself since becoming a wealthy young lady.'

'I'm glad you called.'

'Good. How are you feeling? What have you been up to? And tell me about this young man you're seeing?'

'Mum! How on Earth do you know I've been seeing someone?'

She cackled down the line. 'A mother knows these things. Besides, one of the African tribeswomen told me I should contact you. She said you were going to be needing me soon.'

'Oh?'

'Precisely my thoughts, angel. So spill the beans.'

After telling her all about Luigi and the photoshoot and all the fake Freds, she sighed down the phone.

'What? Why did you make that noise?'

'What noise?'

'A deep sigh, like you don't approve.'

'It's not that I don't approve, Katie sweetheart. It's that, well, I have a feeling in my stomach, and it's not a good one. I just don't want you to get hurt, that's all. Have you spent the night together yet?'

I shook my head.

'Okay, okay, you don't have to tell me,' she laughed.

'No, it's okay. But no, we haven't. That's one of the things that's bothering me. We've been out five times and not once has he made a move. We've kissed, of course, but not the passionate, earth-shattering kiss you would expect in the early days of a new romance.'

She sighed again.

'Well? What do you think?'

'Akwasibah told me to warn you.'

'About what?'

'I don't know. All she said is that you should be careful.'

'Well, that's totally useful - not.'

Mum sighed yet again as I poured the hot water into the cup.

'What do you think I should do, Mum?'

'I don't know, angel. I'm not really in a position to advise you on anything, these days. All I know is that coming into such a large amount of money will bring you heartache, whether you're prepared for it or not. Akwasibah thinks someone is after your money. Whether it's this Luigi or not is another question. It could be anybody. It could be someone you've not even met yet. One thing she did say, that was comforting, was the fact that you are surrounded by such good friends, who love you very much. She said they will always be there for you.'

Smiling, I nodded. 'Well, that I do know. Thanks, Mum.'

'Don't thank me, thank Akwasibah.'

'But what else did she say?'

I took a sip of strong black tea while I waited for her to reply.

'That you'll be making a long journey soon.'

'I will?'

'Yes.'

'Well, I have been talking about going back to the Azores and over to New York to check out my new apartment. Maybe that's what she means.'

'I'm sure it is, but she told me that it would be a journey of deep thinking.'

'O...kay.'

'But enough of all this. Did you go to see your father?'

After explaining all about my trip to Newcastle and catching up on the rest of our news, I put the phone down and sat down at the breakfast bar, my shoulders slumped forward as I pondered the mumbo jumbo that Akibah woman had said. Who was she anyway? And what right did she have to go sticking her nose into my business? It was probably all a load of old tosh anyway.

oOo

'You ready for our double date tonight?' Jo asked happily down the phone later that day.

'Of course! What are you going to wear?'

'I thought I'd wear my slim black trousers with that gold blouse I bought from Lisbon.'

'Ooh, nice, that'll look lovely.'

'What about you, Kate?'

'Honestly, I have no idea. I seem to be totally useless when it comes to dressing myself, these days. I can't understand why.'

'Perhaps you ought to hire a stylist,' she laughed.

'Oh, God! Really?'

'It's not like you can't afford it. But I was actually joking, Kate! Jeeze! What's going on in your head at the moment? You seem to be all over the place?'

'Yeah, I know. I can't put my finger on it. I just feel a bit, I dunno, disjointed, I suppose.'

'Oh, really? That's not good. Maybe you need a holiday? Get away from all the madness for a bit. Is everything okay with you and Luigi?'

Shrugging, I flopped onto the sofa so that I was laying down, looking at the floor.

'I don't really know. It seems to be going great, but I feel like something's missing, you know? But I'm fine, I'll be fine. We're going to go out tonight and have a great time. I can't wait to see you with Paul. How are things with the two of you?'

Her laugh was contagious. She was clearly smitten.

'Amazing Kate! I can't believe I've met such a wonderful man. He's so caring and fun. I think I'm falling in love with him,' she said quietly.

'Awww Jo, that's wonderful. I'm so happy for you.'

'Thanks, hon. The other thing about him is that he loves Carly and she loves him too. They get on so well. I never realised how important it was for her to have a man around the house. I'm thinking about… about asking him to move in.'

My squeal almost shattered the glass vase beside me.

'I'm SOOOOO happy for you! And it's all because of me,' I laughed. 'If I hadn't have fallen and got a concussion, you might never have met in the first place.'

Jo laughed so loud I had to pull the phone away from my ear.

'Are you there?' Jo suddenly asked.

'Yep, right here,' I sighed. 'I'm just so happy for you. All my friends have found true love - you, Julianne, Liz, Anna, Zara. You're all with the men of your dreams.'

'Hey, don't sound so sad. You met the man of your dreams too, remember? Well, kind of.'

'Exactly, I guess I'll never really know if he is, will I?'

'Oh, Kate, don't go down that road again. You really need to get past this whole Fred business now. You do realise that, don't you?'

I tried to stop them but I couldn't, and suddenly my eyes filled with tears and I sobbed like a baby.

'Kate, are you crying? Look, stay put. I'm coming right over. I'll bring my clothes with me, and I'll get ready with you tonight. Just stay there. I'll be as quick as I can.'

oOo

We sat on the sofa for what seemed like ages, Jo with her arms around me as I cried. Letting it all out. Everything. All the pent-up emotions that had been threatening me for years. I cried for losing Fred in the first place; I cried for wasting years trying to find someone that doesn't really exist; I cried for Uncle Sam and for the hundred and forty-seven million reasons he left everything to me. I cried for my dad, my mum and for that silly Akibah woman or whatever her name was. I even cried for Jo, who'd lost her love so many years ago and was now ready to love again. And finally, I cried for Luigi, who'd lost a little brother in a fire. A fact I'd been ignoring because all I cared about was finding a boy I'd only seen once, nearly twenty years ago. Then the tears stopped, and I looked up to find the most beautiful angel looking at me.

'Is that better?' Jo stroked my shoulder like only a mother can.

Nodding, I blew my nose on the snotty wet tissue I'd been using to wipe my eyes.

She let out a little chuckle and went and fetched a new box.

'Here, use these.'

'Thanks, Jo. Thanks for everything. You're the best friend anybody could ever dream of,' my bottom lip trembled slightly.

'And so are you. Come on, don't cry any more. I don't think there are any more tears to be had, anyway. Not now. Not today. Look at you, you're all puffy,' she said as she pulled me up and led me to the mirror above the mantelpiece.

'Oh, God,' I cried. 'I look absolutely hideous.'

Shaking her head, Jo grabbed my shoulders from behind and looked at my reflection. 'You're a little puffy, that's all. You could never look hideous. We've got a few hours, we can sort this out,' she smiled.

. . .

oOo

Never dismiss the usefulness of cold slices of cucumber.

Jo carefully placed them over my closed lids and instructed me to lie on the sofa and enjoy the music while she made us yet another cup of tea.

She'd gone out to her car to grab her favourite CD. I'd heard it a million times before, but this time, I savoured it. The sounds of world music drifted into my head, making me think of my mum and how happy she was in Africa.

A combination of music styles from around the world, including Africa, the group was called Beautiful World, and it was so relaxing, I could feel myself dropping off.

After twenty-minutes, Jo turned the volume down and nudged me to sit up. Removing the cucumber from my eyes, she handed me her little handbag mirror with a smile.

'I told you we could sort this out.'

Looking at my reflection, I grinned. It was as if the crying had made the colour of my hazel eyes ten times brighter and the puffiness was entirely gone.

'You're a genius.'

'All in a day's work, my love. Here, I made camomile tea, I figured it would help to calm your nerves.'

'Thank you,' I grinned. 'You know, I'm actually really looking forward to tonight now. Now that I've got all that out of my system. I almost feel re-energised.'

She squeezed my knee and took a gulp of tea just as a faint commotion could be heard outside.

'Oh, God, I hope it's not those photographers trying to get in again.'

'Photographers?'

'Yeah, paparazzi - they've tried to get into the grounds a few times to get pictures of Tiffany. Luckily they haven't been quite as desperate to get pictures of me. I think my fame is waning a little,' I smiled, standing up to gaze out the window.

A madwoman was shouting at the security guard, but he kept shaking his head. Clearly, he wasn't going to let her in, thankfully. I wondered who she was but thought nothing more of it as I turned away and sat down, the mug warming my cold fingers.

'Shall we go and work out what you're going to wear tonight?' asked Jo casually as she leaned back into the soft sofa.

'Yes, let's!' I laughed, standing up as soon as I sat down.

We rushed towards my wardrobe, giggling as we pulled open the doors and started rifling through everything.

But a knock on my front door made me jump.

'I wonder who that is?'

'Not expecting anyone, then?'

I shook my head. 'Not really, but sometimes Zara, Tony or Tiffany pop by for a cup of tea. Maybe it's one of them. I'll be right back. You carry on looking,' I returned downstairs to the front door.

'Oh. Is everything alright, erm, Steven?' I asked the security guard who had been at the gates just moments before.

'I'm sorry, Miss Robinson. I tried to stop her, but she just keeps insisting that she won't leave until she's spoken to you.'

We both glanced back towards the gate where, standing on the other side, was a woman with bright red and black hair held up with a garish orange headscarf. She wore black leggings with black ankle boots and an orange parka which she was huddling into.

'Miss Robinson! Kate Robinson!' She yelled, waving when she noticed me.

'Do you know who she is, Steven?'

'Says her name is Gina. All she says is that she has something essential to talk to you about. I'm not going to let her in, unless you want me to, of course. Alternatively, I can call the police if you like.'

'No, there's no need for that, thank you. Erm, okay. I'll come over in just a moment.'

Steven nodded with a nervous smile as I stepped back indoors to put some shoes and my coat on.

'Jo, I won't be a sec. I've just got to pop out to the front gate!'

'Okay, I think I've got the perfect outfit for you!' she yelled back. I laughed and closed the door behind me.

Approaching the gate, the woman looked nervous and a little crazed. I gulped, hoping to God she didn't have a gun underneath that coat. What was I doing? Perhaps Steven should ring the police.

'Miss Robinson, I'm sorry to bother you, I really am. But I really, really need to speak to you about Gavin.'

'Gavin?'

She nodded avidly.

'Who's Gavin?'

She looked at me as if I was the mad one.

'Gavin, the guy you've been... dating.'

'I'm sorry erm, Gina, but I think you have me confused with someone else. I'm not dating anyone called Gavin.'

Suddenly she opened her coat, and I stepped back in absolute terror.

I needn't have worried. Hidden inside was just a magazine.

'Gavin,' she said, pointing to a photo of Luigi and me, eating in a restaurant just a few days earlier.

'That's not Gavin, that's Luigi.'

But Gina shook her head. 'Nah, it isn't. It's Gavin, and he's my husband.'

My mouth went dry, and all I could do was stand there, dumbfounded, not saying a word.

'Maybe I should come in?' she asked.

I nodded at her and then looked over towards Steven. With a nod, he unlocked the small pedestrian entrance and Gina followed me back to my house.

'Jo, could you come downstairs please?' I yelled from the bottom of the stairs.

She came happily hopping down, carrying a couple of dresses, but when she caught sight of my face, she dropped them on the floor and rushed to my side.

'Kate?' she whispered.

'This is Gina. Lui... Gavin's wife.'

'Gavin? Who's Gavin?'

'Luigi.'

'Huh?'

'Apparently, Luigi is Gavin.'

'What? What is going on here?'

I led them both into the living room where the three of us sat down.

Gina suddenly stood back up and took off her coat. Sitting slowly back down, she smiled nervously. 'You have a lovely home.'

'Thanks.'

'Hang on a minute. Who are you?' Jo said, sternly.

Clearing her throat, Gina looked from Jo to me and back again.

'I'm Gina Foster, and I'm married to Gavin Foster. Here, look,' she said as she plunged her hands into her enormous zebra print handbag and pulled out a small photo album. Opening it, she revealed several wedding photos of her, wearing the most hideous meringue of a dress, next to a man wearing a blue suit. There was no doubt about it. It was Luigi.

My hand covered my mouth, and I looked up at Jo, whose face was one of extreme disgust. I guess she didn't like the dress.

'You're telling me that your husband has been pretending to be someone else to begin a relationship with my best friend?'

Gina nodded.

'But why? Why would he do such a thing?'

'The money,' I whispered.

Gina nodded.

'How long have you been married to him, Gina?'

'Thirteen years. But we've known each other since we were like, five or something.'

'So you knew him when he lost his brother in the fire?'

'Huh? He never lost any of his brothers in a fire. They all came to the wedding. Look,' she said as she turned the page and pointed to another photo of her with Luigi, or Gavin, or whatever his name was, with a bunch of other men, who all looked remarkably similar.

'Did he ever go to Skegness?' I asked through gritted teeth.

'Skegness? Yeah, we used to go all the time,' she said with a smile.

'In fact, I've got more pictures of when we were kids and went on holiday there. You see, our parents were best friends, and we used to rent caravans there. Look, there's me with Gavin when he was about twelve or thirteen, I think.'

I couldn't bear to look, but I did. There, standing with a mousy-haired skinny little girl was a boy I'd never set eyes on before.

CHAPTER 34

I'm ashamed to admit that I cried for days after Gina left. I refused to see the scum bag, Luigi, Gavin, whatever - and I asked Tony and Paul to deal with him when he came to collect me for our 'date'. I think Jo slapped him, too, but it was all a bit of a blur.

Eventually, Jo had to go home to her daughter, and I had to force the rest of my friends to leave me alone. I told them I was okay. They knew I wasn't. But they also knew I needed time on my own to sort out my head. I tried to call Mum, but mobile phone signals weren't particularly good where she was so I couldn't get through. I'd hoped she'd call me back, but I was still waiting, four days later.

Sitting on the sofa, with a duvet over me and a mass of take-away boxes around my feet, I felt ashamed of myself. I wasn't this person. I didn't react to things this way. I was strong, wasn't I?

Thinking back to the last time my mum had called, I remembered everything that Abika woman had said. It was so obvious now. She'd practically warned me about Luigi. He was after my money. And he'd gone to such ridiculous lengths to fool me - even arranged for his very first letter to be sent via Rome. Jeez.

All he'd wanted was the cash. It was clear as day. And I'd been too bloody stupid to notice. Too convinced by his ridiculous lies that he was the one. The one I'd been searching for my entire life.

I was such an idiot.

I flicked the channels for the thousandth time that morning (and it was only - I glanced at the clock - 9.22am) and settled on Heir Hunters, which made me laugh out loud as I blew my red nose and dropped the snotty tissue on the floor, on top of the mountain of other snotty tissues down there.

The sound of the phone ringing didn't bother me anymore. It had been ringing on and off for the past three days, and I chose to ignore every call. The only person I'd speak to was Mum, and so far, there had been no call from Africa.

When the constant banging on my front door began to drive me insane, I had no choice but to go and open it.

'Surprise!'

'Mum,' I cried, falling over myself to get to her.

'How? Why? What? Oh my god. I can't believe you're here. I'm so happy to see you. Where's Nick? Are you staying for long? Oh, Mum,' I cried, breaking down in tears for the umpteenth time that week.

'I know, I know, my angel. Now let me come in, and we'll talk it all over.'

Pushing me backwards, I noticed her do a little wave to someone outside. Taking a quick peek, I spotted Tony standing with his arm casually draped over Zara. Both smiled sadly at us before they walked back indoors.

'Well, this is all very swanky, isn't it?' she marvelled.

'No, not really. It's just a bit different from the African bush, that's all mum.'

'Well, you can say that again. Where's the kitchen? I'm parched.'

Dropping her only bag onto the floor, I led her through and immediately put the kettle on.

'Tea okay?'

'Oh, you sit down, my angel, let me do it. Now, tell me. I want to know exactly what happened?' she asked as she opened every cupboard door trying to find some cups.

'It was just as your friend said it would be.'

'My friend?'

'Yeah, Akiba?'

Chuckling, she threw back her head. 'You mean Akwasibah?'

'Yeah, that's it. Akwasibah. Everything happened just as she said it would. I should have listened. I should have known. Why did I do it? Why did I follow such a pathetic little girl's childhood dream?'

Mum walked over to me and put her arms around me, pulling me close, like only a mother can. She held me so tightly that I felt safe and comforted. It felt like her touch made everything instantly better.

'There there, angel. It's not the end of the world. You were taken advantage of by a cruel man. Unfortunately, it happens all the time. The difference with you,' she said, as she pulled back and touched the end of my nose with her finger (just like she used to do when I was tiny), 'is that you will learn from it and won't let anyone take advantage of you again. This whole experience will make you stronger. I promise you that.'

'Thanks, Mum. But it's not just about Lui- Gavin. It's about my stupidity for believing that I could hold onto a dream and make it come true. A dream that was so far-fetched and idiotic in the first place. I feel like the world's biggest idiot and the worst part? Everybody knows about it. It's like everyone in England knows what a foolish moron I am. I don't feel like I can step out of my front door... ever... again.'

'Oh, pooh, nonsense. Nobody thinks you're a fool at all. Remember when your story first came out?'

I nodded shyly.

'Remember people's reactions?'

'Not really,' I pouted, not wanting to think about it.

'They all thought it was incredibly romantic, and they were all rooting for you. They all wanted you to find him. So many women were living vicariously through you, my angel. Don't you realise that?'

I shook my head like a little girl.

'How do you know all this?'

She smiled sheepishly. 'I've been keeping up to date with everything.'

'What do you mean, you've been keeping up to date with every-thing, exactly?'

'I have my ways.'

'Mum?'

'Oh alright,' she said, putting the kettle back down onto the worktop. 'I got a friend to send me all the magazine articles, newspaper clippings and recordings of everything with you in it.'

'Oh my god, Mum, really?'

'I'm sorry. I couldn't help it. You're my daughter, I didn't want to miss anything. I wasn't snooping or anything, I promise it wasn't like that.'

A giggle erupted from the depths of my stomach and suddenly came out of my mouth with hardly any warning.

Mum stopped talking and stood, staring at me.

'You're not mad?' she asked gingerly.

Shaking my head, the laughter continued to come. 'Of - course - not,' I stuttered. 'Oh, Mum, I'm happy. I'm so glad you did this.'

'You... are?'

Nodding in between deep breaths, I watched her face soften as a smile lightened her face, and soon we were both howling with laughter. Not really knowing why, but knowing that we needed it. We really, really needed it.

CHAPTER 35

A few days later, Mum threw a party. She called it the 'FAF
Party' (Forget About Fred), and she invited everyone that
mattered. The only people who were missed were my dad, of
course (but that would have been a bit awkward), and Liz and
Jorge (who couldn't leave the Azores at such short notice), who
phoned just before it started, to give me a massive phone hug. It
was almost like they were passing me their energy through the
phone, and it gave me such a buzz that when I opened the door to
my first guest, I nearly knocked Tiffany onto the floor.

'Oh WOW, you're obviously feeling a little better?' she laughed
as I grabbed her hand and led her through into the kitchen, where
Mum was ready with the fruit punch she'd insisted on making - it
went perfectly with the rest of the seventies-style buffet she'd
prepared, including mushroom vol-au-vents, pineapple and cheese
on sticks, pigs in blankets, cheese straws and melon balls among
other things.

She'd gone a bit mad, using the excuse that she hadn't had the
chance to make party food for years.

'Party food isn't exactly popular with the African tribes I live
with, dear.'

'Tiffany, I'd like you to meet my mum, Angela. Mum, this is...'

'Tiffany Chantelle,' Mum whispered, approaching her with her
arms outstretched. 'What an honour to meet you. I loved you in

Into The Dark Lands. That was such a powerful performance from you. I watched it about twenty times.'

'You did?' I asked, surprised she'd been able to watch a movie that wasn't actually that old.

Nodding, she turned to me with a grin. 'We stayed in the city a couple of years ago, and there was a makeshift cinema there. Into The Dark Lands was the most popular film they showed. I hadn't realised how much I missed the movies, so I kept going back. I think I drove Nick insane.'

'Oh wow, that's lovely, Angela. Thank you,' said Tiffany, who was genuinely moved.

'Here, you must try my special fruit punch. It's got a bit of a kick to it,' she said as she handed the pink juice to her in a champagne glass.

'Oh gosh,' Tiffany coughed. 'It certainly does. But it's absolutely delicious. You could market this. You'd make a fortune.'

I glanced at Mum, who blushed slightly.

'Mum's not really interested in money. She lives with various different tribes in deepest Africa.'

'Really? That's amazing. You must tell me more about it. I'd love...'

I left them chatting as more guests arrived.

Soon, the house was full of laughter as my dearest friends surrounded me with love and support as I tried to forget the exploits of a man I had found myself falling for.

The wine and fruit punch flowed as Mum regaled everyone of tales of the African bush and of the many witch doctors she'd met over the years. She had them literally hanging on her every word. It was weird how she'd changed since I was a child. She was more confident, more outgoing and even more beautiful. Africa suited her. Or perhaps it was Nick. Or both. Either way, I was so proud to call her my mum.

Stepping down into the lounge much later on, balancing several cups of coffee on a small tray, I overheard Tony telling everyone about Luigi - Gavin's - pathetic exit out of my life.

'...and then Jo slapped him hard across the face. He stumbled backwards on the step, falling right into Steven, the security guard on duty, who shoved him right out the gate where his wife was waiting for him with a look of death on her face. Gina, wasn't it, Kate?' he asked as I placed the tray on the coffee table. Leaning over and nodding, the blood rushed to my head. Feeling a little dizzy, I closed my eyes for a second, just as Mum arrived with the cream and sugar. Noticing, she caught my arm and gently led me to the sofa where I sat down.

'You okay, honey?' asked Tiffany.

'I'm fine,' I smiled. 'It's just the alcohol.'

'Did you eat anything?' Mum asked, looked worried.

'Actually, no. I guess I forgot.'

Mum rushed straight up the steps to the kitchen, returning with a small plate piled high with food. Then she stood over me, making sure I ate every bite. I felt like a child again, as someone asked about the magazine article that was due out in a few weeks.

'Kate doesn't have to worry about that. I've made some, er, rather drastic changes so that Luigi doesn't get any coverage - other than a little box at the bottom of the page warning other women about him,' Julianne grinned.

I smiled gratefully.

'I've also reduced the spread significantly. I realise now how I used Kate to help sell magazines, and I'm absolutely disgusted with myself,' she said, seemingly rubbing a tear from her eye. 'I hope you'll forgive me.'

Shaking my head and swallowing the last sausage roll, I said, 'There's nothing to forgive. I understand what happened to me was big news and I'd rather you had more coverage than any other magazine.'

'You are such a sweetheart. Do you know that?'

I chuckled.

'You are, Katie,' Jo reiterated, as everyone else nodded.

'Thanks, guys, that's sweet. And so are all of you. I love you guys, but I've decided to leave you all for a while.'

'What?' Jo almost yelped as I nodded and looked at my mum, who patted my hand.

'I've decided to leave England, just for a while, to try and sort myself out.'

'But where will you go?' asked Anna with a look of horror plastered across her face.

'The Azores, New York and Toronto.'

'Are you going on your own?' asked Tony.

I nodded.

'But how long will you be gone?' asked Zara.

'I haven't decided yet, but I was thinking maybe a few months,' I shrugged, taking a gulp of hot coffee. 'I need to go over to the Azores to see how Liz is getting on, see if she needs my help with anything. Then I really do need to head over to New York and Toronto, to check out my new homes over there. It just seems like the right thing to do. I think it will help me to find me again if you know what I mean.'

'Sure we do,' said Mum as she patted my hand again.

'But we'll miss you,' Jo cried as she rushed to my side to hug me tightly.

'I'll miss you, too. But I need to do this.'

'I know, and I understand. You will call, won't you?'

'Of course.'

'And, if you need me, you know I'll be on the first plane, right?'

'I know.'

'I'll contact the solicitors in New York and Toronto and tell them to expect you,' Tony said, with a sad smile.

'Thanks, Tony.'

'When are you leaving?' hiccupped a red-faced Tiffany, who'd drunk a little too much punch.

'Saturday.'

'Saturday?' Jo almost shrieked. 'But that's only two days away.'

I smiled nodding. 'I wanted to leave tomorrow, but Mum convinced me that I'd need a little longer to prepare myself.'

'And speaking of which, I must head on upstairs and pack. I have an early flight to catch in the morning,' said Mum as she lifted herself off the side of the sofa and stretched her arms and legs. 'It has been wonderful to meet you all,' she said as the others all stood to say goodbye. 'I'm delighted that my angel has so many wonderfully supportive close friends. I shall return to Africa happy in the knowledge that she will never be alone.'

The ocean was even bluer than I remembered. So was the sky, even though the sun had not yet risen wholly above the horizon. It was so peaceful.

Glancing down from my private balcony, I watched the yoga teacher and seven others on the immaculate lawns below. As they practised the downward dog and the upward leopard (or whatever the poses were called), I smiled. Liz and Jorge had done the most fantastic job in turning Casa Linda into a real health and beauty retreat. Apparently, bookings were on the up, and they'd even been approached by several celebrities who were looking for somewhere to recharge their batteries without the worry of the paparazzi hiding in the bushes. And that was even before the official launch. It was amazing.

Walking downstairs to get some breakfast, I passed a couple of therapists who stopped to say hello and to thank me for creating such a perfect place to work. It gave me a buzz, even though I was quick to explain they should thank Liz and Jorge, not me. They're the ones who had done all the hard work. I'd merely provided the house and the finances. I still couldn't quite believe what they'd achieved in just under two months.

The breakfast room was stunning. Everything was white. White walls, white floors, white tables and chairs, white curtains. Even the plates were white. I smiled as I took one of them and slowly inspected the buffet. The usual continental style breakfast ingredients sat beside a plethora of gluten-free and lactose-free options that looked divine. Cartons of almond milk, soya milk, rice milk and oat milk were piled high next to large jugs of both skimmed and semi-skimmed. Teas of every variety, including green rose, vanilla rooibos, white and Moroccan were placed among the more usual English and Earl Grey. I chose the latter, along with a large croissant with plum jam.

Choosing a spot next to one of the windows, I sat down and took a sip of tea, relaxing back into the chair contentedly. As I ate, I watched the yoga class come to an end before turning my attention to some of the other guests in the breakfast room. It was slowly filling up with men and women of all ages. All looked relaxed and healthy. I smiled as Jorge walked into the room, grinning at his guests, with whom he spoke briefly before he spotted me sitting alone.

'Kate!' he rushed towards me. 'How you finding everything? Is room okay? Breakfast good, yes?'

I nodded energetically, his positive aura bouncing off me.

'Everything is absolutely perfect, Jorge. Thank you. I am so proud of what you and Liz have achieved here.'

He reddened a little and shook his head. 'It is Liz,' he nodded with a sparkle in his eyes. 'She is amazing. Her ideas. All this, her ideas. I am very lucky, eh?'

I laughed and patted my mouth with the cloth napkin. 'You're right, she is amazing. And you are fortunate to have found each other. And I am fortunate to have you both running this place. Thank you.'

Jorge blushed again, as a member of staff appeared in the doorway, trying to catch his attention.

'Oh, duty calls,' he smiled. 'I must go. You tell me if you need anything, anything at all.'

'I will, I promise. Thank you.'

He nodded with a grin and rushed away.

oOo

I'd been there almost a week when Liz and Jorge took a day off. We drove around the island and were tempted to go swimming in a stunning little cove but, as it was January, it was far too cold. We had lunch in a spot that overlooked almost the entire island. It was absolutely beautiful. It was there that the couple delivered their news.

'We're having a baby!' they'd squealed together.

'You are? Eeeeeeeeeeek,' I jumped up and hugged them both. 'I can't believe it. A baby, awwww I'm so happy for you both.'

'We just had confirmation from the doctor this morning. You're the first person we've told,' sighed Liz as she leaned back and let the sun warm her face, which was relaxed and tanned. She looked like a completely different person to the one I'd known in England.

'You look radiant, Liz.'

'Aww, thanks, Kate. I feel amazing. I can't quite believe it yet, though. That I have a little baby growing inside me.'

'I can imagine. It must be surreal.'

She nodded as Jorge returned from chatting to the owner of the restaurant, an old school friend.

'Are you alright, amor?'

Liz nodded and reached up to squeeze his hand as he sat down. Looking at each other, their faces completely lit up. This was a couple seriously in love.

I sighed happily for them, and she turned to look at me. Tilting her head to one side, she whispered, 'Kate, when are you going to forget about him?'

Taking a swig of cold water, I tried to think of something to say, but nothing would come, so I shrugged. She shook her head.

'This boy has captured your attention for far too long. He doesn't exist anymore, Kate, you've got to let him go.'

'I know, but it's not as easy as that.'

She raised her eyebrows. 'Yes, actually, it is.'

I shook my head and looked away.

'Don't do that. I know you. He's still in there,' she patted my chest. 'Trouble is, he's not out here. He never will be. It's time to move on and find your true soul mate.'

'Like Jorge?' I asked with a smile.

'Yes, exactly like Jorge. He has lots of single cousins,' she grinned. 'I'll introduce you at the wedding.'

'Wedding?'

'Yes, didn't I tell you? We must have told you? We finally set a date.'

'You did?' I grinned. 'When?'

'Next year. 20th of June. I could have sworn I told you because you and the girls are my bridesmaids.'

'We are?' I squealed again.

'I'm sure I told you. I wouldn't forget something like that.'

'Maybe it happened in the middle of the whole Luigi episode?'

'Yes, that's right. I called you one day to tell you, and then that ignorant bastard did that to you, and then comforting you was far more important at the time.'

'Oh, Liz... I'm so sorry. Comforting me shouldn't have been more important than announcing your wedding date and asking me to be a bridesmaid. I'm truly sorry.' I felt tears welling up in my eyes. This was precisely why I needed time to sort myself out. Why I needed some alone time. I well and truly needed to rid my brain of Fred.

CHAPTER 37

I'd never heard so many honking horns in my entire life. They seemed to come at us from every direction. As I looked out the window of the yellow cab, I clenched every one of my muscles in expectation of being hit by another car.

This was New York and, apparently, this was the norm. That's what the taxi driver told me, anyway, when we arrived at my new address on East 57th Street.

'Enjoy your stay in New York,' he grinned as I climbed out, letting him remove my bags from the boot.

'I'm sorry,' I asked, but which building is it?'

The overweight but charming driver gave me a lazy smile and pointed just two doors down.

'That's the one. Very swanky. See ya,' he yelled as he hopped back in the car and drove off, narrowly missing a couple of other yellow cabs in the process. Both leaned on their horns in protest.

'Let me help you there, miss,' said a middle-aged man in a rather fancy suit.

Unsure what was happening, my grip tightened on my bags as he smiled warmly at me.

'Miss Robinson?'

'Oh, how did you know?'

'We were told to await your arrival this evening. Your apartment awaits.'

'It does?'

By then, I was tired, hungry and bewildered.

'Please follow me, Miss.'

Doing as I was told, I followed him into a pretty standard looking building on the outside, into the most exquisite lobby.

'Er, are you sure we're in the right place?' I asked, almost hyperventilating.

The man's face softened, and he turned to smile at me. Placing the bags down, he said, 'You're Miss Kate Robinson, owner of Apartment Number 28? Inherited from Sam Simões, I believe?'

I nodded nervously.

'Then you're in the right place. Welcome to your new home, Miss Robinson. My name is George, and I'm the head porter at the Thomas Residence. You can call on me for anything, anything at all.'

'Oh, thank you, George,' I answered, immediately feeling at ease.

'I've been instructed to give you your keys,' he said as he leaned over the little front desk and handed me an envelope. 'Would you like me to help you up to your apartment?'

'I don't think so, thanks. I can probably manage, I'm sure you're busy enough,' I smiled.

'Not at all,' he said as he picked up my bags once again, and we walked towards the elevator.

As we waited, I glanced around at the impressive surroundings, all done out in white and grey marble, with several large sofas in the centre. It was more like a hotel than a residential building.

Still feeling a bit nervous, I looked down at the floor and waited for the door to open. As it finally did, the most gorgeous guy with short blond hair stepped out, almost bumping into me.

'Oh my, sorry honey,' he drawled in the most wonderful Texan accent. 'Hey there, George. Now, who is this fine young lady with you this afternoon?'

'Evening, Mr Scott. This is Miss Robinson.'

'Why, Miss Robinson, I've heard so much about you. It's a pleasure to meet you, at last,' he said as my mouth dropped open.

'Er, it's a pleasure to meet you too,' I said, holding out my hand as he shook it warmly. 'Please call me Kate. But, h...h...how have you heard about me?'

He blushed. 'Of course, Kate. I was a friend of Sam's. I'm so sorry to hear of his passing. Such a nice man, he was.'

'You knew Sam?' I asked excitedly.

'Why, of course, Andy and I used to cook for him every time he was here.'

'You did?'

Nodding, he looked at his watch. 'Shoot, I'm gonna be late. Kate, it's a pleasure to meet you. You must join me for dinner. Tomorrow, my place, eight o'clock. See ya there.'

And like a massive whirlwind, he was gone.

George leaned over and pressed the button after the door had closed.

He grinned at me. 'Mr Scott is a fine young man, Miss Robinson. You'll be safe with him. I can see you'll be good friends. Shame his boyfriend Andy just left him though,' he said as he smiled at me knowingly.

Oh right. That explains it.

'What's his first name?' I asked.

'Mr Scott?'

I nodded.

'Freddie.'

'Freddie?' I repeated incredulously.

oOo

George left me outside the door to my new apartment. 'If you need anything, anything at all, just let me know, Miss Robinson, okay?'

'Thank you so much, George,' I said as he stepped back into the elevator. I stood watching him as the doors closed, and it descended back towards the ground floor.

Turning, I realised there were just two doors on this floor. Taking the keys out of the envelope, my hands trembled as I unlocked mine. Pushing it open, I gasped, shocked at the sheer size of my new home. Half expecting something just a little larger than my lounge in Wimbledon, I could barely contain myself as I stepped forward into a vast open-plan room - the kitchen at the far end, and a living room at the other.

Giggling, I threw my hand luggage on the floor and rushed over to the nearest window where I could see a glimpse of greenery lit up not too far away. Was that Central Park? Looking down, I saw hundreds of people scurrying along the street and cars honking as they drove quickly through the city's streets. It was New York! I was in New York!

It hadn't quite dawned on me until then. Suddenly, memories of all those chick flicks I'd watched with Jo and Carly came flooding back and, with a massive grin, I couldn't wait to see what the city that never sleeps had to offer.

Unfortunately for this twenty-nine-year-old, however, sleep was exactly what I needed. Food first, then sleep. It had been a very long day. Unable to get a direct flight from the Azores to New York, I'd opted to fly to Lisbon first and then on to the States.

My stomach grumbled just as I contemplated whether to skip dinner or not. Clearly, that wasn't an option, so I grabbed my warm coat and handbag and rushed back out the door. I'd have a proper look around the apartment tomorrow.

George pointed out the nearest diner where I'd rushed straight into and ordered the grilled chicken Caesar wrap, which was enormous. Luckily, my stomach hadn't complained as I'd polished it off, followed by a cappuccino. Completely satiated, I just sat and watched some very interesting-looking people come in and out, enjoying being entirely alone for the first time in a long while.

Soon though, as my eyes began to feel heavy, I paid the bill and walked back down the road towards my new home at the Thomas Residence, where hopefully, a comfortable bed awaited.

oOo

The sound of a police siren going right past the building woke me with a start. Opening my eyes, it took me a good minute to remember where I was. Sitting up and stretching, I looked around the bedroom and smiled. I'd barely even noticed when I'd taken off my clothes and fallen into bed the night before, but the large room was beautifully decorated in creams, beiges and golds. It was quite classical in design, with slightly poofy swags and tails decorating the windows, but I liked it. It suited the place.

Climbing out of the massive bed, which could quite comfortably sleep four, I wandered into the bathroom and sat down for a pee before undressing and stepping into the enormous walk-in shower where gold and beige mosaic tiles twinkled beneath the falling warm water.

As I slowly began to wake up, thoughts of the previous three weeks filled my head. The impending baby and wedding, days spent lazing on the beach (but wrapped up from the chilly air), hours spent contemplating life, while attempting the downward zebra and other yoga moves on the lawn, overlooking the ocean and the hours I'd spent with Liz having massages, facials and manicures together. I'd had a blast, and Fred had only visited my mind on a couple of occasions. It was working. Leaving the UK for a while was doing me a world of good.

Unfortunately, the only time I'd been attracted to a gorgeous man was the previous evening. It's true, Freddie was perhaps the most handsome man I'd ever laid eyes on, and he was well and truly gay. Maybe destiny was playing her hand. Perhaps she was finally telling me that the only Fred ever to come into my life would be this beautiful gay man. I sighed, but not the kind of unhappy, miserable sigh I had been plighted with over recent years (and beyond); no, it was a contented sigh. I was happy. Simply happy.

Throwing on some jeans and a warm sweater, I hadn't even noticed the time. I'd slept for sixteen hours! Shows how much I needed it. I pulled on my cold weather boots, checked out the rest of the apartment (a further two large bedrooms, two bathrooms and a cute little indoor courtyard) and headed out to find the nearest supermarket.

George smiled when I stepped out of the lift. 'Good day, Miss Robinson. Sleep well?'

Nodding, I replied, 'Wonderfully well, thank you, George, but perhaps a little too long,' I answered glancing down at my watch.

'Nonsense. Can I help with anything this afternoon?'

'Yes, please. Could you point me in the direction of the nearest supermarket? I really need to fill the fridge and cupboards for my stay.'

'Of course,' he said as he pulled out a map of the city and showed me exactly where we were, and then gave me directions to several in the vicinity.

'Perhaps you'd like me to call you a cab?'

'That's okay, I'll walk. See you later.'

George nodded with a grin and tipped his hat. He was such a nice man.

New York was everything I expected and more. The atmosphere was electric. There was something about it that was really special. The way people jostled amongst each other as they walked through the streets, the endless river of yellow taxis that flowed between each and every pavement and the way the buildings towered above you were mesmerising. Tonnes of hop-on, hop-off sightseeing buses kept driving past with smiling tourists pointing and taking pictures. I grinned, and my stomach grumbled at the same time. There was so much happening that I had almost forgotten to eat again. As I was enjoying strolling through the streets so much, I decided to grab a hot dog from a nearby stand. After all, I couldn't very well come to New York and not do that, could I? I shivered, watching my breath as I waited.

It was worth the wait – my hot dog was absolutely delicious, but with all the different toppings I made such a mess of myself, but I didn't care. It's not like I had anyone to impress. So I carried on walking, slowly munching on the huge sausage sandwich, ketchup and mustard smothering my chin, as I admired the city that surrounded me.

I took no notice of where I was going, just kept walking down one street after another. Not once glancing at the map. I was utterly lost in the moment until I stumbled upon several pretty horses and carriages.

'Hey there,' said a really pretty woman about my age.

'Hi.'

'Would you like a ride?' she asked as she brushed the mane of the white horse which stood nearest to me.

'Erm, I hadn't really thought about it, to be honest.'

She smiled. 'English?'

I nodded. 'Yes, just arrived yesterday.'

'Welcome to New York.'

'Thank you,' I grinned while deciding whether to go for it or not.

Why not. I was in New York, I had to do everything while I was here.

'Okay then, I would.'

'Great! Hop on.'

Stepping up onto the carriage, the brunette handed me a warm blanket before she climbed onto the seat in front and motioned for the horses to start moving.

I couldn't help but grin.

'So, is this your first time in the Big Apple?'

'Yes, although I actually own an apartment here.'

She turned, her eyebrows raised. 'It's your first time here, yet you own an apartment?' she asked.

'It's a long story,' I smiled, before continuing. 'Basically, I inherited it.'

'Awesome, good for you.'

'Thanks. How long have you lived here?' I asked as we entered Central Park and grinned.

'All my life. Born and bred New Yorker, I am,' she smiled, turning to look at me. 'My name's Ashley, by the way, and these beauties here are Suzanne and Eliza,' she said, pointing to the two horses.

'It's great to meet you, Ashley, Suzanne and Eliza. I'm Kate.'

'Nice to meet you too, Kate. Well, I guess we should do the tourist thing,' she grinned and started telling me all about places that surrounded the park as well as areas within it. I learned that John Lennon used to live in a lovely old building called The Dakota, the Wollman Rink runs from October to April and then becomes the Victoria Gardens; The Pond is the perfect place below street level to while away a few hours (especially if you're into birds); around 250,000 people ride on the carousel every year and the Sheep Meadow is an area of fifteen acres that admits some 30,000 people every day between May and October and has seen concerts, demonstrations and political movements over the past hundred years.

After about forty-five minutes, we were back where we began, and Ashley pulled the horses and carriage over to the side of the road, where I paid her and said goodbye, but not before petting Suzanne and Eliza and then getting out of the way so a loved-up Italian couple could climb aboard. I watched as the horses trotted away. Ashley smiled and waved, and I opened the map George had given me to find the nearest supermarket. It was time to do some shopping and head home. I had to be at Freddie's soon.

CHAPTER 38

'Katie, darling!' yelled Freddie from the other side of the door as I knocked and laughed at his reaction. The door swooped open, and he pulled me forward and gave me two air kisses.

'I've been looking forward to this all day!' he squealed. 'I don't know if George told you but,' he placed his hand dramatically on his chest before continuing, 'my Andy recently left me,' he paused again, 'and so a much-needed heart to heart with my new British friend is just what I need.'

'Well then I'm glad to be able to help, Freddie,' I smiled as I walked into his apartment and admired his décor. The open plan lounge and kitchen was the same layout as mine, only his had a lot more colour and was decorated in a much more contemporary style.

'I took the liberty of opening a bottle of champagne - I hope you approve,' he said as he poured us both a glass of Mumm rosé.

'Yes, perfect,' I grinned as he handed it to me.

'Cheers, my darling,' he whispered as we clinked glasses before we linked arms and walked over to the enormous red sofa that dominated the room. 'I knew we were going to be friends the moment I set eyes on you in the elevator. Now,' he said, placing his hand on my knee, 'I want to know everything,' he winked before taking a long sip of bubbly.

'I want to know everything too,' I laughed. 'Like how a true Texan gay man winds up living in such a fabulous apartment in central New York?'

'That would be down to my dearest mother and father, who were so incredibly embarrassed to have a gay son that they shipped me off to live as far away as possible as soon as I was of age,' Freddie explained. 'New York seemed like the most appropriate place, and they were right, of course. It's where I met Andy,' he smiled before the corners of his mouth began to turn downwards and his lips trembled.

'Oh, Freddie, I'm so sorry. What happened?'

oOo

Masculine-looking, handsome and yet incredibly camp. That summed up Freddie and I loved all of that about him. We became instant buddies, spending every spare minute together. He was like my soul mate. It was such a shame he was gay, of course it was, but this was meant to be. Destiny had brought us together and had made me realise how silly I was to wait all this time for Fred when Freddie was the one I needed.

During our first evening together, he had poured his heart out to me, telling me all about his beloved Andy, the man he'd spent seven years of his life with. The man he had hoped to spend the rest of his life with, too. But it wasn't meant to be. Andy had been unable to resist the charms of a well known Scottish actor who flitted between London, Los Angeles and New York. Naturally, Freddie was devastated.

The following evening we'd got together again, and this time he was the shoulder for my heavy heart. We drank several bottles of champagne and ended up falling asleep on the sofa in front of the TV, where we'd bonded over episodes of Hart of Dixie, both swooning over George, Wade and the town's mayor, Lavon.

It was precisely what we both needed. Followed, of course, by shopping.

. . .

oOo

'You can't possibly be serious?' I asked, standing in the changing rooms wearing the most ridiculous orange and brown floral gown.

Trying so hard to keep a straight face, Freddie could hold it no longer and cracked up. But not before taking a picture of me with his phone.

'Freddie!' I squealed, rushing forward to take a peek. 'You're cruel making me try this on.'

'Cruel perhaps, but it is hilarious don't you think?' he giggled as I eventually stopped struggling for his phone and gave up, walking back into the little booth to take the dress off.

'Okay, okay,' he gave in. 'I promise not to be cruel again. Here,' he said as I opened the door, in my bra and knickers, with my eyebrows raised.

He was holding up the most exquisite lace red dress, I blushed and grabbed it from his fingers.

'I told you I had the best taste in clothes,' he teased. 'That's why my mother chose New York. So she could come over for shopping weekends with me. It's the only time she accepts me for who I really am,' he sighed. 'I wanna see the moment you have it on.'

Seconds later, I pulled open the door and stepped forward, feeling more beautiful than ever before.

'Wow,' he said with a wolf whistle, admiring me as I stood in front of the large mirror.

The midi-length sleeves helped to elongate my arms, and the dress reached just below my knees, making my legs look long and sleek. Even I could see that the colour made my eyes pop. It was true, he did have exquisite taste in clothes.

'Freddie, you're incredible,' I whispered. 'I don't blame your mother at all. You're amazing.'

'I sure am.'

I laughed. 'I don't ever want to take it off.'

'Well, I'm afraid you're gonna have to. Otherwise, the staff will have to call security.'

I rolled my eyes and turned to him. 'What else have you found?'

He grinned sneakily, rubbing his chin with his fingers before leaning sideways into the other changing room and pulling out a pair of blue jeans.

'Jeans?' I asked frowning.

'Not just any old jeans,' he said, handing them to me.

'What's so special about them?'

'I'm not telling. You'll just have to try them on and find out.'

Smiling, I took them out of his hands and turned, glancing at the mirror one more time before pulling myself away and back into my changing room.

'Oh, try them on with this,' he said, opening the door and handing me a purple blouse.

The jeans were like silk against my skin, fitting like no other pair of jeans had ever fit me before. I mean, let's face it, jeans are one of the most challenging items of clothing to buy, right? But these, well, they were just - perfect. I slid the blouse over my head and tucked it in before opening the door and stepping back out. Freddie sat on the sofa, grinning triumphantly.

'I told you.'

'They're amazing,' I said as I rubbed my thighs, looking in the mirror.

'How did you know the exact size?'

'Really? Honey, I'm gay.'

'Oh yeah, right,' I smiled.

'Thank you,' I mouthed to him in the reflection.

He rubbed my arms and grinned. 'My pleasure, Katie. Next stop, the shoe store,' he winked, and I squealed.

oOo

'You sound different. So relaxed... happy,' Jo said, on the phone, several weeks later.

'I am. This trip is just what I needed, Jo.'

'I think it's more than the trip - it's Freddie, isn't it?' she said, and I could almost hear her smile down the phone.

I nodded. 'Yeah, I guess it is. Who knew that all I needed was a gay best friend?'

Jo laughed loudly. 'I just hope he hasn't replaced me,' she joked.

'Replace you? Never! No-one could ever replace you, Jo. I miss you.'

'I miss you too, hon. When do you think you'll come home?'

Shrugging, I stood up and moved the curtain so I could gaze outside. 'Honestly, I really don't know. I do love it here, and I feel at home, you know?'

'But you are coming home, aren't you?'

'Yeah, of course. How's Carly doing?'

'She's great, got a boyfriend apparently, but don't change the subject. It sounds like you don't want to come home.'

'It's not that, Jo. It's just that I feel different here. There are no newspaper reporters following me, people in the street don't care who I am, and I haven't had to read a single begging letter since I arrived.'

'Well, of course, I understand that, sweetie. But you belong here with your friends - don't you? Oh, gosh, I'm sorry. I don't mean to drag you back, I just miss you, that's all. But if you love it there and you want to stay then, well, you should stay I guess,' she said sadly.

My heart sank. I missed her. I really did. I missed all of my friends. But I just felt so much lighter in New York.

'Thanks, Jo. I miss you all so much. I haven't decided what I'm going to do yet. Besides, I still have to go and see the apartment in Toronto.'

'You just do what you feel is right. And whatever that is, I'll support your decision, I promise. If you do decide to stay over there, I'll just start taking more holidays to New York, that's all.'

'Yay!' I squealed. 'I certainly hope so. I hope you all do.'

'We will. Well, I'd better let you go. What are you up today?'

'Going to see the Statue of Liberty with Freddie.'

'Wow, that sounds fabulous. Have fun, hon. Talk again soon?'

'Absolutely. Give Carly my love. I'll call you soon. Love you. Bye.'

I put the phone down and sat down on the sofa. I missed her so much but was I ready to go home? No. When would I be prepared to go back? Honestly, I really didn't know.

CHAPTER 39

I'd never been to a gay bar before. I hadn't entirely known what to expect, so when Freddie took my hand and pulled me through the door of the coolest club in the world, I actually held my breath.

He'd laughed so hard when he had seen my face when he'd announced where he was taking me that night.

'Don't be such a prude, honey. It's only a gay bar. You've got nothing to worry about,' he said as he rifled through my limited wardrobe and finally opted for those amazing jeans and a bright sequinned top. When I went to put on my black boots, he shook his head dramatically and pointed to my black sandals.

'But it's freezing out,' I cried.

'Tut tut, girl. Style over the weather - always.'

Reluctantly, I'd put the sandals on and grabbed my new black leather jacket.

He grinned. 'Are we a great team, or are we a great team?'

I nodded. 'So, a gay bar? You're taking me to a gay bar. Why?'

'Honey, you're not the only one that needs to get laid.'

Clearly, my face said it all as he almost fell over laughing.

'I guess you have a point,' I whispered as we left the building, waving to George and grabbing the nearest available cab.

The bar was heaving, the music was loud, and the dance floor was full of mostly men dancing together. Although it seemed a bit weird at first, I soon got used to it. Several people waved to Freddie from a distance, and I followed him towards the bar where he smiled seductively at the super cute barman as were the majority of the guys there.

'Hey, Freddie. Haven't seen you around for a while. How're things? Where's Andy?' he asked.

Freddie pouted as he leaned on the bar. 'He left me.'

'Oh poor you,' the barman shouted above the deep thud of the bass before he started mixing drinks. We watched as he proceeded to throw bottles around like Tom Cruise in Cocktail. Eventually, he poured two purple cocktails and placed them in front of us.

'On the house,' he yelled.

Grinning, I yelled thanks before tasting what was most definitely the tastiest cocktail that had ever passed my lips. Freddie leaned over the bar and stroked the guy's face before taking a sip.

'You're a doll, Adam. Thanks.'

We turned around and looked for somewhere to sit. But it was too full, all seats were taken, so we just hovered around the dance floor, people watching.

'You okay, honey?' Freddie asked, more than once in the space of about ten minutes.

I grinned at him and nodded. 'I'm good. It's a great place.'

He nodded. 'I know, right?'

Looking over his shoulder, a handsome dark-haired man in his forties stood watching us from the corner of the room. I shifted from one foot to the other, turning away for a moment. There was something vaguely familiar about him, but I couldn't put my finger on it. Glancing back, he nervously took a sip from his drink before he put it back on the bar and made a swift exit. Odd.

Several cocktails later, Freddie had found a seat for me while he proceeded to flirt outrageously with several hot guys, both on the dance floor and at the bar. I giggled whenever he made a move and watched in awe as all these guys seemed to hang on his every word. If he wanted to pull, he could pull. But, towards the end of the night, he only had eyes for me. Sweeping me off my feet, he dragged me to the dance floor where we boogied away for an hour before we finally decided to head home.

'I thought you needed to get laid?' I laughed as we started to leave the club.

'Honey, I ain't leaving you for a second,' he put his arm around me with a warm smile, and we climbed into a cab that just pulled up outside.

'Come on, back to mine for a coffee before we call it a night.'

I threw off my sandals and fell onto the sofa, closing my eyes for a second as Freddie made us a cup of 'proper coffee'. Having lived in Rome for a year, back in his early twenties, he'd developed a taste for the 'really good stuff'.

Opening my eyes, I focussed on a picture on the wall. My heart seemed to thump out of my chest as I jumped up and rushed over to it. With my mouth wide open, I turned to look at Freddie as he waltzed from the kitchen to the sofa, with two black coffees in his hands.

'What's wrong?' he said, quickly placing the cups on the table and rushing to my side.

'It's him,' I said, pointing to the picture.

'Who? Andy?'

I nodded.

'What about Andy, honey?'

'He was there at the club.'

'What? What are you talking about?'

Holding his hands, I pulled him back to the sofa, where we plopped down.

'He was standing at the back of the club, earlier this evening. He was watching you. He seemed really nervous and then he left, really quickly.'

Freddie's nostrils flared, and his lips quivered as his hands flew to his mouth.

'My Andy?' he whispered.

Nodding, I squeezed his knee, and we just sat, saying nothing for a while. Eventually, a little sob came out of his throat.

'Oh, Freddie, I'm so sorry.'

He smiled and shook his head, reaching forward for our coffees.

'No, I'm fine, absolutely fine,' he insisted. 'I'm over him. I won't let him do this to me again,' he handed me my cup and leaned back.

I squeezed his knee again and smiled. He wasn't a very good liar.

oOo

'Katie,' Freddie yelled down the phone, two days later. 'Katie, honey, I need you,' he repeated.

'I'll be right there,' I said, hopping out of bed and throwing on my dressing gown and slippers. I didn't even wash my face or brush my teeth. I just knew from the tone of his voice that something was wrong.

Opening his door, with tears flowing down his cheeks, he practically fell on to me, sobbing.

'Oh Freddie, what on Earth is it? Are you okay? What's happened?'

'It's Andy.'

'What's happened to him?' I asked, imagining him lying dead in the New York City morgue or something.

'He wants me back.'

'What?'

Freddie pulled me indoors and dragged me to his bedroom, where we sat on the bed. He then stood up, pacing up and down, then sat down again, continually fidgeting.

'Stop!' I yelled.

He stood still and turned to look at me. His beautiful face was tear-stained, his eyes a little puffy.

'Right, tell me exactly what happened?'

Taking a deep breath, Freddie quietly sat down on the little blue chair in the corner of the room and sighed.

'He showed up late last night, drunk. He said he was really sorry, that he'd made a massive mistake, that he loves me and wants me back.'

'And what did you say?'

'I told him I didn't care what he thought, that I was over him.'

'But?'

'But then I faltered...'

'And?'

'And then I let him stay the night.'

'Oh Freddie,' I sighed, getting up and going over to him to give him a long hug.

'Oh Katie, you do give the best hugs in the world, you know?'

Leaning back, I looked into his eyes, and beneath the tears, I could see real happiness.

'Do you really want him back?'

He bit his bottom lip and looked away momentarily before turning to face me and nodding.

'Yes,' he cried.

'Do you really love him?'

'I do.'

'Can you forgive him?' I asked tentatively.

'I... I want to forgive him.'

'But do you truly think you can?'

Slowly, he nodded, and I hugged him tightly.

'Then you must take him back. He must be an extraordinary man, Freddie.'

'He is, honey. I know he fucked up big time, but he's my soul mate.'

'Hey, I thought I was your soul mate?' I laughed.

'Well, of course you are,' he smiled. 'But Andy is my second soul mate.'

'Then you should be together. If you're sure he's the one, then I can't wait to meet him.'

Freddie clapped his hands together. 'We arranged to meet at Starbucks at ten. Will you come?'

'Don't you think you should go alone? You have a lot to talk about. I don't want to cramp your style.'

'You could never do that, honey. Okay, I'll go alone, but I want you to come down after an hour, okay?'

'Sure, I'll be there at eleven. I promise.'

oOo

Freddie was right; Andy was perfect for him in every way. A beautiful person, inside and out. It was clear that he was deeply sorry for his mistake and I could tell that he would make it up to Freddie, probably for the rest of his life. They were made for each other. Even I could see that.

So, when I saw them together, I knew it was time for me to leave. Freddie needed time with Andy, and I needed to move on with my life.

'No, no, no, no, no,' cried Freddie when I told him. 'You can't leave.'

I nodded, smiling. 'I have to, Freddie. I still have to go to Toronto, and then I need to get back to my life in London.'

'But you have a new life here, with us.'

'Freddie you are the sweetest man I've ever met and I love you to bits, but I've put my life on hold for long enough. I need to sort things out. But I'll be back, I promise. Although London is my home, so is New York, now. I've decided to flit between the two cities, so you'll see a heck of a lot more of me in future.'

'Really?' he sighed. 'You promise?'

I nodded. 'I promise.'

He hugged me tightly.

'You don't need me to come to Canada with you?'

'You need to be with Andy, right now. I'm okay on my own, I need to spend a little time alone. I'll be fine.'

'Okay, if you insist. But you'd better come back real soon, honey.'

Two days later, Andy and Freddie waved me off from JFK Airport. I was alone again, but totally relaxed and looking forward to what the future would hold.

oronto. A great city filled with the friendliest people on Earth. It didn't take me long to figure that out. It started with the flight attendants, who were like long lost friends, chatting about anything and everything, asking about me - loving my accent. Then the taxi driver, chatting about anything and everything - again, loving my accent. Then the person I'd arranged to meet to pick up my keys. She was just lovely, very chatty and helpful, giving me her phone number, should I need anything at all.

And then, when I popped into my local supermarket, the staff busied all around me, making sure I found everything I needed.

Every single person I came across seemed genuinely delighted to meet me. They were full of smiles and joy, and it was totally contagious. For the next week, I wandered around on my own, sight-seeing, full of the joys of spring. I visited the CN Tower, where I almost had the knickers scared off me on the Edge Walk. I had palpitations just thinking about it. But I had to do it. Since becoming friends with Freddie, my perspective on life had changed. I'd become braver, more willing to do the kinds of things I would always have been terrified of doing before. So, while there, I also took up the opportunity to grab a helicopter ride over Niagara Falls. It was breathtaking, thrilling and oh so loud.

After two weeks of enjoying everything the city had to offer, I had made up my mind about the apartment and what I should do next. I would let it out, long term, and return to London to finally proceed to stage two of my life. With all my money, I had to start investing wisely. So as soon as I got back, I'd make an appointment with a (real) financial advisor and see where I should be putting my cash. Then I would start dating again. I would no longer look for black-haired, blue-eyed ghosts; I'd allow myself to casually date anyone that took my fancy. Freddie had taught me that.

'You must find your own soul mate, other than me, of course,' he'd smiled. 'And if he is short, with ginger hair and freckles, so be it. But to find him, you must start dating. And if that means going out with a hundred frogs, then so you shall.'

I'd laughed at the time, but soon realised he was absolutely right. When it finally dawned on me, I'd chuckled for about an hour - in the comfort of my three bed Toronto apartment, of course. Freddie had become my fairy godmother and when I'd realised that, I'd called him to tell him so. He'd laughed so hard down the phone. The next day he'd emailed a picture of himself, dressed up like something out of Cinderella. How I loved that guy.

So, with my bags all packed, I hopped into the taxi and headed for Toronto airport, where I'd done the whole self-check-in business, which never failed to confuse me. Afterwards, I spent a little time wandering around the shops, buying some perfume for Jo, a cute teddy bear for Carly (even though I knew she was getting a bit old for that kind of thing), chocolates for Anna and John, the latest copy of Canadian Vogue and some Canadian tea for Julianne, maple syrup for Tony and a Canada teapot for Zara. I'd already sent Liz and Jorge a beautiful print of Niagara Falls - I just knew it would go really well in their living room. All my purchases were held by the shop, who assured me they would be on my flight when I left.

Happy I hadn't missed anyone, and as it was already early evening, I decided to head to the bar for a little drink.

Sitting on a barstool, the barman turned and flashed me a wide grin.

'Hey,' he said. 'What can I getcha?'

'Erm, I think I'll have a glass of white wine, please.'

'One white wine, coming right up,' he smiled, grabbing a bottle from the refrigerator below the bar. Pouring it in front of me, he looked at me and squinted. 'Do I know you?' he asked.

'I don't think so.'

'Yeah, I've definitely seen you before. Hm,' he said, placing the wine in front of me and rubbing his chin. 'Are you famous?' he laughed.

I shrugged my shoulders. 'Not really.'

'Ah, you've intrigued me. Clearly, you are well known. Come on, spill the beans,' he laughed.

Throwing my head back, I laughed aloud. 'Really? You really want to know?'

'Absolutely,' he said, leaning forward slightly as he started drying some wet glasses. 'I'm all ears.'

'Yes, I'm sure you are,' I chuckled and started to tell him all about my brief encounter with the British press.

'Yeah, I remember now,' he said mid-way through. 'I knew I'd seen that pretty face before.'

'Really? How come? I'm sure the news didn't spread all the way across the Atlantic Ocean.'

He shook his head. 'No, it didn't. But I spent several months in London recently and I read all the papers while I was there.'

'Oh, God, really?'

He nodded with a chuckle.

'So, what have you been up to since then?'

'I spent a little time in the Azores, nearly two months in New York, and a brief two-week spell here, in Toronto, and here I am, ready to go home.'

'I must say you look very relaxed. You had a good time?'

'Very. It was exactly what I needed.'

'So what happened to the guy then?' he asked.

I laughed. 'What guy?'

'You know, the guy you were searching for?'

'Oh, I guess I've come to realise he just doesn't exist. Not any more, anyway.'

The barman frowned.

'What?'

'You really think so?'

Nodding, I suddenly realised it was the first time I'd talked about Fred for ages, and it was the first time the pang had gone. Those butterflies I always used to get in my stomach, at the mere mention of him, were no longer there. I grinned. Finally. I was over him.

FRED

It was time to go home and face the music. I'd left England over a year ago and not once had I been in touch with any of my friends. The only way I could move on was to completely cut off everything about my home country. I refused to even read the news.

Twelve months of travelling the world. India, Malaysia, China, Australia, New Zealand, America and Canada. I'd loved every moment and every second spent was another second to help me forget. The pain I had caused. The pain I had felt. The humiliation. I took a deep breath and walked into the airport. It was now or never. I had to get back to my life.

With my bags safely checked in, I headed straight to the bar. I needed a drink, something I hadn't done since, well, since D-Day. That's what I'd been calling it, anyway.

Approaching the bar, I saw the back of a brunette with an attractive figure as she stood up and walked in the opposite direction. Something about the way she walked was vaguely familiar, but I shook it off and went and sat down in the same seat.

'Hey,' said the bartender.

'Hey yourself. Can I get a beer, please?'

'Sure. Any particular brand?'

I shook my head, 'I haven't had a drink for months, so no, any will do. I'm sure they'll all taste the same, anyway.'

He nodded and handed me a Bud.

'Cheers,' I said as I let the cold liquid flow down my throat. Immediately, my muscles seemed to sigh in relaxation.

'Oh, that's good,' I smiled.

'So, how come you haven't had a drink for a few months?'

'Well, now that's a long story.'

'All I got is time, buddy,' he said, leaning on the bar.

'I haven't talked to anyone about it, actually, not anybody at all.'

'Hey man, it's good to talk, you know?'

I laughed, 'Yeah, you're right. I stopped drinking about twelve months ago after I got really drunk at my stag do.'

'Stag do?'

'I mean my bachelor party.'

'Bachelor party? So where's the bride?'

I raised my eyebrows, 'Now there's the thing. I called off the wedding.'

The bartender sucked air through his teeth and cringed as I continued.

'I'd always known she wasn't the one, but I figured I had to get on with my life, you know?'

He nodded.

'I was ready to go through with it, I was going to marry her, have a family. Live happily ever after,' I chuckled. 'But then... BAM.'

'Bam?'

'Bachelor party.'

'What happened?'

He was clearly intrigued.

'I saw her. She was at the club. Man, she looked just like her, you know?'

The bartender shook his head and leaned forward, 'Nope. You lost me, man.'

'Oh, sorry. The thing is, I've always been in love with this other girl, and I always hoped to find her one day, you know? But I never did, so I decided to settle for someone else. That's when I met my bride to be, Katelyn. She was a real sweetheart, but she deserved to marry someone who was madly in love with her. I wasn't. But it didn't really hit me until my bachelor party when I went back to a hotel with another woman. That woman, man, she could so easily have been the girl from my childhood. The girl I saw when I was just a kid. We'd spent just minutes together, but I knew then that she was the girl for me.'

'What happened?' he whispered, hanging on to my every word.

'I was on holiday with my mum, some caravan park we went to once or twice before she died. There was this kids' disco. It was silly, you know? But I was only twelve, and so I joined in. And there, on that dance floor, was where I saw her. The most beautiful young girl, hazel eyes, brown hair. She was the prettiest thing I ever saw. It was like it was just her and me, you know? And then she was gone, her dad came and got her. I followed her, rushed over to a nearby garden and picked a daffodil,' I chuckled. 'Then I ran over to her to try and give it to her, but she had to go before I got the chance. I never even spoke to her. Not a word. Not a single word.'

The barman stood with his mouth wide open. 'Did you never go back? Never try to find her?'

'My mum died, and I was sent to Wales to live with an elderly uncle. I never got the chance.'

'Flight BA 092 is now boarding. Please make your way to Boarding Gate...'

'Oh, that's my flight. Shit, I'm running late. I gotta go. Keep the change,' I yelled as I threw a few notes onto the bar. 'Thanks for listening!' I rushed away, just noticing him pick up the phone in an apparent panic.

As I approached the boarding gate, I realised I was the last to board the plane.

A pretty blonde flight attendant was on the phone; her eyebrows knitted together before a huge grin appeared on her face. 'Right, okay, Danny, I got it. And yes, he's right here. I'll sort it. Yep, I'll see you tomorrow. Bye,' she carefully put the phone down and looked at me with a cheeky smile. Was I missing something?

'That was Danny.'

'Erm, okay.'

'Danny was the bartender you just left.'

'Oh shoot, did I not leave enough money?' I said, thinking either that or I'd left something behind. I patted down my pockets but seemed to have everything in check.

'Nope, nothing like that at all. Not to worry. I'd better get you on board.'

Totally confused, I wondered what was going on.

The blonde woman grinned at me and checked my passport.

'Erm, we've had to change your seat, Mr Jones.'

'You have?' I was a little annoyed because I'd booked that seat on purpose, as it had a bit more legroom.

'Yes, you've been upgraded,' she grinned, 'to First Class.'

'First Class? I've never travelled First Class before.'

'Well then, I do believe you're going to have an extraordinary flight, Mr Jones,' she winked as I walked through the gate, leaving me excited yet confused.

As I approached the aircraft, another pretty attendant flashed me a huge smile. 'Good evening, Mr Jones. I believe you've been upgraded to First Class?'

'Yes, I think so.'

'Please follow me.'

I gingerly followed closely behind, looking at the wealthy travellers already in their seats. I smiled nervously until she stopped and pointed to my seat. Wide-eyed, I still couldn't quite believe I'd been upgraded, and my heartfelt like it was in my mouth. I imagined someone suddenly appearing out of nowhere and loudly accusing me of stealing their seat or something. So I quickly sat down, letting her see to my bags.

As I turned to look at my nearest traveller, my breath literally caught in my chest, and my skin went numb. I'd never had palpitations before, but my heart felt like it was about to jump out of my chest.

'Mr Jones, are you alright, sir?' asked the attendant, who looked at me with concern.

I slowly nodded with a smile.

'Danny, the barman, did this, didn't he?'

She grinned and nodded, putting a finger over her mouth as if to say, 'Shhh, don't tell anyone'.

I nodded and laughed. Tears unexpectedly sprang from my eyes and rolled down my cheeks as the girl in the next seat suddenly turned to look across at me. I swear my heart stopped beating in that very second.

Her expression mirrored mine and slowly, very slowly, the most beautiful smile began to creep across her face.

'Marc?' she whispered.

Nodding, I wiped my eyes, completely embarrassed.

'It's you,' I whispered. 'You're the girl from Skegness, aren't you?'

She covered her mouth with her hand and slowly nodded her head in utter disbelief.

'You're... you're... him?

I nodded. 'I'm so sorry about before. I hope you'll forgive me for leaving you like that.'

She looked so confused, and my heart literally felt like it would break.

'I was supposed to be getting married... until you.'

She held her breath and shook her head. 'You didn't, did you?'

I shook my head, knowing I could finally be happy. I had finally found the woman of my dreams. The woman I'd fallen in love with, all those years before.

THE END

"Don't be such a prude."

"I...I'm not a prude," Aggie stuttered as she pushed her long, mousy brown hair behind her ear and glanced around at the other shoppers on the high street.

"Oh, come on," Coco laughed. She grabbed her best friend by the arm and gave her little choice but to enter the famous sex shop.

Feeling her face blush a deep shade of aubergine, Aggie stumbled beside her, hiding as best as she could.

Coco, on the other hand, was in her element, picking up bras, panties, feather boas, sequinned bodices and...

Aggie gasped aloud when she saw her best friend pick up a vibrator before it dawned on her that Coco was merely teasing her.

"Can we go now?" she whispered as her best pal hooted with laughter.

"Go?" Coco giggled, "but we only just came in."

"I'm just not...not...comfortable."

"Jeeze, Aggie, it's about time you got over your nerves in places like this. It's just a sex shop, they sell lingerie and fun stuff for the bedroom. You're not an eighty-five-year-old Vicar's wife—you're twenty-eight for God's sake! Live a little. Come on, look at this," she said as she pulled a blood-red basque covered in feathers from the rails and held it up to her best friend's slim physique.

Mortified, Aggie gulped, and her nostrils flared.

Realising the extent of poor Aggie's embarrassment, Coco relented and immediately put it back with a shake of the head.

"Okay, okay. Just give me a minute to pay for these things."

"I'll see you outside," Aggie muttered as she tried not to trip over her own feet to get out of there as fast as she could.

The cold immediately hit her as she walked outside, so Aggie rubbed her hands up and down her arms and crossed the high street. She waited around the corner near a popular newsagent, avoiding eye contact with everybody, her embarrassment still evident on her flushed face.

Five minutes later, Coco emerged with a huge grin on her face and another large pink carrier bag in her hand. Aggie watched as her friend's smile faded, her head turning one way and the other as she scoured the crowds for her best pal.

Aggie waved from across the street as she stepped out of the shadows.

"I thought you'd buggered off and left me," Coco shrieked and tottered toward her in three-inch heels perfectly suited for a shopping expedition. "Come on, let's grab a coffee."

Arm in arm, the two women walked toward Starbucks, just a few metres further down the shop-lined street.

"I'm dying for a cappuccino," Coco added.

Aggie pushed open the door. Warmth and an inviting aroma of coffee enveloped her as she waited for Coco, who struggled with all the carrier bags. An attractive man in his forties rushed forward to help.

"Let me give you a hand," he said in such a smooth tone that Aggie's knees almost buckled. Men never rush to my aid like that, she thought while Coco relished the attention.

"Thank you," she breathed. "You're very kind."

"It's nothing. Can I buy you a cup of coffee?"

Coco stopped momentarily before she smiled, that beautiful bright smile that would cheer up many a toothpaste advert, and shook her head.

"No, thank you, I'm here to have coffee with my friend. Perhaps another time?"

The man, who had a head full of thick silver hair, nodded with a cheeky smile, then reached into his inside pocket, removing a silver cardholder. He withdrew his business card and placed it into Coco's front jacket pocket.

"In that case, I shall wait for your call."

And then he was gone. Aggie stood, still holding the door, with her mouth wide open.

"Shut the door will you, love? You're letting the cold air in," said an old lady to her side.

"Oh, sorry," Aggie muttered. She quickly shut the door and followed Coco to the only available table in the corner of the cafe.

"Sit down, hon. I'll get these. What do you fancy? Your usual?"

"Erm...yes please," Aggie replied as she struggled to remove her bulky coat, almost hitting a nearby person in the face. Once it was off, she sat down with a sigh.

Several minutes later, Coco returned with a cappuccino and a soy caramel latte.

"Thanks," Aggie smiled.

Sighing contentedly, Coco sat down and pulled out her flashy smartphone.

"So. Will you ring him?" Aggie asked.

"Ring who?"

"That guy?"

"What guy?" Coco asked.

Aggie rolled her eyes, "That gorgeous older guy who just gave you his card."

"Oh him. I don't know. Maybe."

"Maybe? But he was...was...so handsome, so dreamy. If not a little old."

"Yeah, I suppose," Coco murmured as she proceeded to flick through her text messages. "Oh look, I've won another competition."

"What this time?"

"Oh, just some makeup. Shit," she shrieked all of a sudden, "I mean, seriously OMG".

Aggie jumped. "What? What on earth is it?"

"Aggie, honey. Did you check your messages this morning?"

"No, why?" Aggie replied.

"You need to check your email. Now."

"Why, what's going on?" she asked.

"Just do it," Coco said, clapping the elaborate case of her mobile phone shut before she gave her friend a slightly sad smile.

"Please just tell me, Coco," Aggie replied as she delved into her handbag and tried to retrieve her own phone.

"Oh, alright then. I got an email from Amelia Hornblower. The library is closing down."

"Wh...wh...what?" stuttered Aggie.

"I'm sorry honey."

"Wh...wh...when?"

"At the end of the month," Coco added.

"But why wouldn't they tell me? And why does Amelia know about this before me? She doesn't even work there."

"Honey, Amelia is the town gossip. You know that. She knows you're going to fart before you do. What will you do?"

"I don't know. I didn't have any idea this was going to happen. I thought the library was going well," Aggie cried.

"Oh honey, even I knew it was having financial difficulties. I mean who really cares for a library that specialises in nothing but mythology?"

"I do," Aggie whispered.

"Oh babe, I'm so sorry, I didn't mean it."

"What am I going to do?"

"Don't worry," Coco placed her hand over Aggie's, "We'll figure something out."

"I didn't even know I had a Great Aunt Petunia."

"She was your Grandma's younger sister, Aggie. I must have mentioned her once in a while when you were little. Don't you remember?" said her mother.

"No," Aggie replied.

"Well, she certainly seems to remember you, for some reason, because she's left you the old corner shop in her will."

"What? What corner shop?" Aggie asked as she shifted the phone to her other ear while she balanced several books under her right arm and walked across the room.

"The one underneath her flat where she used to work."

"Why on earth would she leave it to me? It's just weird."

"Weird? But darling, you should be happy. You won't have a job to go to in a week. At least you can do something with the shop."

"A shop? What on earth am I going to do with a shop?" she reiterated, trying and failing to stop the books from tumbling to the floor.

"That's enough, Agatha. You should be grateful to your late Great Aunt Petunia for this opportunity."

"Mum, I am grateful. Really I am. Sorry, it's just with the library closing down and me losing my job, I'm just not myself. I'm sorry," Aggie said as she crouched down and tried to pick up the books.

"I understand, sweetheart, I really do, but this could be the perfect opportunity to get you back on your feet. I know it's not your dream job, but it's a job all the same."

"I know, Mum. I just can't imagine being a shopkeeper, that's all."

"Well, whatever you do, that shop belongs to you now, whether you like it or not," her mother stated.

"Thanks, Mum."

"I'll talk to you soon. Love you, sweetheart. Toodle pip. "

"Love you too, Mum. Bye."

Aggie put the phone down and tried to remember her mother talking about her Great Aunt Petunia as a child but she just couldn't. She must've been too young. Way too young.

Before she could continue packing away the beloved books she'd spent several years caring for, her mobile rang again.

"You'll never guess what. No, you won't guess. I've won a holiday for two, and I'm taking you with me," Coco shrieked down the phone so loudly that Aggie had to hold it at arm's length.

"Huh? What are you talking about? You've won a holiday?"

"We're going to Las Vegas!" Coco yelled.

"What?" Aggie asked in shock.

"We leave in two weeks," Coco replied.

"Coco, what on earth are you talking about?"

"Honey, I entered some random Twitter competition to win a five-day trip to Vegas, and I won. I want you to come with me."

"You want me to come with you to Las Vegas?" Aggie asked.

"Yes," Coco shrieked again.

"In two weeks?"

"Yes!" Coco replied.

"I can't come to Las Vegas in two weeks," Aggie decided. "I've just lost my job, I've inherited a corner shop, and my life is insane right now. I really can't Coco."

"Of course you can and of course you will."

oOo

The breakfast buffet was more significant than anything Aggie had ever seen. In fact, it appeared to be more of a banquet than a meal to be eaten in the morning hours. It was famous, after all. Almost anyone and everyone who had ever visited Las Vegas knew about the fantastic champagne breakfast buffet at the ridiculously grand hotel.

"I can't possibly drink any more," sighed Aggie before she swallowed the last drops of her third rather large glass of champagne.

"Nonsense, of course, you can," Coco said as she nodded at one of the many waiters who seemed to appear out of nowhere to pour the fourth glass.

"Cheers, my dear. Now come on, let's hit the buffet one more time," said Coco.

Holding her full, slightly rounded stomach, Aggie only semi-reluctantly stood up and headed back toward the food for the third time.

"I'm going for Chinese this time. What about you?" Coco asked.

"Hm?" Aggie murmured, not really taking much notice of the question.

Coco ignored her and wandered off, leaving Aggie to decide over the massive selection of hot and cold meats, seafood, pasta dishes, salads, vegetables and much more. But she'd had her fill with savoury stuff, so she turned her attention to the sweets. A creamy chocolate mousse, topped with a generous serving of softly whipped cream caught her attention.

Back at her table, Aggie spotted Coco being chatted up, yet again, by a particularly good looking guy in his early twenties. She couldn't help but notice the manliness of his square jawline, not to mention the twinkle in his eye as he looked down at Coco. She always received attention with her caramel-coloured skin, a mass of honey brown curls, huge blue eyes, and naturally dark pink bee-stung lips. The only thing that prevented her from being a supermodel was her height or apparent lack of it, Aggie thought. Coco was only five foot one. Not that she let it hinder her from doing anything. She often chose to wear at least five-inch heels—even when she was just nipping out to the corner shop.

In other words, Coco was the exact opposite of Aggie.

She sighed and turned her full attention back to the chocolate mousse at the exact time that a very attractive guy in his early thirties appeared beside her.

"Erm, excuse me, Miss," he said.

"Huh?" Aggie muttered as she looked at him.

"You dropped your jacket," he smiled, pointing to the floor behind her.

Her heart began to flutter as she watched him lean over before he stood up and put it back on the chair.

"Oh, thank you very much," she said, her cheeks changing colour.

"You've, erm, got a little cream..." he pointed to her top lip.

She blushed an even deeper shade of red and wiped her mouth with the back of her hand. The young man grinned and walked away. Aggie looked down and noticed the huge amount of whipped cream she'd wiped away.

She lost her appetite all of a sudden and pushed the offending dessert away.

"Not gonna eat that? It looks delicious," said Coco as she put down yet another plate of sushi on the table.

Aggie shook her head, "I thought you were having Chinese?" she asked.

"That guy recommended the sushi," Coco smiled as she pointed across the room to the young man with whom she'd been chatting.

"Oh, okay. I don't know where you put it all," Aggie sighed.

Coco grinned, "I'm lucky I've got a high metabolism." She pouted before placing a large piece of tuna sashimi into her mouth with the chopsticks.

Aggie blushed and shook her head.

"Want some?" Coco offered.

Aggie shook her head, dabbing her mouth with the cloth napkin for the third time.

"I think I've had enough. So who was the cute guy?"

"Just some guy who wanted to go out with me tonight," she answered as if it happened every day. Probably because it did.

"Oh."

"I turned him down," said Coco, before she put another piece of sushi in her mouth.

"He was handsome."

Coco swallowed the fish before she replied, "A bit young for me."

"He was probably the same age as you!"

"Exactly...too young. Enough about me anyway, I thought I saw someone chatting you up," Coco teased.

"Not really, he just picked up my jacket from the floor...and then told me I had a cream moustache."

"Oh, oh well. Better luck next time, hon."

"Yeah, I don't think there'll be a next time. I just don't have the kind of appeal that you have, Coco."

"Nonsense. You're beautiful. You just don't seem to see it."

Aggie looked across the table at her friend as if she was looking at a little green man.

"I'm serious! I'd kill for your poker-straight hair, perfect skin, and height."

"But not my thin lips, flat chest, and sticky-out cheekbones," Aggie almost whispered.

"Oh Aggie, there's absolutely nothing wrong with your lips, chest, or cheekbones! Honestly, woman. I do believe you've got body dysmorphia or something. Your problem is that you hide from the world. Even when you're out and about, you just want to blend in with the crowd or sink into the floor."

Aggie glanced around and pulled herself more upright in her chair.

"What you need is a makeover and some confidence-building lessons. In fact, let's go out on the town tonight, and I'll do your hair and makeup. Ooh, we could go shopping first and get you a new outfit."

"No, I don't think so," Aggie whispered.

"You're doing it again," Coco shook her head.

"What?" Aggie asked.

"Trying to sink into the floor."

"No, I'm not."

"Then let's go shopping!" Coco exclaimed.

Aphrodite's Closet is available from most online book retailers.

FREE DOWNLOAD

Willow Tree Farm

Nestled among a thicket of weeping willows deep in the heart of Dartmoor, lies a house like no other. A house defying the laws of logic—and gravity for that matter. Some might even say it had a mind of its own. They wouldn't be wrong.

Affectionately known as Willow, this house has been an integral part of the Winterbourne family for over 400 years, and it is very, very protective of the Winterbournes, so woe betide anyone who dares to wrong this family of witches…

Compatible with all reading devices.

Exclusively available, and never before published.

Get your FREE COPY of Willow Tree Farm when you sign up to the author's VIP mailing list. **Get started here:**

www.suzyturner.com/free-book

ABOUT THE AUTHOR

Suzy Turner wrote her first chick lit novel in her early twenties, but it wasn't until much later that she decided to focus on writing full time. It was during a visit to Canada in 2009 when the ravens within the dark eerie forests of British Columbia called to her. The story of Lilly Taylor was born soon after and the first novel in The Raven Witch Saga was created. Suzy has since published several more urban fantasy books (under her pen name SG Turner) and contemporary women's novels.

Having lived in Portugal since childhood, Suzy, who is originally from Yorkshire in England, loves to travel. She finds inspiration wherever she goes. Old decrepit buildings, graveyards, cathedrals and castles are just a few of the things that can be found within the worlds of her urban fantasy books, and her contemporary women's fiction novels are filled with fun friendships, ordinary people in extraordinary circumstances and quirky characters you'd want as friends.

Suzy lives in the Algarve with her husband, three cats and a dog, where she does yoga every morning and bookish stuff for pretty much the rest of the day!

For more books and updates, visit www.suzyturner.com

ACKNOWLEDGMENTS

Huge thanks to Jill, Brittany, Mary, Lucy, Sharon, Mindy and Helene for reading and correcting my very first chick lit novel. I was so nervous about what you would think and you all made me truly believe I could do this. I'm hugely grateful to you all. Thank you to my editor, Andrea, for all your hard work. And a very special thanks to all my friends, social networking pals and readers for the constant support you always provide.

And of course to Michael, my very own soulmate. I am so blessed to have met you when I was just sixteen years old. Thank you for being such a constant support throughout the many years that I've messed about with this book!

This book is about finding your soulmate and so
I dedicate this book to the love of my life
oOo Michael oOo